A
**BUTCH
BLISS**
NOVEL

Also by Harry Bryant

In & Out
Hidden Palms

SNAKE ROAD

HARRY BRYANT

51325 Books

This book is published by **51325 Books**, a division of Firebird Creative (Clackamas, OR).

Flow like water across stones . . .

Book Design by Firebird Creative.

First **51325 Books** edition: April 2020.

This one is for
Elmore Leonard

SNAKE
ROAD

CHAPTER 1

I was queuing for a hot dog at the corner of Ventura and Las Mercados when the black sedan pulled up and scared off half the line. The couple in front of me closed the gap that had suddenly opened, and he made some joke about illegal immigrants. She laughed politely, but she looked away. She met my gaze and offered a tiny shrug. *What's a girl to do?* it said.

She was wearing a gauzy wrap over a bikini top and a short skirt. He was wearing white socks with his cork-soled sandals. One of them was dressed for being seen at the beach, and the other one wasn't.

I shrugged back. I wasn't going to offer any suggestions if she couldn't see for herself. The white socks were a dead giveaway, frankly.

"Hey," someone said. I could see the front edge of the sedan out of the corner of my eye. I wasn't going to turn my head any farther. "Hey, asshole."

Sock Dude looked. His lady friend rubbed the back of her neck as she stepped a little ahead of him, turning her body slightly so she could move out of the way if she needed to.

Sock Dude, on the other hand, didn't have the same instinctive sense of danger.

"You talking to me?" he asked. He screwed up his face, like that was going to help, but all it did was highlight the narrow space between his eyes. He looked about as ferocious as a wet weasel.

The driver of the car said something, and the man's expression changed. "What?" He frowned. His eyes darted toward me. "Him? You want to talk to him?"

I took a couple of steps forward, until his outstretched finger nearly touched my chest. "I'm just getting a hot dog," I said.

"He's—ah—" Sock Dude curled his finger up as he took a step backward.

His lady friend was looking at me. She had hazel eyes, and strands of brown hair hanging down from the careless bun atop her head. They framed her face nicely.

I gave her a smile. Letting her know I wasn't worried.

Tourists like it when the locals smile at them. It makes them feel like they belong.

The sedan's tires rubbed the edge of the sidewalk as the car crept forward. I heard the back window slide down. "Get in the car, Bliss." A woman's voice.

I looked over my shoulder. You always look when a woman says your name.

The windows of the sedan were tinted, which made the interior of the car darker than the rest of the world. I couldn't see much of the woman, just the curve of her jaw and the cut of her business suit. Both were impressive.

"I'm getting a hot dog," I said.

"You can get one later," she said.

"I'm hungry now," I said.

She said something to the driver, who looked like a piece of marble with sunglasses taped on, and he rolled the car forward again.

"Horatio," the woman called out, directing her attention to the guy working the hot dog cart.

He was trying his best to ignore the black sedan, but he flinched when she said his name.

"Everything up to date?" she asked. "Licenses? Permits?"

Horatio looked down the line at me, silently pleading with his eyes.

I sighed. "And just like that," I said. "A man's appetite disappears." I glanced at the hazel-eyed woman. "Enjoy your visit to LA," I said. "The food's good, even if the atmosphere is a bit sketchy."

I stepped out of line and turned toward the sedan. "Get in," the driver said, jerking his head toward the back of the car.

I had barely gotten into the car when the driver sped away from the curb. The sudden motion slammed the door shut behind me, and I slid around on the cool leather seats. The woman had already moved over to the other side of the car, otherwise I would have fallen into her lap, which would have spoiled their spooky government agency vibe.

While I got myself situated and put my seat belt on, I checked out the woman. Her hair was black, and she had it pulled back and formed to her head in a rigorously precise shape. Her face was as angular as her attitude, and her lipstick was a muted red—several steps away from cherry red, but not so far as to be drained of color. She wasn't wearing any rings, and I caught sight of a watch peeking out from the sleeve of her dark blue suit jacket.

"Where are we going?" I asked.

She made her own examination, and briefly, the corner of her mouth twitched as she finished. "You owe me a favor," she said.

"I do?"

I didn't know this woman, though if I had to guess from the car and the outfit, I didn't want to know her.

"A couple of months ago . . ." She let it hang there.

And here it is, I thought. *The other shoe.*

I had been involved in a little trouble over the summer. About an hour north of LA. When it was all over, I had gone to Oregon for a few weeks, where I had gotten some private surfing lessons. I was a good student, and the instruction was excellent, but the weather turned eventually. The sky lost its luster, the waves had gotten mean, and it had been time to come back to LA.

Where everyone had moved on to more interesting stories.

Well, almost everyone.

I leaned forward and glanced down at her shoes. Black wedges. Closed toe. Hard to tell if her toenails were painted, though I would bet that they were. And I knew where she had them done.

"Hot Passion Excess?" I asked, nodding toward her feet.

She leaned forward and slipped off one of her shoes. She was wearing sheer black stockings under her immaculately tailored pants. I caught a glimmer of silver when she flashed her stocking-covered foot at me. "Iridescent Moonlight Frolic," she said.

"That's a nice shade," I said. "Really sets the mood."

She slipped her shoe on again, and I leaned back against the seat. Marble Face was staring at me in the rearview mirror. Or maybe his head was stuck at an odd angle. It was hard to tell with the sunglasses.

"You two probably don't swap tips on toenail polish, do you?" I said.

"We don't."

"Must make all that idle caught in traffic chit-chat sorta tough."

"We find other things to talk about."

"Waxing?" I asked.

He kept staring at me.

I glanced out the window instead, watching as he merged into the bumper-to-bumper joy that was the 10. He worked his way over to the leftmost lane, and the sprawl of central LA slowly crawled by us. We were heading south.

"I need you to deliver a package for me," the woman said.

"What sort of package?"

"The people who will receive your package will give you a receipt. You will bring that back and deliver it to a third party."

"Yeah, I'm familiar with this routine," I said. "And no, I'm not interested."

"It's not like that," she said.

"It's always like that," I said. "Especially when you tell me it isn't." I shook my head. "I did my time. And then some. I was never a mule then, and I'm not going to be one now."

She was silent for a minute, and when I looked over at her, she was regarding me with a cool stare, as if she was considering how long she was going to wait before she stopped asking nicely.

"Okay," she said.

And that was it. I let the silence stretch between us, waiting for her to say something, and eventually, I broke. "*Okay* what?" I asked.

"It doesn't matter," she said. "You don't need to know."

"Know what?"

"Are you going to take the package?"

"No."

"Then we're done here."

"Are you fucking kidding me?"

"Mr. Bliss, it's adorable that you think you're entitled to some sort of explanation, but I don't owe you a damn thing. You're a convicted felon. I shouldn't even be having this conversation with you."

"And yet here we are." I waved a hand at the freeway outside the car. "I was doing just fine a little while ago. Looking forward to one of Horatio's dogs. And now . . . ? This is bullshit. Who are you working for? DEA? INS? The DA's office?"

She shook her head. "It doesn't matter, Mr. Bliss. It really doesn't." She leaned forward to speak to the driver. "Derek? Go ahead and take the next exit. We'll let Mr. Bliss off."

"Hang on," I said. "You can't just throw me out of the car like this."

"We can't?"

"No, damnit. You can't. This is—"

"Is the neighborhood too rough for you?"

"No, the neighborhood isn't rough. That's not the point."

Derek changed lanes, heading back toward the righthand lane where the exit was.

"No, wait, wait," I said. "Wait a minute."

Derek stared at me in the rearview mirror. The car stayed in its lane.

I exhaled noisily. "What kind of package?" I asked.

A ghost of a smile touched the woman's lips.

"Not yet," she said. "You have to say 'yes' before I tell you anything more."

"I hate this game," I said.

"It's more fun than the one the DEA plays."

"They know better. We've already had a chat about how they don't want to play any games with me."

She shrugged. "Maybe they won't play with you. Maybe they'll ask someone else—"

"Leave her out of this," I said.

"Out of what?"

"Whatever it is that we're doing—or not doing. I can't tell. But you leave her the fuck alone."

"What are we doing?" she asked. She raised an eyebrow, and I swear she tucked her tongue against the inside of her cheek.

"Delivering a package," I said. My hand clenched on my knee. "And bringing back a receipt."

"There. See? Not so hard."

"Fuck you," I said.

"Careful," she said. "I've seen some of your films. Don't be giving me any ideas."

She laughed when I blushed and turned away. I watched the scenery scroll by until I was done being bent out of shape by what she knew about my past—both recent and not-so recent.

I heard her move around on the leather seat. A yellow file folder dropped onto my lap. "Which will it be, Mr. Bliss?" she asked. "The package or the girl?"

Inside the folder were two pictures. One was of a young woman standing on a beach, a surf board tucked under her arm. The sun was setting the sky on fire, and the wind was blowing her hair. It was taken with a telephoto lens, and the light was all wrong to see her face, but I knew those shoulders and the lean shape of that body. How many times had I watched her stare out at the water like that? We had surfed like the summer might never end.

With a sigh, I tucked the picture of Dolly behind the other picture in the folder.

It was a long snake, curled up in a white file box. It was some kind of python—pale green, with yellow eyes.

"What is this?" I asked.

"It's Operation Trouser Snake," she said. "That's the package."

CHAPTER 2

Derek dropped off I-5 near the US-Mexico border, and he cruised around an enormous parking lot that embraced a sprawling outlet mall along Camino de la Plaza. There hadn't been much chit-chat during the ride—after I agreed to the job, there hadn't been much to talk about.

Derek wheeled the black sedan next to a sad looking station wagon and stopped. He put the car in park and sat still, his dark glasses making it impossible to tell if he had gone to sleep or if he was staring at me in the rearview mirror.

I looked at the station wagon instead. It needed a wash—in fact, it needed an entire makeover. It had been blocky and out of fashion when it had debuted decades ago. There was never going to be a time when this look was retro. I looked around the rest of the parking lot. We were as far away from the outlet mall as we could possibly be without being in Mexico proper.

"Well, this doesn't look suspicious," I said.

"It's fine," she said. "No one will look closely at that car."

"Are you kidding me? It's exactly the sort of car they're going to look at."

She rolled her eyes. "Derek? Would you show Mr. Bliss to his car?"

He made a noise like a piston grinding, and the car bounced when he opened his door and got out. He opened my door and stood there, a block of stone in a hot parking lot.

The light was bright after riding in the car, and I blinked heavily.

"The photos," she said as I got out of the car.

"What?" I was still holding on to the file folder. "I don't get to keep them as souvenirs of our time together?"

"You don't get to keep them."

"Not even as a friendly reminder of your heartwarming concern for my well-being?"

"You don't need a reminder, Mr. Bliss."

"No, I don't suppose I do."

I put the file folder on the seat between us. Her hand moved to take it, but I pressed it down with my fingers. "You're playing someone," I said. "This isn't just a favor."

She gave me a professional smile, and I saw a glint of something in her gaze that might have been actual warmth. "I'm protecting valuable assets," she said.

"You know I don't give a shit about your assets," I pointed out.

She looked at me for a minute and then dipped her head slightly. "You might," she said.

"Convince me."

She shook her head. "Not today. You don't need to know."

I weighed my options—there weren't many, to be fair—and finally decided I didn't want to play her enigmatic spook game. Too many layers of deceit and bullshit. It wasn't my style. Too much work. It was exhausting.

"I'm going to give you a code name," I said. "In light of your ridiculous Operation Trouser Snake."

"It's a good operation name. No one will take it very seriously."

"To their detriment, right?"

She gave me one of the enigmatic spook shrugs. See? Way too much work.

"Frolic," I said. "After your toenail polish. That's what I'm going to call you."

She gave me a genuine smile—one that made me almost regret being a jerk about things. Almost. But not quite. "I like that name, Mr. Bliss."

"Might make for a decent TV show," I said. "*Frolic and Bliss.*"

"Might be a decent way to spend an afternoon, too," she said.

I thought about that for a second and then shook my head.

"Less emotional baggage with a TV show," I decided.

Her laugh followed me out of the car. I pretended to adjust my shirt, so that I could swallow the stupid grin that was threatening to spill out of my mouth.

Derek remained inscrutable. If he noticed, he gave no sign. "Package and directions are in the back," he said. He held out a tiny metal ring with some keys on it. When I reached for the ring, it slipped out of his grip and fell to the ground.

I looked at the keys and then at Derek. His mouth moved the tiniest amount. Just enough to let the word "asshole" slip out. He got back in the sedan, and I watched the car pull away. Frolic didn't drop a window and give me one of those smoldering looks that femme fatales roll out when they are leaving the frame.

One of the keys unlocked the back, and inside, I found a frayed military-green surplus blanket covering a boxy shape. I lifted the blanket and found a white file box, just like the one I had seen in the picture. It was taped shut, and there were holes along the top and sides. I nudged the box with a knuckle, and it felt like there was something inside. Gee, I wonder what it could be?

There was a file folder next to the box. Inside was a single piece of paper with a couple lines written on it. I scanned the writing. It was an address and a phone number.

I read it again.

The address was in Tijuana.

"Shit," I said.

The tape came off without much effort, and when I had enough of it off to open the lid of the box, I peered inside.

"Shit," I said again.

The snake was much bigger in real life than in the picture.

☆

I drove the station wagon closer to the mall, and parked in the middle of a row of other unremarkable cars. Much better than that conspicuous last slot at the ass-end of the parking lot. I fumbled with the keys, trying to figure out how to lock up with the car without looking like I was breaking into it, and then I went into the air-conditioned mall.

I wasn't about to drive that old clunker across the border with nothing in the back but a cardboard box under a blanket. I might as well stroll up naked with the snake draped around my neck.

How about a cavity search, sir?

Oh, I was hoping you'd ask.

Inside the mall, I bought a duffel bag, a couple of shirts, and several packages of underwear. I stopped at the food court for a hot dog.

Two, in fact, since it was past lunch and I skipped breakfast. Not intentionally. It was just how the day had gone.

It had been quiet these last few weeks. There had been the one job, back in the spring, for the producer guy I had worked with in my former life. After that, I had been in Oregon, and I had missed the story in *The Las Angeles Times* about the ex-porn starlet who had been caught up in a murder cult. Well, there were some dead bodies too, which always makes a salacious story juicier.

Anyway, it turned out the producer guy who had hired me was, in fact, still married to the missing starlet, and part of the reason I had gone north was to avoid his wrath at the publicity. Turned out that he was quite pleased. *Fucking genius,* he had told me later. *Everyone talked about it all summer. I've gotten a dozen offers on her life story already.*

Hollywood. Nothing was too weird or morbid for the jaded executive set, who were like rabid dogs for something more tawdry and watchable than the prime-time train wreck that had captivated viewing audiences the year before.

The producer offered me a bonus. I had demurred, not eager to get caught up in the same greediness as the rest of the starry-eyed hopefuls. He had insisted. I waited a couple of seconds—long enough to assuage my diminishing standards—and then caved. It's how the game is played. The bridge to the moral high road has been out for a long time in Hollywood. There's crazy, which is still bankable to the right demographic and with the right spin, and then there's outright lunacy. People get a whiff of the latter, and they stop returning your calls.

That's when the rumors start. Given my career trajectory over the last decade, I didn't need more rumors.

Other than a couple of weekend gigs, there hadn't been much going on. I didn't mind that, but Mrs. Chow—my erstwhile landlord, even though the bungalow on the back of her lot was mine, free and clear—had started to harangue me about getting out of the house. Too many early morning visits from her and her tiny Pekinese.

The dog wasn't allowed in my house—not after what he did last time—but Mrs. Chow had a tendency to ignore boundaries. This morning, Baby Baby had been running back and forth under my window, barking at who the fuck knows what. Sunbeams. Dragonflies. God, that dog was annoying.

I had thrown on some clothes and gone down to Wilie's, where I did my morning tai chi routine with a couple of the regulars, followed by an hour with the bag and rope. Afterward, a shower and a half hour or so of listening to Willie talk through the investment section of the paper. Eventually, I wandered off, taking the long way home so as to watch the late summer beach bunnies cavort along the boardwalk. And to get a dog at Horatio's stand.

A pretty good day, all in all, until I got to the hot dog stand.

I finished the first of my mall-bought hot dogs, and regarded the second one with some dismay. It looked like a grey earthworm that had been fried in a microwave, and the bun was more like cardboard than processed white bread. No amount of mustard, onions, and relish was going to mask the terrible taste of processed food that had been smothered in plastic and then flash-frozen.

For a moment, I almost missed prison food.

A gaggle of giggly young women at a nearby table provided a distraction from the not-real food on my plate. The quartet was matched in designer tops and short skirts. You could almost tell their home zip codes from their hair styles, and their nails were all shiny with the latest shades.

As I watched, one slipped a tiny bottle from her oversized purse. She dumped the contents into a cup emblazoned with the rictus grin of one of the burger chain mascots. She snapped the plastic lid back on the cup and shoved it toward the woman sitting on her left. The woman shook her head, and I heard her say something about driving, but most of her words were drowned out in a chorus of mean-spirited peer pressure.

The prudent one made a face at the harassment from the other three, but she picked up the cup and sucked delicately from the straw. The others—who had clearly been hitting the sauce and soda for awhile—whooped and laughed.

Gee, it wasn't hard to guess where they were headed.

I gave the dead earthworm in the sawdust box a decent burial in the trash and left the noisy food court. Watching college-age women get drunk before they went into Tijuana for some south of the border action wasn't going to get my packaged delivered. For all I knew, Frolic had someone watching me, ready to snap an entire roll of film that could be sent to the DEA.

The agency hadn't been thrilled about the story in *The LA Times*, even though their name hadn't come up. I had kept things vague when I had called Al Tonkin at the City Desk from a pay phone in Monterey. Al was the one who had done the digging and asked all the questions. It was the DEA's own damn fault for not running a tighter operation. Of course, no government agency likes being slapped about for being sloppy, and shit always trickles down. Going to Oregon had been an attempt to avoid the trickle down.

No, if Frolic was DEA, then she was fucking her own people, and while I wouldn't be surprised if that was how government agency spooks played with each other, I felt like she was working another angle.

I didn't know what she was up to, which meant the best approach was to cover my end. It's like Mr. Chow always said: *The man who knows his place is never surprised.*

I wandered past a cavernous pet store, stopped, and went back. No amount of industrial air freshener could hide the fact that too many cats and dogs and ferrets and what-not were living in cages. There were fish tanks, bird cages, and large aquariums that housed reptiles. A gangly kid, wearing a t-shirt with the store's logo on it, was peering myopically through a set of unflattering eyeglasses at the fish tanks.

He was making notes on a clipboard, and I thought someone should rescue him from the drudgery of counting fish. I went into the store and approached him.

"More than twenty?" I asked

"Wh-what?"

"How do you keep track of the ones you've counted already?"

"I'm not counting fish," he said sullenly.

The page on his clipboard had a long list of fish, and beside many of them were handwritten numbers.

"My mistake," I said. I reached for my bill roll and peeled off a twenty. "You know anything about snakes?" I asked.

"I, uh, yeah," he said. "A little."

"I need something better than that," I said.

"I'm—I'm not sure—"

I dropped another twenty on top of the first one.

"—yeah, okay, I can be your expert," he amended nervously.

"Great. Come with me."

"Out . . . out of the store?"

"Do I look like I have a snake shoved down my pants?" I asked.

It was the wrong choice of words. Somewhere, Frolic was laughing.

The kid blushed and started stammering. His eyes flicked back and forth between me and the pair of cashiers at the front of the store.

"It's not like that," I said. "Look. I've got a snake in a box in my car. It's big and green, and I don't know what the fuck to do with it. Can you help me out?"

"In the parking lot?"

"Yeah. Just right outside."

He hesitated.

"Look, do you want me to bring it in here?" I asked. I waved toward the gals at the cash wraps. "Should I ask one of them about it?"

"No, no," he said. "I'll come out. I'm—I'm your guy." He tucked his clipboard under his arm, and waited for me to lead the way.

His name was Mike, and he was impressed by my snake.

"*Morelia viridis*," he pronounced after looking at what was in the box in the back of the station wagon.

"Uh huh," I said. "And if I was, say, trying to impress someone who wasn't a snake-ologist—"

"A herpetologist," Mike said. "That's what's they're called."

"Okay, great. Say I was talking to a pretty girl. Maybe she came into the store. Maybe she doesn't know shit about snakes. I'm not going to call it a *morelia*—what did you call it?"

"*Morelia viridis*," he said.

"Yeah, that. I'm not going to say that now, am I? No, I'm going to call it a . . ."

Mike got my prompt. "A green tree python."

"Really?"

He shrugged. "That's what it means. *Morelia viridis*. It means green tree python." His spine stiffened. "It's descriptive," he said, as if he was personally offended by my lack of enthusiasm.

"Okay, fine. Green tree python. I can dig that."

The snake, annoyed by all the talking we were doing, slithered about in the box. Its angular head was larger than its body, and its eyes were cold and unblinking.

"They're from New Guinea," Mike said. "Parts of Indonesia."

"Rare?" I asked.

"Not really." He rubbed his ear with a long finger. "This one is a few years old, I guess, judging from its size. I've seen them at the zoo. They can get pretty big."

"Aggressive?"

He let out a snort. "Only if you're a mouse."

I was distracted by a sound of laughter. I looked up and caught sight of the quartet of young women from the food court. They were walking through the rows of parked cars, but they didn't seem like they had a destination in mind.

"How much?" I asked Mike absently. An idea was starting to form in my head.

"For the snake?"

I nodded.

"We don't buy animals," he said. "Not from private collectors."

"No, how much for this snake on the open market?"

"I dunno. A couple hundred dollars, maybe," he said. "But I don't—we don't do that sort of thing."

"Fair enough," I said. I said. I peeled two more twenties off my roll and put them down next to the box. "Can you put it in my duffel bag?" I asked.

"What?"

I had been watching the ladies from the food court, and his confusion snapped my attention back. "Can you put it in my bag?" I repeated. I unzipped the duffel and dumped out the shirts and underpants. "Are you a mouse?" I asked.

"No," he said brusquely.

"So put it in the duffel for me already."

"I don't know, Mister—"

I peeled off another twenty. "Jesus, kid. There's a hundred bucks to lift a snake out of a box and put it in a duffel bag. Stop busting my balls about this."

"All right, all right."

Mike picked up the cash and shoved it into his pocket before he reached into the box. The snake lazily started to loop itself around his arm as he lifted it out the box, and it seemed like it was a lot longer than a few feet. Mike carefully lowered the snake—tail first—into the open mouth of the duffel bag. The snake kept coiling around his arm, but the kid was quick enough that he got the snake in the bag without too much trouble.

"Thanks, kid," I said, clapping him on the arm. "Now, beat it."

He didn't need to be told a second time. As he hustled back to the safety and boredom of his fish-counting job, I pulled the tags off my shirts and unpackaged my underwear. I dumped all the clothes into the bag and zipped it up before the snake could protest. I snagged the paper with the Tijuana address on it, and slammed the hatch shut on the old station wagon.

Hustling across the parking lot, I caught up with the quartet as they finally figured out which car was theirs.

"Excuse me," I said politely, the duffel bag slung over my shoulder. "Maybe we could help each other out."

CHAPTER 3

MY NAME REDUCED TWO OF THEM TO GIGGLES, BUT THE others—the mostly sober one and the one with the stash of mini bottles—smiled politely and listened as I made my offer: I would be their driver for their trip into Mexico.

"There and back?" The designated driver was hopeful.

"There and back," I said. "What's the point of going to Tijuana if everyone can't have a good time, right?"

This made perfect sense to the giggle twins. "Now you can party with us, Steph," one of them said to the designated driver. The other one whooped with delight.

The stern one was glaring at me. She was trying to figure out my angle. "Come on, Pen," the first giggle twin whined. "Let's go already." She was wearing an oversized top that somehow managed to show off the diamond piercing in her navel while simultaneously slipping off first one shoulder and then the other.

"Why do you want to ride with us?" the one called Pen asked.

"Because I don't want to walk the whole way," I said.

The other giggle twin laughed at that. Noisy, braying laughter. The sort of noise that would increase in volume as the evening went on, and not in a pleasant way. At some point, her aggressively displayed cleavage wouldn't be enough of a distraction.

"What's in the bag?" Pen wasn't done grilling me. She didn't like how everyone's attention was on me and not her.

"Underwear and some shirts," I said.

"No drugs." She said it matter-of-factly. Not a question.

"Who walks drugs into Mexico?" I asked. Rhetorically.

"I—I'd feel better about this," Steph said quietly. "I probably shouldn't have drank—"

Pen cut her off with a flap of her well-manicured hand.

"Sixty bucks," she said.

"I'm not asking to be paid," I said.

"No," Pen clarified. "That's what you need to pay." She thought about it for a second. "Each of us," she amended.

I felt the snake move in the bag, and I shifted the duffel against my back, hoping the ladies hadn't noticed the bag moving. "Well, good luck getting into Tijuana," I said. "And if you do"—I looked at Steph—"don't let them talk you into drinking more. Getting popped on the way back is much worse. In fact, you should probably just stay in the car the whole time. Under a street lamp."

Stephanie paled, and even the noisier of the two giggle twins quieted.

I let them eyeball each other.

Waiting was easy. I had years of practice. I doubted any of these ladies had ever waited more than five minutes for anything.

Pen wanted to huddle up and talk about it, but that meant showing indecision in front of me and that wasn't going to happen. The louder of the twins kept opening and closing her mouth like a thought was starting but failing to get all the way down to her throat. Steph had already decided my plan was the right one, and she folded her arms, signaling that she was ready to get on with matters. The other woman—the one with the pierced navel and the slippery top—kept sniffing and playing with her nose.

"She's high," I said to Steph, nodding toward the one with the sniffles. "Did you know about that?"

"What?" The giggler gave me a blast of wide-eyed outrage.

"Are you holding?" I asked her.

"I'm—what are you talking about?" Her voice went up to a tinny shriek.

Pen crossed her arms and gave me a withering glare that probably worked on college boys who were trying to get into her panties. Her left leg was vibrating, which undercut the steeliness of her glare.

This is a bad idea, I decided.

"Have fun, ladies," I said. I hitched the bag up on my shoulder and walked off.

The situation was all wrong. There was a lot about it that made me uncomfortable—the car, the destination, the package. I didn't know who the station wagon belonged to. I didn't know who was waiting for me in Tijuana. Even though my new pal and snake expert Mike didn't think it was illegal to be carrying around a green tree python, it still seemed like I was asking for trouble.

Or, maybe it was all a lot less complicated than I was making it out to be. All I had to do was drive the car across the border, drop off the snake, and come back. Easy, right?

Frolic had leaned on me, but there hadn't been an overt threat. Derek hadn't taken out his gun (which I'm sure he had). He hadn't gotten excited about busting my legs or anything. Frolic had called it a favor, and I knew damn well she was underselling it, as well as not telling me everything. But if this delivery was really important, she wouldn't have sent me off so ill-informed.

Maybe it was just a simple favor.

Nah, it was a means to an end. Unless the snake had swallowed something it shouldn't have, it was a peace offering. A gift. An overture. Delivered by an anonymous messenger, who didn't know any of the players. Who couldn't be compromised because they didn't know anything. Just a stupid mule, and the less the mule knew, the happier everyone would be.

Drop off the snake. Get a receipt.

Therefore, following that line of thinking, the station wagon probably wasn't going to blow up. I wasn't going to get popped at the border. No one would notice . . .

"Hey, Bliss."

I stopped and turned around. The foursome had come to a consensus.

The bag squirmed against my back. The package was getting restless. *Right there with you*, I thought.

"Okay," Pen said. "You can drive us."

They were all about the same height, but Pen's heels made her just a bit taller. Her clothes were just a little better—the silk of her blouse was finer, and the tailoring was slightly more flattering—and her diamond earrings were larger. Without saying a word, everyone would instinctively know which zip code she was from, and how much farther up the hill she lived than her companions.

The tone of her voice—the way she made it sound like she was doing me a favor—curled something in my gut.

"Sixty bucks," I said, suddenly inclined to make a point. Why? You know as well as I: some people approach the world as if they own it. You want to remind them, now and again. Not that it makes any difference, but you try anyway. For your own sanity.

She waved her hand. "No, no. Forget that. You don't have to pay us."

I pointed at her. "You do."

"What?"

"Just so we understand each other. Sixty bucks. I drive you and your friends into Mexico. You pay me sixty more when I drive you back."

Pen fumed, her foot doing a brisk staccato against the pavement. Steph said something too quiet for me to hear, and Pen nearly bit her head off before getting her temper under control. "Fine," she growled at me.

"Fine," I said.

Steph had the keys, and she raised the fob and clicked it. A red Mercedes sedan flashed its lights and chirped.

I stared at the car.

"What?" Steph asked.

"Maybe we should take my car," I said.

"Don't push your luck," Pen snapped. She had taken three twenties out of her tiny purse. She stalked up to me and slapped her hand against my chest. I grabbed the cash before it could flutter away when she removed her hand.

Up close, I had a chance to examine her face. There was a hint of amusement under her mask of annoyance and outrage. When she spun on her foot and walked away, her motions were exaggerated enough that I would notice.

She's going to be trouble, I thought.

"No," I said as she walked around to the front passenger side of the Mercedes. "In the back." I indicated the giggle twins. "With those two."

She gave me the death glare again, which slid off me as readily as it had the first time.

"And you"—my finger paused on one of the twins—"lose the top before we get to the border. And if you can handle making out with your partner there, all the better."

They stared at me.

I explained it to them. "I'm driving four sexy—and slightly drunk—women into Mexico in a bright red Mercedes M Class. One of you is probably holding on to some coke"—I held up a hand to forestall any protestations—"and I don't care which of you is, but we're going to sell these border guys a story that'll give them something to masturbate to later, when they get off shift. Which is all they're going to think about when we roll past, okay? It's Hot Tarts & Hot Wheels. That's what we're selling."

Steph giggled, and then quickly covered her mouth as if embarrassed to have been caught having fun. "That sounds like a porn film," she admitted.

"As a matter of fact, it was," I said.

My third film. Bobby Banger had been the lead. He played the Driver. The producers were looking to make a name for themselves, and they had cast a lot of fresh faces, gambling that one of them was about to take off. They got lucky. Bobby's career took off like a rocket after *Hot Tarts & Hot Wheels.*

Me? I had been Stud in the Trunk. It was another year before I got a role with an actual name attached to it.

At the border proper, I was as invisible as you'd expect in a car filled with half-naked drunk co-eds making out with each other. More so when I explained to the nearly drooling idiot staring through the driver's side window that the one in the middle—*yes, the one with the agile tongue who was fiercely rubbing against the large breasts of her friend, that one*—she was my niece. *Yes, I was their chaperone. Wasn't I the good uncle?*

Which meant—in the feverish fantasies these border guards were imagining—I wasn't fucking any of them. But someone had to, right? That's where it all went, and since I wasn't in the picture, they would cast themselves.

Not now, of course, but later, after they waved us through.

Ah, yes. Have a good time. Welcome to Mexico.

No one asked about the duffel bag stuffed under my legs. I'm not even sure any of them saw it. Would you?

"That was fun," Cathy sighed as we cruised past the obvious tourist traps.

I glanced up at the rearview mirror, and offered her a smile. She was the one without the top. The other one—the noisy laugher—was Marsha. They had introduced themselves shortly after we had left the parking lot, a sure sign everyone was on-board with the evening's plan.

In the corner of the mirror, I caught sight of Pen glaring at me, and I couldn't tell if she was pissed that the plan had worked or that she hadn't been included in the fun. *No one wants to play with the bitchy ones*, I thought. Important life lesson.

"Where are we going?" I asked.

"You're the one driving," Pen snapped from the back seat.

I ignored her, and looked over at Steph—well, *Stephanie*, though she didn't want to be a bother about it. Stephanie toyed with her hair for a second, and then pointed at a building covered in garish neon. "There," she said.

"You sure?" I asked.

She nodded. In the back seat, Marsha bounced up and down, clapping her hands.

There was a lot beyond the club, and a guy in a black shirt and big sunglasses wanted twenty American before he'd let me on the lot. I gave him a bill, and he pointed at the back of the lot. When I shook my head, he shrugged and didn't move. I gave him the rest of the money Pen had thrown at me, and his mood changed.

"He's going to rip us off," Pen said as I eased the car toward a spot at the front of the lot.

"No, he isn't," I said. I turned the wheel sharply, and eased the Mercedes into a space where we could see the street. "We're VIPs. We're going to spend money at his club. They're going to be nice to us. We'll have a good time, stagger home, and tell all our friends about this place." I turned off the car. "The third or fourth time you come down? That'll be when they rip you off, when they know what you're worth."

Stephanie looked like she might throw up.

"Okay," I said. "Pep talk over. Have fun!"

Marsha and Cathy were out of the car in an instant, leaving Pen alone in the back seat. She leaned forward, her hand outstretched. "Give me the keys," she said.

"No," I said.

"You're going to drive off as soon as we're inside," she said, displaying a level of cunning I hadn't expected.

"Where would I go?" I played the innocent.

"Back across the border."

I gave Stephanie a wide-eyed look. "Why would I do that?"

Pen snapped her fingers. "Come on, asshole. Give me the keys."

"No," I said again. "I'm not going to leave you here."

"I don't believe you."

"I really don't have any interest in being caught with a hot car."

"That's such bullshit," she sneered.

"I don't need the hassle," I said. "And grand theft auto is—trust me—a hassle."

Stephanie gave a curious look, her eyebrows elevated. She had figured out what I wasn't saying. Pen, on the other hand, was oblivious.

"You're just going to sit in the car while we're in there partying and having a good time?"

"No," I said. "I've got my own idea of a good time."

"While driving around in my car."

"I'm not going anywhere in your car," I said.

This was one of those conversations that was going to go round and round forever. Pen was well practiced at it, and I imagined she usually stamped her foot and held her ground long enough for the other person to throw in the towel. While, in principle, I wanted to be as obstinate, who was I trying to impress.

"Look, I get it," I said. "But I'm not giving you the keys. You're going to be in even *less* shape to drive back to the US in a few hours."

"We'll be fine," Pen said, but there wasn't as much fire in her tone as there had been.

"I'm your designated driver," I said. "Just leave it alone."

Pen narrowed her eyes, still fuming, and this might have gone on for some time, but Stephanie was getting restless. "Come on, Pen," she said. "Marsha and Cathy have already gone in. This isn't what we came down here for. I trust him. Let's go and have some fun."

Pen leaned forward, her hand held out again.

I cut her off before she could start. "Hang on." I pulled the key out of the ignition and showed it to her. "There's the ignition key and this is the security fob for the doors. How about I give you the fob and I keep the key?"

"You can key into the car without the fob," she pointed out.

"Then I'll keep the fob and you can have the key," I said.

"Fine," Pen said. She snapped her fingers impatiently. I worked the key off the ring and put it in the center of her hand, which folded over it like a Venus Flytrap over a lazy fly. "We'll call you when we're ready," she said.

I cleared my throat. "Call me?" I asked.

"Oh, for fuck's sake." She rolled her eyes. "Stephanie, give him your number."

"I don't have a phone," I said.

"What kind of moron are you?" Pen asked, but she didn't give me a chance to answer. "Just give him your phone," she said to Stephanie. And then, with a loud sigh of disgust as if this was just *another* example of how *shitty* the world was at not doing *exactly* what *she* wanted, she huffed her way out of the car—slamming the door behind her—and stomped off across the lot.

Stephanie, somewhat apologetically, extricated a tiny red object from her purse. "It flips open," she explained, and I did just that with the oblong object in my hand. A tiny screen showed me the time on one side. Back in LA, it was coming up on rush hour—that long stretch of time between mid-afternoon and sunset when no one went anywhere quickly.

"Right, right," I said.

She put her hand on my knee, and then pulled it away almost as quickly. "She's not always like that," Stephanie said.

"Yeah, she probably is," I said.

Stephanie tried to brush off my response with a tiny movement of her shoulders, but she wasn't fooling anyone. She put her hand on the back of her neck and ducked her head. Embarrassed by the whole thing.

"Have fun," I said, nodding toward the club. "I'll be here when everyone has had enough."

"Will you?" she asked, and when she raised her head and looked at me, there was real concern in her eyes. All the things she had imagined going bad in the last few years were going to be manifestly real when she and her friends staggered out of the club. It would be her fault, of course, because she was the one they had picked to babysit them—which had been a bullshit set-up from the get-go, and they all knew it. They had ceded responsibility for everything to her because it was never their fault. But Stephanie had gone along with it all, because Pen and her friends were important. They were popular. They could make her life better, couldn't they? Stephanie wanted to fit in. She wanted to be liked. All she had to do was make sure this party wagon to Tijuana didn't turn into a nightmare. How hard could that be?

"Yeah," I said. "I'll be here." She kept staring at me, wanting something more than words, and so I gave her a little glimpse inside. That same sort of glimpse I gave the assholes in the yard at Tehachapi who didn't believe me when I said I wasn't going to move to a different seat in the cafeteria. The place inside which Mr. Chow had shown me how to find.

Blood and thunder and the end of the fucking world as they know it, he had said. He had poked me in the chest with his finger. Making sure he had my attention. *They asked nicely, and you tell them no in the same tone. But that's where it ends. Show them why. What they do next is their choice. Tell them that. It's your choice, motherfuckers. But everything that comes after is all mine.*

During my time inside, there had been a couple of idiots who thought I was bluffing. *There'll be one in every crowd,* Mr. Chow said, *but that's okay. It's how the rest learn the rules.*

CHAPTER 4

I SAT IN THE CAR AWHILE AFTER STEPHANIE AND PEN WENT into the club. The duffel bag was on the passenger seat, and its sides kept bulging in and out, a slow ripple that ran the length of the bag. The green tree python was exploring his new cage. They weren't venomous and they didn't bite. They wrapped themselves around their prey and squeezed. I didn't know if they squeezed so hard that bones shattered or if they squeezed so tight their prey suffocated. Either way, when their prey was dead, the python slowly swallowed it, like a low-rent magician hoping no one would notice as he made an egg disappear at a kid's birthday party.

Eventually, the bag stopped moving and the ladies didn't come back out, and so I figured it was time to do what I needed to do in Tijuana. I slipped Stephanie's phone into a back pocket, grabbed the bag, and got out of the car. I beeped the locks and then dropped the fob into my other back pocket. The folded slip of paper with the address and phone number I kept in hand.

As I wandered across the lot, the lights atop the leaning metal poles flickered on, bathing the half-empty lot with unnatural light. Off to my left, the sun was slipping away behind the confusion of buildings that lined the main thoroughfare into Tijuana, leaving nothing but an orange stain spreading along the rooftops.

The guy watchdogging the lot didn't get up from his plastic lawn chair when I approached.

I told him the street name of where I wanted to go.

He shrugged.

"Not your department, right?" I said.

He shrugged again, and went back into whatever zen space he lived in to make the job of sitting on his ass tolerable.

"*Gracias*," I said.

I had better luck with the first cab I waved down.

The address wasn't that far—a mile or so farther down the road and two blocks off the main drag. It was a block that looked like it was struggling toward the last century. The tallest building was three stories high, and the narrow windows on the upper floors gave no indication if it was residential or office space. The ground floor had that universal industrial warehouse charm to it. There weren't any windows, and I spotted a narrow loading dock halfway down the block. There were three doors along the long side of the block, and metal numbers were nailed above each door. None of them were the number I was looking for.

The cabbie didn't offer to stick around when I got out of the car, and I watched his car rumble up the block and turn left. On the other side of the street, it was all much livelier. There were shops and bars, including a taqueria which was where all the locals ate. Tables overflowed along the sidewalk in either direction, and every seat was taken. People were talking loudly, and I could hear music struggling out of cheap speakers within the restaurant.

The address I was looking for was two doors closer. It looked like a bookstore, and I ambled across the street to check it out. It was one of those eclectic shops that wasn't interested in carrying the popular stuff. The window display was filled with leftist manifestos, Communist rants, and what looked like naturalist poetry books written by retired revolution-aries. A small stack of garishly-covered science fiction filled up one corner. It looked like the sort of place where it would be difficult to tell the difference between a book club meeting and a opposition party planning session.

The bag hung heavily in my left hand, swaying slightly as the contents shifted.

I watched people drinking and laughing for a few minutes, watching to see if anyone cared about a tanned touristy-looking fellow with a duffel bag, standing around like he was lost. No one cared. I took a final glance over at the warehouse. Nothing moved in any of the windows of the upper floors. It was all very quiet.

My timing was off. Frolic had picked me up around noon. It had taken us a few hours to get down to the border, and now, it was well into happy hour (though it's always happy hour in Tijuana). If there was a timetable on this delivery, I had blown it. Hell, it had probably been blown before Frolic had even decided to track me down. Which meant that either no one was actively waiting for me to show up, or they had been waiting all day and, by now, were probably in a real shitty mood.

I was starting to feel an edge of that mood myself. *Get on with it*, I thought, and I pushed open the door of the bookstore.

A bell over the door tinkled as I entered, and a thin man with black-rimmed glasses and a brown cardigan looked up from behind the narrow counter. "*Hola*," he offered.

"How's it going?" I replied.

He gave me a nervous smile, which could mean a lot of things, all things considered.

The store was cramped, but what little bookstore wasn't? The aisles between the shelves were narrow. There were stacks of books rising up like mushrooms, and more books were stacked on top of the bookcases. A grey and white cat lounged on an old overstuffed parlor chair that had faded to a color somewhere between grey and mildew. The store smelled like wet socks, moldy paper, and fruit that should have been thrown out a long time ago. A tiny thread of smoke struggled up from an incense burner parked precariously on a stack of unjacketed hardcovers. It wasn't doing the job, unless it was the source of the old fruit smell.

"Can I help you find something?" The clerk spoke English, having cleverly deduced that I was from out of town.

"You got any Thoreau?"

His eyes opened slightly at my question, a tiny glimmer of life coloring his face. He leaned to one side and pointed toward an aisle on my right. "Down there," he said. When I started in that direction, he cleared his throat and pointed at my bag. "Would you mind leaving that up here?"

"Not at all." When I put the bag on the counter, it squirmed uncharacteristically.

The cat hissed from its chair.

The clerk stared at the bag, blinking steadily. "Oh," he said.

"Yeah," I said.

He picked up the receiver on an old rotary phone and started dialing.

I glanced at the cat. Obviously *Oh* and *Yeah* were the sign and countersign. Good guess on my part, right?

The cat growled, its claws rippling against the threadbare seat of the chair.

The clerk glanced at me nervously while he waited for someone to answer the phone. I thought about checking out the store's selections, but I didn't want to leave the bag alone with the cat. I feigned interest in the row of worn paperbacks along the front of the counter. Some were in English. Most of them were in Spanish. They were a mix of mysteries, horror, and fantasy novels. All with lurid covers of half-naked women being chased by ghosts, shadowy men, or weird monsters that were half-goat and half-crustacean.

"Ah," he said when someone answered. He spoke rapidly in Spanish. Listened, and nodded, and then nodded again. "Okay," he said. I caught a little bit of what was being said. *There is a man here with a bag*—me—and the clerk was asking if I should wait or go. He got an answer that he liked, because he stopped looking like he was about to vomit, and he hung up the phone.

"Okay," he said, looking at me.

"Okay," I said.

"The middle door," he said, pointing out the front window of the store. "Across the street, there. You see?"

I looked, and saw. "I do," I said.

"Knock twice, and then go in," he said.

I grabbed the paperback with the goats wearing crab armor. "How much?" I asked.

"Take it," he said.

I offered him the smallest bill on my roll—a ten—but he just shook his head. "I can't make change," he said. "Not US."

I left the bill on the counter anyway. "Nice shop," I said. I slipped the paperback into my back pocket, and lifted the bag from the counter. The cat hissed again, and I smiled at its righteous indignation. How dare I bring a snake into a bookstore?

The street was still empty, and the light and noise from the taqueria was growing bolder as the sky darkened. I crossed the street and went to the middle door. I knocked twice, and then tried the knob. It was unlocked.

It was dark inside, and my attention was drawn to my left, where a band of light was shining under a closed door at the far end of a hallway. Before my eyes could adjust more to the gloom, the door to the street slammed shut behind me. Someone shoved me forward. I rolled with the push, but stopped short of banging my face against the cheap drywall.

"¡Tire la bolsa."

I shook my head. "I'm not dropping the bag," I said.

"Imbécil—"

Something hard poked me in the back—like a stick or the barrel of a gun. When I didn't flinch, it poked me again. Mid-back, on my right side. Useful information, because now I knew where the guy was standing and how tall he was.

When I looked over my shoulder, I could make out the general shape of a guy a couple inches shorter than me. He was close. It had to be a pistol he was poking me with. Otherwise, he'd be standing farther back. "You gonna shoot me?" I asked.

"Right here?"

He called me an idiot again. He raised the gun, like he was going to point it at my face instead of grinding it against my kidney.

I didn't wait for him to finish. I pivoted, sweeping my right arm over his. Classic tai chi move—scooping air and bringing it down to lift your spirit. His arm was trapped against my side, and while he was still trying to pull free, I slammed my head forward, hitting the brittle part of his nose with the hard part of my head. He made a funny choking noise, and his legs got all rubbery. I let go of his arm, and as he slipped free, I stripped the gun out of his hand.

He wasn't quite done yet. He wobbled for a second, caught himself, and then came at me. I cracked him across the face with the butt of his gun, and that took the rest of the fight out of him. He collapsed, whimpering.

I walked down the hall, and pushed open the door at the end.

The room contained a pair of beat-up metal desks and an old sofa that leaned like it was missing its back legs. There were two guys in the room, and they were dressed like they were hoping to be extras in a gangster movie: hoodies, white t-shirts, work pants slung low, name brand sneakers with the laces all puffed up. They had guns like the other guy, which they pointed at me when I walked into the room.

I let them look at me, waiting for them to realize that I was holding the gun I had taken from their pal by the barrel. Unless I was going to pull some crazy Hong Kong style stunt of spinning the gun in my open hand and then firing it blind with my pinkie finger, I wasn't any threat to them. "*No problema*," I said.

We stared at each other for a few seconds, and I felt some of the tension bleed out of the room. Neither lowered their guns, but their stances relaxed the tiniest bit. I walked over to the nearest desk and put down the gun and the bag. "I'm the delivery boy," I said as I backed up a few feet. "I'm supposed to drop this off. That's all."

They both thought about that for a minute, and I thought maybe we were going to put the guns away and get down to business, but then the guy from the hall burst into the room, ruining the calm atmosphere I had carefully cultivated.

There was blood on his face, and he started yelling and pointing. When neither of his pals started shooting, he darted over to the desk and snatched up his gun. The weapon made him braver, and his tone got uglier. He wasn't a handsome fellow to start with—he was missing some of his lower teeth, and a scar made his left eye droop—and the blood caked around his nose didn't help.

I noted that he was careful to stay out of arm's reach, though.

One of the other guys lowered his gun and started yelling at Droopy. The third man—the one who came off as the calmest, which was, I suspected, nothing more than a facade for some serious twitchery—backed away from his pal. Making sure he wasn't in the line of fire in case people started shooting.

That's when I started to get nervous. If Twitch was worrying about getting shot accidentally, what did that mean for me? Maybe I should—

The bag rolled over on the desk, and a gun went off.

Everyone flinched, and we all shut up for a second. But only a second. The man in the middle turned and started yelling at Twitch, who replied with equal gusto. Droopy yelled at both of them.

I watched the bag on the desk. It was thrashing and jerking. There was a bullet hole in the bag.

"*Problema*," I said. Not that any of them were listening to me.

CHAPTER 5

THEY KEPT YELLING AND GESTURING WITH THEIR GUNS, AS IF all the talk and posturing was going to make a difference. The bag finally rolled off the desk, leaving behind a red smear, and that put an end to all the jabber.

Twitch lowered his gun, and the guy in the middle followed suit. Droopy kept shoving his gun in my direction. He was still pissed about our interchange in the hall.

"That's the problem with dick measuring contests," I said. "Someone always has the shorter dick."

His face darkened—a decision was being made in his brain—but he was brought up short by a word from the guy in the middle of the room. Droopy resigned himself to grinding his teeth and giving me a death glare, but I ignored him.

It was the guy in the center of the room who was in charge.

That guy retrieved his phone from a pocket. Whoever he dialed answered quickly, and he spoke rapidly and obliquely. Keeping his language vague. *There's a problem with the delivery.*

"*Muerto,*" I offered.

Phone Guy glared at me. "*La serpiente está muerta,*" he admitted, and then he followed up with some noises that didn't sound like a real explanation. Twitch had the good grace to look embarrassed during this part of the call.

Phone Guy shifted back and forth as he listened. "OK," he said. His eyes darted from me to Droopy and then to the stain on the desk. "OK," he said again.

I gave Droopy a genial smile. "Okay," I said. Much like my conversation with the bookseller across the street. *This is all going to be fine. There's no problem here.*

Droopy sneered at me. His hand was still tight on his gun.

"OK," Phone Guy said again. His gaze hopped around the room again: me, Droopy, desk. "OK," he said one more time, and this time his gaze went to the desk and Droopy. Not me.

I didn't like the omission.

"No snake," he said, pocketing his phone. "No deal."

"OK," I said. My response surprised him. "Look, I'm just the messenger," I explained. "I don't care one way or another. My job was to drop it off. Get a receipt. And then I—"

"A what?" Phone Guy interrupted me.

"Receipt," I said. "Something that says I brought you the snake."

"You didn't bring us a snake," he said.

"I did," I said. "Twitch over there shot it."

He looked over at the guy in the corner of the room, who firmed up his mouth and shook his head, like he had no idea what I was talking about. He muttered something and I caught Phone Guy's name: Julio.

Julio shrugged. "He didn't see a snake," he translated for me.

"Yeah, I caught that," I said.

Julio looked at Droopy. "You see a snake?" he asked.

Droopy's gaze flicked down for a second. He half-raised his gun when his gaze came up. "*No hay serpiente*," he said.

"No snake, huh?" I bent—which made everyone flinch—and picked up the bag. I dropped it on the desk, and we all stared at the bloody hole in the side. "You want me to open it?" I asked.

"It doesn't matter," Julio said.

"It does to me," I said. I unzipped the bag, and reached in like I did this sort of thing every day. I grabbed a coil of the slack snake and pulled out a length of bloodstained tree python, along with one of the cotton briefs I had bought. The damn snake had gotten tangled in my underwear. I kept hauling until all of it was out of the bag, in case any of them weren't sure what we were looking at. One four foot green tree python, deceased.

"Here you go," I said, dropping its bloody length on the bag. "One *morelia viridias*. As ordered."

Julio wanted to be pedantic. "It's dead. We didn't ask for a dead snake."

"It wasn't dead when I walked in here," I said. "It wasn't dead when Short Dick here decided to rough me up in the hall. It wasn't dead when you and Twitch were waving guns at me."

Julio dismissed all of my words with a wave of his hand. "We're not paying you for a dead snake."

"I'm not asking you to pay—wait, what?"

Frolic had said something about a "receipt." This guy thought he was supposed to—

Julio rubbed two fingers together—the universal sign for cold cash. "Yeah," he said. "What did you think—"

"I'm just the messenger," I said lamely, as I tried to figure out what angle I had missed.

Twitch said something and Julio shook his head. "*Mensajaro*," he said.

"*¿Mensajero?*" Twitch echoed.

"*Imbécil*," Droopy said.

"It's starting to look that way, isn't it?" I said.

I casually let my hands touch the snake. Let them slide along its length. Looking for the tail.

Julio snorted. "*Imbécil*," he said. He looked at Twitch, who went for the full belly laugh.

Droopy, on the other hand, wasn't feeling the mood. He was still pissed about what I had done to his face. All this hilarity wasn't fixing his ego. He raised his gun, and in rapid-fire Spanish, started listing his grievances. I caught idiot—*imbécil*—again. He was angry about his nose. He wanted to return the favor. And then some.

Julio listened as Droopy went on, a wry smile on his face, and when Droopy finally ran out steam, he shrugged. *So do something about it*, his shrug said.

We all stood there for a moment, thinking about what was going to happen next, and then Droopy sealed it. "OK," he said.

I had a firm grip on the snake's tail when I pivoted. The snake whipped off the table, and I smacked Droopy in the chest with it. His eyes were wide—he had had a split second to realize what I was doing—and his gun went off. The bullet went somewhere; I distantly heard it ricochet off the concrete floor. He was wrestling with the snake when I ran into him, and all three of us went down. We squirmed and wrestled on the floor, the snake tangled between us. I grabbed Droopy's ears and banged his head against the floor a few times. When he let go of his gun, I grabbed it, leaving him glassy-eyed and snake-tied.

There was gunfire as I rolled against the side of the desk. I peered under the barrier and spotted Twitch's legs. He was standing in a spread-legged stance on the other side of the room. That was a target I could hit. I fired twice, and Twitch spun around with a loud squawk.

I slid to the other end of the desk and took a peek. Julio had bolted. I saw the door on the other side of the room closing on its own accord. Was he splitting or running to find some friends?

Droopy was starting to come around, and cuddling with a dead snake was more than he was ready to deal with. I thought about putting a bullet in him so that he'd shut up, but that would complicate an already fucked up situation. Twitch was down, but he was still twitching. Julio had the right idea. I took a couple of deep breaths, and then scampered for the door I had entered through earlier. A couple of rounds hit the walls around me as I reached the door. Incentive to keep moving. The door to the street wasn't locked, and I went through it without slowing down.

Once on the sidewalk, I shoved the gun into my pocket and pulled out my shirt to cover the bulge. I ran a hand through my hair, realized there was blood on my shirt sleeve, and rolled up both sleeves as I quickly walked across the road.

The first dinner rush was over, and several of the tables at the taqueria were empty. I smiled at a trio of well-dressed ladies as I walked by. Don't mind me; just passing through. But I had a better thought after I passed them, and I doubled back. There was an open table behind them—closer to the restaurant— and I sat down, angling my chair so I could see the warehouse without directly facing it.

The women at the table had been drinking for awhile, and they gave me a once-over. Two of them did a more critical assessment, and some chatter went back and forth. No one said *imbécil* and they thought my flushed appearance made me quite rugged. I smiled and nodded, as if I didn't understand a word they were saying, and when the waitress showed up, I fumbled my way through an order for a couple of margaritas and fish tacos.

"And some fizzy water, please," I called out as an afterthought.

Blood is a pain in the ass to get out of clothing if it dries.

Never run, Mr. Chow said.

We were in the yard, watching a bevy of guards separate a pair of inmates who had bumped each other one too many times during a "friendly" basketball game.

The guilty run, he said. *An idiot runs. Cops are like cats. They react to movement. The little bunny freezes when he's been spotted out in the open. Why? Because he disappears.*

No, he doesn't, I said. *He's right there. Out in the open. He's probably not even camouflaged.*

You and I can see him, Mr. Chow said. *But we aren't hunters.* He touched his cheek. *Our eyes are in front. We are always looking forward. Predators have eyes on the sides of their heads. They're always looking around. They see movement. They don't have good depth perception. Everything is flat to them.*

He nodded toward the game. *Wee Wee over there is playing ball. Knuckles, however, is playing a different game, and Wee Wee—well, Wee Wee doesn't have eyes on the side of his head. He can put a ball through a hoop, but the guy with the sharpened spoon on his left? He doesn't see him coming.* Mr. Chow tapped his head again. *Especially with that detached retina.*

The guards pulled the two men apart. There was blood on Wee Wee's uniform, as well as his lips and chin. One of the guards was shouting into his rig, calling for medical assistance. The other guards getting nervous. There were five of them, but there were three times that number of inmates in the yard.

It's going to go bad, I said.

Mr. Chow shook his head. *No,* he said. *You still don't see the game that is being played, do you?*

The guards flicked out their riot rods as they tried to watch all the inmates at once. Guards on the wall were shouting at the inmates milling along the edge of the makeshift basketball court. Telling them to back away. Get down on the ground. Assume the position. Mr. Chow and I were over on the weight benches, a good distance from the ruckus, but we both sat very still.

Off to our left, the main doors burst open, and dozen guards came barreling into the yard. Riot rods out. Guns drawn. Big and loud and serious. Inmates were shouting too, and everyone was looking at the court. Waiting to see what was going to happen. There was blood in the air, after all.

Back by the doors, something moved. An inmate, his jumpsuit stripped down to his waist so that his white t-shirt was clearly visible, stepped away from the wall where he had been standing. He slipped through the doors before they shut.

See? Mr. Chow said. *If it isn't in front of us, we're liable to not notice it. Especially when there is something else to look at.*

Mr. Chow spent the last years of his life in the California Department of Corrections and Rehabilitation for fraud. That's where we met. I was in for drugs, and, later, for violence in the prison shower. I hadn't done any of the things I was incarcerated for, but that's what all misunderstood inmates say, right? Mr. Chow, on the other hand, had done many things the State of California and various agencies of the federal government would like to pin on him, but the best they could do was wire fraud and tax evasion. Enough to send him up to the facility at Tehachapi, where, they hoped—off the record, of course—a different sort of justice would be meted out for old Mr. Chow. Accidents happen all the time, even in a medium security prison stashed away in the picturesque Sierra Nevadas.

Mr. Chow was a smart man and knew a lot about a lot of things, including the odds that a naive ex-porn star who had been made an example of by a righteous LA DA with broader political plans would survive his incarceration. *Eighteen to one,* he had told me later. There had been a pool—there was a pool for everything, frankly, even though no one had any money—and he cashed out after the incident in the shower with Lando Turk. The Double Zees ate a lot of his markers for that one.

Mr. Chow was always accomplishing three things in the space of one action.

It was only after we were both out—me, for having served my time; him, so that CDCR wouldn't have to deal with the medical costs of having him linger on a long time as the cancer chewed him up—that I came to realize how time spent in the California penal system had been a solution to an existing problem. He hadn't gotten caught because he had been stupid; he had gotten caught because it made his life easier. Meeting me had been a happy accident—near as I could tell—and Mr. Chow, even after death, was always gracious about the happy accidents in his life. That didn't make him any less of a manipulative asshole, but, at least, I always knew where he and I stood.

Mr. Chow left me a tiny bungalow in the back corner of one his Venice properties. Mrs. Chow lived in the main house, and I took her shopping once or twice a month. When she wasn't managing the half dozen salons the family owned from West Hollywood to Venice, she badgered me about getting a job or a girlfriend or both. I didn't need a job. My adult entertainment days were well behind me, and the skills I had picked up while in the cosy embrace of the California penal system weren't exactly resumé-friendly. I did the occasional favor for friends and friends of friends. Money came my way. It was almost like a job, and I got to set the hours, which was nice.

Mr. Chow's oldest son managed the convenience stores that made up half of the family empire, along with a handful of custom car shops which were where his passion lay. The youngest son managed a building full of accountants, which may have seemed like a lot less to handle, but I had heard they can get unruly if the numbers don't line up. The middle brother was a chef, and Angel—both the joy and terror of Mrs. Chow's life—was finishing up a law degree at UCLA. All in all, a nice and respectable family with respectable businesses.

Well, sure, the patriarch had ties to Hong Kong triads, but since he's dead now, why ruin the Chinese-American success story with old lies and unconfirmed rumors?

Shortly after my margaritas arrived, Julio came out of the warehouse. He glanced up and down the street, and when he didn't see anything obvious, he wandered toward the end of the block. When he got there, he looked up and down the other street. He didn't see anything, and he came back, passing the warehouse door. He looked over at the taqueria as he went by, but his gait didn't change.

He saw the ladies—he was as much a man as I, after all— and maybe he realized there was someone sitting behind them, drinking a margarita, but he didn't notice. The ladies were more interesting, even though they weren't what he was looking for. He got all the way to the end of the block before he pulled out his phone and made the call he wasn't looking forward to.

I winked at one of the ladies—the one on the right with the dusky eyes and the mouth that kept curling into a smile. She made eye contact, and wet the edge of her glass with her tongue before she drank. I raised my glass in appreciation, and settled back to wait for my food.

A few minutes later, a Honda with large wheels and steel rims roared up the street. It slammed to a stop, and Julio hurried over. For an instant, I caught sight of the other occupants, and then Julio was in the car. The Honda made a lot of noise as it drove away, and the ladies were clearly not impressed. *Poor Droopy*, I thought. *So much compensation.*

He had been driving, and the guy in the back seat had been Twitch.

My tacos arrived, and they were hot and delicious. As I wolfed them down, I thought about the snake. The night hadn't turned out well for him. Shoved in a bag. His head caught in a pair of men's briefs. He had probably been hungry. That's why he had been squirming around.

I felt bad about that, but only until the second margarita kicked in.

CHAPTER 6

AFTER HAVING A QUIET MEAL, I DECIDED TO WALK BACK TO the club. It wasn't far, and I didn't expect the girls to be done any time soon. I dug Stephanie's phone out of my pocket as I walked. It hadn't made any noise or vibrated during the last hour, though when I deciphered the tiny symbols on the screen, I wasn't sure it was getting any service. Pen couldn't call if she wanted to. I slipped the phone back into my pocket and picked up my pace.

Very little of what had happened since Frolic had picked me up made sense, which only heightened my unease. Why pay someone to haul a snake across the border for a delivery that had all the trappings of a drug deal? There had been a lot of hardware and attitude on display—much more than was necessary for a green tree python. It wasn't even poisonous, for crying out loud.

On the one hand, I should call the number Frolic left me. On the other, did I care? What were the possible outcomes of me calling and and telling them the deal had gone sour? Was Frolic going to thank me for my service and shrug it off? Probably not. It was likely that she'd follow through with her threat and tell the DEA where they could find Dolly, but now that I thought about it, the DEA probably already knew where she was. Last I heard, they had her brother, and they were likely to be in contact. So what did Frolic actually have on me for leverage?

Nothing.

And that lack of *something* gnawed at me. During my walk, I kept replaying the conversation in the back seat. What had I missed? By the time, I reached the parking lot next to the club, I had to admit defeat. Either Frolic was a total master at double-speak and ambiguity, or the favor was pretty much exactly as it had seemed: a dumb package drop on a trio of dumb gangbangers. Things had just gotten out of hand.

A different guy was watching the lot, and I nodded as I passed. I stopped by the car and used the fob to open the trunk. I leaned over, keeping my hands out of sight, and popped the magazine out of the gun I had taken from Droopy. After tucking the now-empty gun out of sight, I closed the trunk and went into the club.

No point in sitting and stewing.

Three hours and one tour through the vomitorium later, I managed to herd the ladies out of the club. It took two of us to pour Marsha into the back seat, and Cathy took the middle seat so she could prop the drunk woman up. Stephanie wasn't as bad off, but she was roaming around some deep vale of bitterness, and I put her in the back seat too. That meant Pen was riding shotgun, and as I queued up in the line at the border, she got talkative.

"Do you like women, Butch?" she asked.

"What?" I had been zoning out on the line of headlights ahead of us, idly dreaming about a day that might have been: a couple of street cart hot dogs, a lazy afternoon, and a beer or two before crawling—alone—into a comfortable bed.

"Are you gay?" Pen clarified.

"No," I said. "No, I'm not gay. What the hell are you talking about?"

She turned in the seat and pressed her back against the car door. Her top was a blue silk blouse with buttons up the front, and it was sheer enough to see her bra and camisole underneath. When I glanced over, there was enough glare from the streetlights to see that she had lost both undergarments at some point during the evening.

"No, you're not." She smiled and toyed with the collar of her blouse as I pulled my attention back to the bumper of the car in front of us. "Silly mistake on my part. Sorry."

"It's all right," I said.

"I wondered," she continued. "Because, you know, when we came across the border, Cathy and Marsha were doing all that stuff in the backseat. You never looked. I wondered what kind of guy doesn't watch two hot women fondling each other?"

"I've seen it a couple of times," I said.

Out of the corner of my eye, I watched her fumble with one of the buttons on her blouse. "Yeah?"

"Yeah," I said. I distracted myself with a few questions. *How many cars were ahead of us? How fast were they moving? How long would it take her to get bored with the strip tease and move on to something else?* Not liking any of the answers, I kept my hands firmly on the wheel and looked at her.

Three buttons were undone—which was already quite a display—and if she undid the fourth . . .

"If you pop another button, you're going to show me everything," I said.

"And . . . what's wrong with that?" she asked, fingering the button in question.

"I like a little mystery," I said.

She pouted, but her fingers moved away from the button.

"I tell you what," I offered. "You can undo it right before we get to the border. It'll give the lads a bit of a late night perk-me-up."

"I don't want to show *them* my tits," she said. "I want *you* to look at them."

She had a bit of pronoun confusion going on there, but I wasn't going to school her. No more than I was going to tell her where and when she could flash her tits, though I did approve of her ability to maintain standards, even in her inebriated state.

It wasn't lost on me that earlier in the evening, she hadn't liked me at all, so that was a positive turn. Comparatively speaking, her night couldn't have been as awkward as mine, but it's all a matter of perspective, right? And for a woman like Pen, with her perky tits and fancy car—both of which were probably paid for by mommy and daddy—it was no fun being ignored.

Me, on the other hand? Being ignored meant I would have had that hot dog, that lazy afternoon, and that beer before bed.

"They're nice," I said, focusing on the positive.

"Nice?"

"Yeah," I said.

"That's it? Just 'nice'?" She squirmed on the seat and her face flushed. "They're quite perfect, I'll have you know. Just the right amount of—"

"Stop right there," I said. She started to protest, but I held up a hand to cut her off. "I have, in my time, seen many tits. I have seen small ones, big ones, and enormous ones so huge they could suffocate you if you were given a big hug. I've seen truly perfect tits, tits that pointed in two different directions, and tits that were like missile silos. I've seen small nipples, taut nipples, and nipples the sizes of quarters. I've seen brown tits, pale tits, tits with tattoos of snakes licking the nipples, and tits that were so perfectly spherical they'd make an architect cry. So, yeah, when I say they're 'nice,' I'm not being dismissive, I'm saying that they are nicely shaped, they have a pleasant curve to them which would fit nicely in my hand, and I suspect the nipples would perk nicely if I were to flick them with my thumb, okay?"

She stared at me, and I wondered if I had said too much. Headlights flared ahead of me, and I had to pay attention to the road for a minute. I heard her moving around, and when I could glance over again, she was facing forward in her seat.

The fourth button was undone, as was the fifth. Her blouse hung open, and when she arched her back, one of her breasts slipped out and was fully exposed.

"You can flick it, if you like," she said, her voice in that husky range porn directors could never get enough of.

I reached over and gave her nipple a quick tweak. She shrieked, pulling away from my grip.

"Knock it off," I growled at her.

She pretended to be shocked, and then her hand darted over and reached between my legs. "Hey!" I protested as she got ahold of me. I nearly jerked the car into the next lane as she tweaked me.

Satisfied with her shenanigans, she sank back into her seat, a wicked smile on her lips. "Now we're even," she said.

"How do you figure that?"

She laughed, and curled up on the seat so she could stare at me. I avoided looking at her breasts by noticing how much her short skirt was riding up her hip. "You do like women," she purred.

I gave her a glare, which only made her giggle. "Especially the feisty ones," I admitted.

"I knew it."

"Keep your hands to yourself."

She nodded demurely, but her smile said she was merely biding her time.

The border crossing seemed impossibly far away, and she was so close.

Hot dog. Beer. Bed. I let the mantra run over and over in my head. When I felt my resolve fray, I thought about a dead tree python with a pair of men's boxers on its head.

That didn't help as much as I hoped it would.

CHAPTER 7

I HAD FORGOTTEN TO COLLECT IDs FROM THE LADIES BEFORE we had piled into the car, which made for a brief moment of panic at the border. Fortunately, Pen's nipples—pressed firmly against the silk of her top (she had, in the end, buttoned up three of the five buttons before we had reached the front of the line)—gave the guy in the kiosk something to look at as I dug around in tiny purses. Once we cleared the border, traffic opened up and we slid into the flow heading north.

As we passed the outlet mall parking lot, I spotted the station wagon that I was supposed to have driven. For a fleeting instant I considered taking the next exit and picking it up. *Pen's in no shape to drive her friends back to LA,* I told myself as we streaked past the mall. I was still responsible for them, wasn't I?

I half-expected Mr. Chow to say something, but he kept quiet.

"Where are we going?" I asked after a few miles of riding in silence.

"Westwood," she sighed. She toyed with her seat so she could stretch out. Luxuriating, like a cat. Her fingers drifted toward the buttons on her blouse again. It was more than two hours to LA, and repeating *hot dog beer bed* over and over in my head wasn't going to be enough to keep my mind—and eyes—on the road.

"You going to UCLA?" I asked.

"Uh huh," she sighed. Her hands drifted down to her skirt. She tugged at it as she squirmed briefly, getting more comfortable in the seat. I eyed her efforts, and it seemed to me that the hem of her skirt had gone up an inch or so instead of down.

"What are you studying?" *Eyes on the road, Butch.*

"Biodiversity," she said.

"Like birds and fish?"

"Diversity and extinction," she said, and then she clarified: "Why there are less birds and fish."

"And what do you do with that degree? Work at a zoo?"

"No," she said. "If I'm lucky, I get to travel. There are many places in the world where governments and corporations are doing their best to wipe out species. I work with local universities and ecological organizations to help educate people why we need the birds and fishes—as well as the trees and the rivers and the soil—so it all doesn't end up a barren wasteland that can't support any sort of life."

"Wow," I said.

"What do you do you for a living, Butch?"

"Nothing as interesting as that," I admitted.

"Uh huh," she said. She squirmed on the seat. "You're going to have to do better than that."

"Why?"

"Because I'm going to take off my clothes if you bore me."

I gave her a broad smile. "No, you aren't," I said. "Because then you'll be naked, and you won't know anything about me."

"Maybe I don't want to know anything about you," she countered. She undid one of the buttons on her blouse and stretched.

I swerved a bit, but got back into the center of my lane.

"I don't think you've been to college," she said.

"Why do you say that?"

"Uh, 'nothing as interesting as that.'" She was a pretty good mimic.

I laughed. "Fair enough," I said. "I finished high school. A town out in the Midwest that didn't have many options. I wasn't the sort of student that got scholarships or grants or stuff like that. There wasn't any reason to go to college."

"So you went to work," she said.

"Yeah, more or less."

"Is that when you came to California?"

"Yeah," I said. "It is."

"Thought you'd be a movie star?"

"Isn't that why everyone comes to LA?"

She noticed I hadn't answered her question. "But you didn't have that spark, did you?" she said. "You didn't have that—what do they call it? That certain *je ne sais quas . . .*"

"The what?"

"It's French." She stretched again. Her breasts pushed against the fabric of her blouse. It was a natural motion this time—she wasn't trying to get me to look at her—which only made it that much harder to not look.

"No, I didn't," I said. "I didn't have . . . whatever it was."

"That left bit parts and stunt work, didn't it? *Thug number six. Man at Service Station.* Hoping to get enough dialogue to qualify for a SAG card?"

"You know a lot about how the movie industry works," I said.

"Mom's an actress. Daytime soaps."

"Really?"

She nodded sleepily. "Going on twenty years. Doing her best to not age a day."

"And your dad?"

"Cosmetic surgery."

"What kind?"

She gave me a *Are you kidding me?* look.

"Oh, right," I said. "Sorry."

There were lots of cosmetic surgeons in LA, and they did everything from tucks to lifts to making new faces, but most of the work was all about augmentation. Making things bigger. Everything was bigger in LA. And not just because the camera added ten pounds.

We bantered back and forth for twenty miles or so, and her questions got farther and farther apart. Finally, she stopped asking altogether and her breathing became slow and rhythmic. I held my breath for another mile, and then finally relaxed. There wasn't much traffic through above Carlsbad, and I took advantage of the long stretches of empty road to look at her.

Her face was a long teardrop, and her eyebrows were gentle arcs across her face. Her nose was canted slightly to the left, and she had a few lines at the corners of her eyes, lines I suspected her father would remove for an upcoming birthday present. When she relaxed, her lips were narrow and flat. Her hair was blonde and brunette, streaked in the latest style. It was tousled from the evening, and some of it fell across her forehead. I wanted to reach over and brush it back.

She was a nice-looking woman. They all were, in fact. But Pen seemed like the one who had to work at it. Marsha had her breasts; Cathy had a magnetic personality that kept a group's energy focused and bright; and Stephanie, even as reserved as she was, had a natural charm and grace that would transform her if she would only let it. Pen, on the other hand, was the hard one. Looking at her as she slept, I thought it might not be who she was, but it certainly was the mask she wore all the time.

Something beeped, and I came out of my reverie. The noise was coming from my back pocket. I dug around and retrieved Stephanie's cellphone. The tiny symbols indicated that it had found a cellar network. I thought about the phone number on the paper Frolic had given me.

What did I owe her?

"Nothing," I muttered. But I was curious.

I pulled the folded paper out, and reading by the light of the phone, I punched in the number. It rang a few times, and I was about to hang up when someone answered. They fumbled the phone for a bit, and then, they slurred something unintelligible in a sleep-filled voice.

"It's me," I said. "Your messenger."

I had woken her up. That gave me a little jolt of joy.

"Who?"

"Your—"

We went under an overpass, and static crackled on the phone, eating whatever I was going to say. When we came out the other side, there was a moment of silence on the phone. "—time it is?" The last half of her question suddenly came through.

"Yeah, I do," I said. "It's late, but not too late to check in, right?"

"What are you—" Another overpass, another patch of static. And then there was nothing but dead air on the phone. I listened for a few seconds, played that dumb game of repeating myself a few times, and then hung up the phone.

"This is why I hate cellphones," I muttered. There were more overpasses coming up, and I had to wait awhile before trying again. This time, it only rang twice before she picked up.

"Jesus Christ," she snapped. Much more awake this time. "What is your problem?"

"My problem? You gave me this number." The connection was clear this time. I could definitely hear her annoyance.

"When did I give you my number?" she asked. "Never mind. Even if I did, I certainly didn't tell you to call me at 1:30 in the morning. And who the fuck is this anyway?"

"Your errand boy." That feeling of elation was draining away. There was something different about her voice. It didn't sound like . . .

"I don't have an errand boy. What the fuck? Are you just drunk dialing some random number, asshole?"

"You gave—wait a minute. Did you send someone to deliver a package today? As a personal favor?"

"What?"

"Operation . . . never mind. Is this Frolic?"

"*Frolic*? Oh, fuck off, already." The line went dead.

I stared at the phone, trying to put a face to that voice. It wasn't Frolic, but it was . . . familiar. I checked the paper. I had dialed the right number. So who was it? And why did they not seem to have any idea what I was talking about?

Oh, fuck, was this whole thing a massive joke? Some sort of sadistic payback from the DEA? But why go through all this trouble? Why not haul me in and dump me in a windowless room for a few days? That would be more effective. But to what end? It didn't make any sense.

Frowning, I dialed the number one more time. She picked up immediately.

"Okay, asshole, this is where I tell you that—"

"It's Bliss," I said, interrupting her.

"What?"

"Bliss. That's who is calling you."

For a moment, I thought I had lost the call, and then she spoke again.

"Butch?"

I *did* know this voice.

"Yeah, it's me," I said. "Hello, Angel."

"Jesus, Butch. It's late. Where are you calling me from? It sounds like you are on a cellphone. Are you driving?"

"Yeah, I'm on the 5, coming back from San Diego."

"When did you—wait. Why are you calling me?"

She didn't add the extra word, but I heard it in her voice. After almost a year, why was I calling her *now*—in the middle of the night, while driving on the freeway.

"I was given your number," I said. "It was part of a delivery package that I—uh, well—yeah, it was part of a package deal."

"A package? What sort of package?" She was definitely awake now. I was getting lawyer voice. Cold. Detached. Careful.

"Do you know why I might be delivering a package, Angel?" I asked.

"Are you in trouble, Bliss? Can you talk freely?"

I glanced over at Pen, who hadn't stirred during my conversation.

"Trouble is a relative term," I said. "Are you in trouble, Angel?"

"No, of course not. I was fast asleep before"—she paused a second before finishing—"some asshole woke me up."

I smiled at that. *Especially the feisty ones,* I thought, recalling Pen's question about my predilection toward women. "*Morelia viridis,*" I said. "Do you know what that is?"

She was quiet for a moment. "Some type of reptile," she said finally.

"Green tree python," I said. "I was supposed to deliver one to a guy in Tijuana."

"Shit," she breathed.

"Are you sure about not being in trouble?" I asked.

"Where are you?" she asked, ignoring my question.

I peered at the approaching sign. "About thirty miles south of Anaheim," I guessed.

"Meet me—never mind—where are you going?"

"Somewhere in Westwood," I said. "Hang on." Juggling the phone and the steering wheel, I leaned over and opened the glove box. I rooted around for the car's registration. I found a bottle opener, a can of pepper spray, and a couple of sanitary napkins along with the car's manual and a couple of folded maps. But no registration.

Pen, sensing my proximity, stirred. I leaned back from her side of the car, and held my breath.

Her eyelids fluttered slightly, and she snuggled down more against the seat. Her skirt rode up a little more, and the light from the glove box illuminated the inside of her thigh. I didn't need that distraction right now. I leaned over and shut the glove box, trying not to touch her. She sighed deeply, and slipped back into whatever dream she was having.

Angel's voice buzzed, and I pressed the tiny phone against my ear in an effort to muffle the noise. "I'm here," I whispered.

"What's going on?"

"I'm trying to—just, hold on a sec."

Pen's tiny purse was sitting between the seats. I opened it and found her license. "Here we go," I said. I read off the address to Angel.

"Beverly Hills?" she asked. "I thought you said Westwood."

"Close enough," I said, even though we both knew no one in LA would ever mistake one for the other. "I'll be there in about an hour, okay. Maybe an hour and a half."

"That's really late, Butch," she said.

"You'll be there, won't you?"

"I'll be there," she said eventually.

It was a reasonable guess that the address on Pen's license was her parents' place in Beverly Hills, and an hour after my call with Angel, I turned off Sunset and started winding my way through the maze of streets that was every Beverly Hills neighborhood. Lots of private driveways and expensive homes you could barely see from the road. The streets were empty, which made it easy to find the house I was looking for. It was the only one with a car parked by the curb.

I pulled up behind a green Subaru, and just before I turned off the headlights, I saw the single occupant in the car look over her shoulder. I took the Mercedes key with me when I got out of the car. I let the door close quietly.

Angel met me at the back fender of the Subura. She was the tallest one in the family, and in a decent pair of heels, she could look me in the eye. Her hair, pulled back into a single ponytail, was longer than it had been the last time I had seen her. She was wearing a black turtleneck, a black fleece jacket, and black tights.

"You look like a ninja," I said. "Minus, you know, the head mask thing."

She gave me a once-over as well. "Did you get a tan?" she asked.

"I always have a tan," I said, a peevish note in my voice.

"Maybe it's your hair, then," she said. "Lighter?"

"No, it's the same," I said.

"Huh," she said. She was letting me know she hadn't thought about me enough in the last year to remember any details, but I didn't believe her. Apparently, this was the game we were going to play.

"Who's in the car?" she asked, pointing with her chin.

"Friends," I said.

"You sleeping with any of them?"

"Probably," I said.

Her eyes gave her away: a brief flick to see if I was kidding, and then back to the shadowy figures in the car. "Well, whatever works, I suppose," she said lightly. Much like her tone earlier. Just an opinion. She didn't care one way or another.

"What doesn't work for me is getting shot at," I said, moving past all the feigned indifference.

That got her attention. "Shot at?"

"What's going on, Angel?"

Her eyebrows creased, and she reached out and touched me lightly on the arm. "Are you okay?" she asked, ignoring my question.

"It's 3:00 AM on a weeknight, Angel. I'm not okay. My plans for yesterday were to have a hot dog, maybe a beer, and then go to bed early, because I could. Instead, I got dragged into some shit involving a python and Mexican gangbangers. Oh, and your phone number. You want to tell me how those things are all related?"

She wrapped her arms around herself, and she wouldn't look at me. "It's not what it looks like," she said quietly.

"Oh, good, because it looked like someone was setting me up."

Her head came up, and the gleam in her eyes was fierce. "No," she said vehemently. "You weren't—how did you even get involved?"

"Oh, so that wasn't a random thing?"

"Yes"—she hesitated—"No. It's . . . It's complicated."

"I'm sure it is."

"Can we—let's not talk about this now, okay?"

"I'd like to talk about it now."

"But not here, okay?" She touched my arm again. "Let's go somewhere else."

"Okay. Where?"

She chewed on her lower lip for a second. "What about them?" she asked, nodding toward the quartet in the Mercedes.

"I'm going to leave them here," I said.

"Where is your car?"

"Back at the house. I never got in it yesterday."

She tried to parse that, and I waved her off on the effort. "I'll ride with you," I said. "Just give me a minute with them."

"Okay," she said. I waited, but she didn't move.

"You can wait in the car," I said. "That way it doesn't look like you're thinking about robbing one of these houses."

"I'm not—" She frowned at me. Then, with a flick of her ponytail, she stomped back to her car.

I shook my head, and returned to the Mercedes. I was going to do something lame, like write a note, but when I closed the door, I saw that Pen was awake.

"Who was that?" she asked quietly. "Your girlfriend?"

"She's not my girlfriend," I said. I nodded toward the house behind her. "This is your parents' house, yes?"

She glanced out the window, screwing up her face as she recognized the fence and manicured hedge row beyond. "Why did you bring us here?"

"I didn't know where else to bring you," I said. "Sorry."

She let out a long sigh. "It's okay." She put her hand on the center console, close enough that her fingers brushed my leg. "She's not your girlfriend?"

"No, she isn't," I said.

"Someone you work with?"

"I don't—we've known each other a long time." That seemed easier than explaining my relationship with the Chow family.

She leaned toward me, her face getting close to mine. "Have you seen her tits?" she asked softly.

I swallowed. "No," I said, truthfully. "I haven't."

She picked up my hand and guided it to the rounded curve of one of her breasts and held it there. "But you've seen mine," she said. Her teeth touched her bottom lip as that wicked smile curled her mouth. I didn't pull my hand away, and that was signal enough. She shoved her face against mine, kissing me hard.

I gasped when we broke contact. Only then did I have the presence of mind to retrieve my hand. She sat back, stretching out on the seat. Making sure I could see the tight point of her nipple through the fabric of her dress. "Maybe I'll let you see them again sometime," she said.

Anything I could say in response was going to cause more trouble, and so I kept my mouth shut. I got out of the car, and without looking back, I crossed around to the passenger side of Angel's Subaru and got in.

Angel didn't say anything as she started her car and pulled away from the cub. She didn't have to. I could read her thoughts plainly enough on her face.

I had traded one sort of trouble for another.

CHAPTER 8

We found a Denny's on Wilshire, and Angel picked a booth where she could look out at the late night traffic. A waitress who looked like she was close to perfecting her "strung out junkie" look for an upcoming casting call brought menus and glasses of water. She poured coffee without asking if we needed any, and then stood next to the table, rocking back and forth. As if coming back in a few minutes for our order was outside the realm of possibility.

"Waffle," I said. "No, two. And a side of bacon."

"Hash browns or toast?" the waitress said. Her voice was even flatter than her stare.

"Just the waffles and bacon," I said.

"Mmmkay." She stretched out the letters as she ponderously swung her gaze toward Angel.

"Egg white omelette," Angel said. "Green peppers, tomatoes, mushrooms, black olives. Sour cream and guacamole on the side."

"What kind of cheese?" the waitress asked, unmoved by Angel's specificity. This was LA, after all.

"No cheese."

The waitress swayed from side to side as she scratched our order on her pad. A lot of whole-body effort went into the process, and she finally wandered off, listing to the right. Like an old boat, taking on water.

Angel ignored her coffee and dumped the creamers out of the small dish. Using a spoon, she dished her ice out of her water glass. I used the creamers to change the color of my coffee from black tar to river mud, which was what it tasted like. Angel took a sip from her de-iced water, made a face, and then sat back in the booth. She unzipped her dark jacket halfway.

"It's hard to find good food at 3:00 AM, isn't it?" I said, making conversation.

"Which is why I'm usually in bed at this time of day."

"That sounds nice," I said, and then immediately regretted the words as I realized how they sounded.

She tipped her head and raised an eyebrow. She had her mother's face, but her father's eyes. They could be quite unforgiving. She had his hands too, which had led to some strain in the household, given Mrs. Chow's run as a hand model for Cartier. Angel wore a man's Rolex, and she had tiny diamond studs in her ears. She wore no makeup, and didn't really need to.

I had been released from Tehachapi before Mr. Chow, and I had spent a year or so doing the sort of shit jobs available to an ex-con with no discernible job skills. When CDCR agreed with Mr. Chow's legal team that it was in everyone's best (read financial) interests to let the dying man spend his last few months at home with hospice care, he had tracked me down. I didn't have any paper saying I was qualified to be an in-home assistant, but that hadn't mattered. Mr. Chow wanted me close, and I had moved into the bungalow. After he died, Mrs. Chow made it clear that it had been his wish that I continue living there.

During his last days, I had come to know the rest of the family: Jackie, Tony, Marco, and Angel. The boys and I got along well enough; they knew about their father and I's relationship inside. Mrs. Chow tolerated me, out of respect for her husband while he was alive, and once he was gone, I was useful as an on-site chauffeur. As for Angel . . . well, Mrs. Chow made it abundantly clear I was to stay away from her daughter.

I had '*yes, ma'am*'ed that rule until the funeral.

Angel looked good in black. She always looked good in black.

Like a lost dog, the waitress wandered past our table, coffee pot in her hand. She tried to refill our cups, but there wasn't room for more than a splash in either. She stared at the ice cubes in the creamer dish, a tiny flicker of panic in her eyes—had she done that?—and she forgot all about the ice cubes.

"We're out of black olives," she whispered to Angel.

"Okay," Angel said.

"You want to substitute ham or something?"

"No, thank you. I'll be fine."

The waitress smacked her lips around a "mmmkay" and wandered off again, the coffee pot dangling precariously from slack fingers. Angel stared out the window and I watched the waitress totter toward the counter so as to not stare at Angel. Eventually, she reached into her jacket pocket and took out a cellphone. She put it on the table and rested a long finger on it. "Did one of my brothers give you this number?" she asked.

"No," I said. "They didn't."

"You didn't get it from my mother."

I chuckled. "Absolutely not."

"How did you get it?" Her finger tapped the phone.

I still had Stephanie's phone. I dug it out and put it on the table.

Her eyebrow went up. "When did you start carrying a phone?"

"I'm not," I said. "This belongs to—"

"Your girlfriend?"

"She's not my girlfriend."

"Are you her fuck toy? Is this how she gets ahold of you when she wants a little something?"

"She'd like that idea." I shook my head. "But no."

"It's not your color, so someone else must have picked it—"

"It's not my phone," I said, cutting her off. "It belongs to one of girls. I forgot to give it back."

"One of the girls?"

"Do you want to hear this story, or you want to keep badgering me?"

She crossed her arms. She looked out the window again. A tiny smile quirked the corner of her mouth, a subtle shift in her expression that was a jolt to my heart.

"How long as it been?" she asked. "Since Dad's funeral?"

I shook my head. "No, there was that time around Thanksgiving last year, when I was—"

"'Just leaving,'" she said, and I heard her mother in her tone of voice.

"I was running late," I said.

She nodded absently, distracted by her own recollection of that November afternoon. "We had just arrived, and you were standing there. Right next to where we parked the car. I got out and you said hello, and . . . and the dog started barking."

"That fucking dog," I said.

She hid her smile with her hand.

Baby Baby—Mrs. Chow's yappy Pekinese—and I had a love-hate relationship. He loved to bark at me; I wanted to shove him in a plastic sack and leave him at the curb on garbage day. Hell, it didn't matter if it was garbage day.

"You still seeing . . . what's his name?" I asked, trying to remember the guy who had been driving the car. He was a lawyer with some big Century City law firm. "Bartoloni?"

"Nathan," she said.

"I was close."

"No, you weren't."

I shrugged like it didn't matter one way or another.

Her eyebrows tightened for a second. "Yeah," she said. "I'm still seeing him."

I had gotten the backstory from Jackie. Angel and *Whatshisname* had met when she had been an intern at the law firm where he worked. It had been part of her graduate study. She had another half year or so before she got her JD, but the degree was merely a formality. They were going to offer her a job as soon as she got her diploma.

"I remember the dress you were wearing," I said.

"Butch . . . " She shook her head slightly. "You didn't even see—"

"It was red and black," I said. "I saw enough of it under that coat. It was a great dress."

She continued to shake her head. "And Tony showed up in sweatpants. Mother was not happy." She picked up her water glass and looked at me over the rim. "You were wearing that grey suit," she said. "The same one you wore to Dad's funeral."

"It's the only suit I have," I confessed.

She took a small sip from her water glass. "You had a different tie, though," she said.

"Who wears a black tie to Thanksgiving?"

"Depends on the company," she said.

"I suppose it does," I replied.

I was glad that we were no longer pretending we hadn't thought about each other during the last year. The exhaustion tugging at my eyelids and tightening the muscles in my neck and upper back was slipping away.

"God, you do that so well," she said.

"Do what?"

"Blithely ignore a leading question."

"You didn't ask a question," I said.

"Would you have answered it if I had?"

"Which?"

"See? That's what I'm talking about." She tapped her glass with a finger. "Nathan loves witnesses like you. They bring a cross-examination to a grinding halt. What someone thought was going to take fifteen minutes suddenly takes an hour, and by then, everyone is so bored that no one remembers what's been said."

I didn't say anything. Mr. Chow's legal team had done right by him. They got him home in time to die in his own bed. My experience with lawyers hadn't been as stellar. The DA at the time had had a hard-on—if you'll pardon the expression—for a certain vices, and I had been a poster child for those sorts of ne'er-do-wells. Sure, it was nice to be recognized, but the whole process cooled my enthusiasm for the American legal system.

The waitress brought our food, slapping the plates down noisily on the table. There was a plate for each waffle, and then another one for three strips of flash-burned bacon. Angel got a single plate with her egg-white omelette, which looked like a sickly cloud. Something oozed out the end. Since she had asked for no cheese, I had a hard time imagining what it was.

"Anything else?" the waitress asked. When of us said anything, she dragged herself away, leaving us to our food.

Angel poked at her omelette as if it might be alive. She peeled back the top and we both stared at the sparse assortment of poorly cooked vegetables. There was more gooey stuff that I really hoped was cheese. Angel thought about putting her fork into it, but that was about as much as she was going to commit.

I pushed one of the waffle plates toward her. "Don't risk it," I said. "Go with the tried and true."

"What are the chances the mix didn't come out of a bag?" she asked.

"Oh, no chance," I said. "But I don't need to eat both of them."

She shoved the omelette aside and brought the waffle close. The omelette quivered on the plate, as if it knew it had been rejected.

"I'm sure we can find a better restaurant in an hour or two," I said. "The waffle will tide you over."

"You have some place in mind?" She poured the barest minimum of syrup in each crater of the waffle.

"Around here?" I shook my head. "This is your 'hood."

"Your girlfriend hasn't taken you to her favorite spots yet?"

"We usually order in so we don't have to stop fucking," I said.

She stared at me, trying to read my face,. "Okay," she said when she decided I was kidding "I'll knock it off."

"I'd appreciate it," I said. I grabbed the syrup, since she was clearly done dotting her waffle with it, and poured it liberally over my waffle. I poured the dregs over the bacon, in a futile effort to bring some life back to the desiccated pig.

"That's a lot of fucking," she said, and I nearly choked on my first bite.

She held up her hands after I could breathe again, and we both ate in silence after that. Under the table, her leg vibrated, and she bumped mine once or twice with her foot. I didn't move my leg out of the way. That would have drawn attention to the contact, and, well, after the third time, I figured it wasn't an accident.

"You owe me a story," Angel said when she finished her waffle. She pushed herself into the corner of the booth, up against the glass.

I considered dissembling, but what was the point of being obtuse? She was right about how I could be evasive—survival skills one picks up while inside the penal system—but I knew I wasn't going to get anything out of her without giving up something first. What was the phrase that had been so popular after that movie about the serial killer? The film that made cannibalism hip. *Quid pro quo*, or something like that. Some Latin phrase that an ignorant hick without a college degree wouldn't know anything about.

They had a good library at Tehachapi, but my state-assigned case officer hadn't been interested in my self-directed course in the humanities. Mr. Chow said I could have gotten an online degree from a university in Arizona that was doing a pilot program with prison inmates. I found out the university was looking for government funding, and they wanted to show off their successes as part of that fund drive. *And here's an ex-porn star who got a college degree in accounting during his rehabilitation! 'I'm ready to count beans with all the other bean counters,' Mr. Bliss says in a prepared statement as he is released from incarceration.*

I didn't need the piece of paper. Not with that sort of attention.

"Well, I slept in, like I always do on Wednesday," I started.

"You sleep in every day," she interrupted. "Compared to the rest of the world," she qualified.

"Regardless," I continued. "I slept in. Got woken up by the dog. I went down to Willie's Gym. Over near Pico. I got some exercise, talked about important stuff with Willie for awhile, and then went to get a hot dog for lunch."

"Important stuff?"

I shrugged. "Stocks. Girls. Marlin fishing. You know Willie."

She raised her shoulders to indicate that she did, indeed, know Willie. Every conversation with the man was a breathless interchange fraught with exclamation points, hand-waving, and an overuse of adjectives. "And how was your hot dog?" she asked.

"I didn't get my hot dog," I said.

"No?" She raised an eyebrow. "Is this the part where you stop teasing me and get to the action?"

I tried to look wounded at her judgment about my story-telling skills, but she wasn't having any of it. "Move it along," she said.

"I did not get a hot dog," I said with an air of gravity. "I tried too, though. I really did. I'm down at the boardwalk, standing in line at Horatio's, when this black sedan rolls up. I get invited to go for a ride, and like the dutifully indoctrinated and perpetually cowed post-incarceration citizen I am, I go for the ride. During which, I'm asked to perform a favor."

"A back seat favor?"

"No. Not that sort of favor."

"A favor for a friend, then. What the rest of us would call a 'job offer.'"

"No, they weren't friends."

"Oh, definitely one of *those* favors then." Politely, she kept her eye rolling to a minimum. "Did they threaten you?"

"Are you asking as a concerned listener or as a lawyer?"

"I'm asking as someone who wishes you'd get on with this story."

"They didn't threaten me," I said. "But they did make some threats."

"Very cloak and dagger of them."

"They wanted me to deliver something. In fact—" I dug Frolic's paper out of my pocket, and tossed it on the table.

She picked it up and unfolded it. She frowned at what she saw on the page. "Tijuana," she said, looking me in the eye.

"Yeah, Tijuana." I poked the paper in her hands. "That's where I got your number."

I couldn't read anything in her expression.

"Some guy asks me to deliver a green tree python to another guy in Tijuana," I said, getting to the part I knew she was going to love. "Pretty straight-forward, right? Take this thing there. Drop it off. Say 'thank you very much; I'll see myself out.' And then what am I supposed to do when I'm done?"

"You're supposed to check in," she said quietly.

"And who am I supposed to check in with?"

"The people who sent you," she said.

I poked the paper again. "And since they were so kind as to supply a number, guess what number I called?"

She didn't answer. It was a rhetorical question anyway. We both knew who I had called.

"It gets better," I said.

Her head came up, and her eyes were hard. "And how does it get better?" she asked, leading her witness like a good prosecutor.

"The snake has an accident during the hand-off."

"What sort of accident?"

"The fatal sort."

"So, the snake didn't actually get delivered."

"Well, we were deep in a discussion about semantics and the relative definition of 'delivered' when things . . . things got a little out of hand."

"How *out of hand*?"

I rolled down the sleeve of my shirt. The blood had dried, but no one was going to mistake it for a splash of chocolate sauce.

Angel examined the dark slash on my sleeve. "Yours?" she asked.

"No," I said. "The snake's probably. Maybe Droopy's."

"Droopy?"

"I didn't catch his name," I said. "We were a little pre-occupied."

"With what? A dick measuring contest or something?"

Her phone started vibrating. I barely had a chance to see the name on the screen before she scooped it up and answered. "Hello?" she said as she slid toward the end of the booth. "Yeah, it's me. Hang on a sec." She put her hand over the phone as she stood. "I have to take this."

"Of course you do," I said, graciously excusing her with a wave of my fork.

I watched her go outside and stand in the parking lot. Her head was down—she was doing more listening than talking—and the blank expression on her face reminded me of the stoic mask she had worn at her father's funeral.

"Coffee?" the waitress asked, having magically appearing at my elbow.

"No," I said. "Jesus, where did you come from?"

She stared at me with her lifeless eyes, as if she found the existential nature of my question too unfathomable. The coffee pot hung loosely in her limp grip.

"Just the check," I said. "I think we're done here."

"Mmmmmkay," the waitress said. She didn't move.

"What?" I asked.

Her gaze rested on the abandoned omelette that had been summarily opened like a corpse on a medical examiner's table. "You taking that with you?" she asked.

"No," I said. "Just the check."

"I'm going to have to throw it out if you don't take it."

I thought about telling her that I was going to throw it out regardless, but I knew that revelation wasn't going to mean anything to her. "Fine," I said. "Put it in a box."

She dragged the plate off the table, leaning too close to me as she did, and then wandered off again.

I didn't watch her go. I was too fascinated by the angry conversation Angel was having with someone whose name started with the letters 'N' and 'a.' I wondered what they could be talking about at this time of the morning.

CHAPTER 9

ANGEL FINISHED HER CALL AS I CAME OUT OF THE DENNY'S. She shoved her hands into her pockets and didn't face me.

"Everything all right?" I asked.

"Yeah," she said. "It's fine."

"Okay," I said.

We stood awkwardly in the parking lot, like two kids who knew a date was over but weren't quite sure of the good-bye protocol. Was it a handshake? A hug where no parts of the body touch? Had we clicked well enough for a kiss?

"How's Nathan?" I asked.

She shook her head. "I don't want to talk about Nathan."

"Anything else you want to talk about?" I indicated the restaurant behind me. "We could go back in."

"No, I . . . I have to go, Butch."

"Oh," I said. "That's kind of quick."

"It's . . . I'm sorry—it's complicated."

"Quickies usually aren't complicated." This got a hint of a smile.

"Look, I know it's not fair to run off like this," she admitted. "Especially after what happened to you today, but . . . I'm serious about it being complicated. I don't want to—not right now, okay? You shouldn't be involved . . ."

"I think we're past that point," I pointed out.

She nodded tersely. "You shouldn't be," she insisted. "That's part of what is making things complicated." She took a hand out of a pocket and fussed with her hair—which was not in need of fussing. "Who asked you for this favor?" she asked. "Can you tell me?"

"Honestly, I don't know. A woman. She's connected to a federal office, I suspect. I don't know which one."

"More complications." Angel sighed. "Why did she pick you?"

"That is the sixty-four thousand dollar question, isn't it?"

"Just leave it alone for now, okay?" Angel fished her keys out of her pocket. "Please? Let me figure things out before . . . "

"Are you in trouble?" I asked. For, like, the fifth time.

"No," she said.

"Is Nathan?"

She was a little slower to respond. "No," she said. And then, more quietly: "Maybe."

"We're going to talk about this at some point," I said.

"Yes," she said. "We will. I promise."

"Okay," I said.

We were back to the awkward part. She rattled her keys. Her teeth worked her lower lip. I stood there like an idiot, with a greasy omelette wrapped in tin foil in my hand. "You—you don't have your car, do you?"

"No," I said. "It's back at the house."

She frowned, knowing in advance how tactless her next question was going to be. "Would you mind getting a cab?"

"Yeah, I can get a cab," I said. "On one condition."

Her face froze. "What?"

I held out the tin foil. "I'm not taking this home."

That smile flitted across her face again. "Okay," she said.

She did a little dance, trying to decide if she should snatch the take-out and run or linger a moment longer. She rushed over, snatched the tin foil out of my hand, and distracted me with a quick kiss on the cheek. She moved away before I could return the kiss or try to touch her. "I'll call you soon," she said over her shoulder as she walked quickly to her car.

"I'm looking forward to it," I said. She was in the car and closing the door before all of the words got out of my mouth, and so I doubted she heard them. I just stood there with a smile plastered on my face and my hand raised as she started her car. She backed out of the parking spot, and sped out of the lot onto Wilshire.

She didn't look at me as she left.

I was dreaming about rowing a boat across a stormy sea. The skies were like lead, and the rain was falling in heavy sheets. My clothes were soaked through, and my hands and shoulders ached. How long had I been rowing? I didn't know. A woman sat in the prow of the boat. She was wrapped in a blanket, and the rain had molded it to her body. Her black hair was ink, running down her back. I couldn't see her face; she was looking toward whatever destination I was hoping to reach. But it was still very far away, and the boat was taking on water, both from the rain and from waves that slopped over the sides.

I was so tired of rowing.

A seal breached nearby. It started barking. It wasn't the guttural cough I expected. It was more like the noise made by a small dog. *Bark bark!* It cried. *Bark bark barkbarkbark!*

I started awake. I was tangled in my sheets and I couldn't move my arms. Bright sunlight was trying to force its way through the heavy blinds on the bedroom window. Somewhere nearby, a dog was barking itself silly. I raised my head and read the display on the bedside clock. A little after eight, which meant I had gotten about four hours of sleep.

Bliss! Bliss! The barking went. *The sun is up! So much barking to do!*

"Fuck off, mutt," I muttered. I yanked an arm free of the sheets and tried to rearrange the pillows to block out the yammering.

I was a big fan of more than four hours of sleep a night.

Baby Baby kept at it, though the noise moved away from the window. I heard the front door of the bungalow open, and the noisy fur ball was suddenly in my bedroom. He bounced onto the bed. *I'm going to bark all day!*

I threw a pillow toward the noise and heard a satisfying yip as Baby Baby tumbled off the bed.

That was more like it. I nuzzled down into my remaining pillow, delighted by the silence. There was hope for—

The blinds went up with a noise like a hippo farting, and sunlight rushed into the room. My eyelids caught fire, and I tried to burrow away from the light.

"Wakey wake, Butchy Boy." Having ruined my relationship with sleep, Mrs. Chow smacked me on the ass as she strode out of the room. The woman had unerring aim, even with the sheets tangled around me. "Many errands today."

What day was it? The fucking dog and the sunlight were making it hard to remember. I tried to recall the last few days, and got hung up on the long car ride I had taken last night. The one with the nearly naked co-ed in the front seat. "We—we ran errands last week," I grumbled.

The bungalow was mine, but the property it sat on belonged to Mrs. Chow. Out of respect to her dead husband, she couldn't throw me out, but as long as I was "freeloading"—a term she used often—I would make myself useful. I was her chauffeur when she needed to play matriarch to all the young women working at the family salons. Occasionally, there were other errands, like running supplies from her wholesaler in Orange County, but we had done that last week.

Mrs. Chow said something from the other room. I rolled over and was about to yell at her to say it again, but I swallowed the words instead. Of course she hadn't spoken loudly enough for me to hear her from the other room. She was talking to me, and I was the rude jerk who wasn't in the same room. It was my fault I couldn't hear her. The clan matriarch couldn't be wrong, after all.

Thrashing my way out of the sheets, I skirted the bright pool of sunlight. The bathroom was cool and dim, and I left the door open as I pissed. When she started talking again, I flushed and turned on the shower.

I knew how to play the passive-aggressive game of *Who's in Charge Here, Really?* I had studied with the same master as she had, after all.

The dream about the boat sluiced off me as I showered. It circled the drain, caught in the frothy bubbles of the soap, and slipped away into the vast maze of pipes that ran beneath the sprawl of Los Angeles. I turned off the shower, wiped the last of the water from my face, and pulled back the curtain.

Baby Baby, who had crept in while I was showering, gave a loud bark. I started and nearly slipped in the tub. I grabbed the shower curtain for support, and it tore through several of the rings as I leaned heavily on it. The dog grinned, yapped at me once more, and then fled as I swore at him.

Fucking dog. It was like he was playing *Who's in Charge Here* too.

After drying off and getting dressed, I found a plate with toast and a neatly sliced apple, along with a cup of hot coffee, in the kitchen. Mrs. Chow had left a note too. *You need a girlfriend*, it read. Written in Mrs. Chow's elegant handwriting. *Otherwise, you will starve with what you have in your refrigerator.*

"I was going to go shopping today," I protested to the empty room. I dropped the note in a nearby drawer, where it fell on top of all the other notes Mrs. Chow had left me. Endless variations on the same theme.

I thought about Angel and the dress she had worn at Thanksgiving as I ate the spartan breakfast Mrs. Chow had laid out for me.

We took the M5. I had been without a car for the last few months, and it hadn't particularly bothered me. Mrs. Chow, on the other hand, found it inconvenient that I didn't have proper transportation when it came time to drive her around. One morning, I had found a brand new BMW M5 in the driveway.

The keys had been in it. We used it to run errands that day, and when we were done, Mrs. Chow informed me all the paperwork was in my name. Paperwork that turned out to be a forty-eight month lease, complete with monthly payments that I was responsible for.

I called the salesman at the dealership, and asked if I could bring it back. He laughed at me, and said I should enjoy the car. *The Chows lease all their cars from me,* he said, *and I'm not interested in explaining to Mrs. Chow why this car was coming back.* Regardless, I'd still be responsible for the lease payments. *You might as well enjoy it,* he said. *You're getting the family rate.*

Of course I was.

I didn't like debts like this, but getting worked up about it wasn't going to change anything. Once, I had pushed back when she was making me drive her all over the city. *How long would you have survived in prison if my favorite husband hadn't taken an interest in you?* She had asked. It was one of those rhetorical questions that isn't meant to be taken at face value. It was meant as a reminder. That 'life for a life' bullshit that was going to haunt me forever with this family. Cynically, you could say I was a prisoner. Or, you could look at the positives, like the new car smell and the four hundred horses under the hood.

The M5 was dark blue, and it had a leather interior. There were lots of buttons and dials that did all sorts of things that German engineering thought were critical to riding in comfort. Mrs. Chow rode up front, and Baby Baby sat in her lap. This was the only time he didn't bark in my presence, though he spent the whole ride staring at me. As if he were judging my driving.

I had never suffered from performance anxiety during my film career. You learned, early on, how to do what you needed to do during a scene—more than once, if necessary. You couldn't get hung up about the two dozen people who were watching you. I knew a guy who could hold a hard-on for two or three hours at a time, but he could only do it on a closed set. If he thought anyone was paying too much attention, he'd lose his erection. He'd be worthless for the rest of the day, his mind all twisted up with anxiety. He had been headliner on two films before he got relegated to special guest status—the guy you'd pay to have in a scene or two, just so you could put his name on the box. That worked until audiences figured out that just because someone's name was on the one-sheet, that didn't mean you were going to see a lot of them during the film.

"Jasmine," Mrs. Chow said as we pulled out of the driveway. "And then Lily and Camellia."

All of the salons were named after flowers. While each one did the basic services you'd expect from a fancy salon, each store embraced its flower varietal as part of its unique offering. Jasmine had a perfume counter. Lily—which was tucked down a back street not far from Beverly Hills High—had makeup specialists, and Camellia, in West Hollywood, was attached to a tea house run by the family.

I nodded, and headed north toward Santa Monica. We were going to do the long loop: north and east, and then loop back down through Chinatown to visit Lotus and Orchid and then LA proper to stop at Chrysanthemum. Depending on traffic and how much time Mrs. Chow spent chatting with the staff, "running errands" were going to take most of the day.

We had done this on Friday. It wasn't like Mrs. Chow to hover over the stores. The staff knew their jobs and did them well. I didn't understand why we were making the rounds today, and I knew better than to ask.

Regardless, I could nap in the car while she traded gossip with the girls. Until Angel called me back, there wasn't anything I needed to attend to.

☆

After visiting Lily, I remembered talking nail polish colors with Frolic, and I mentally kicked myself for not thinking of it earlier. When we got to Camellia, I came in with Mrs. Chow. She and the store manager fell into rapid-fire Mandarin as they disappeared into the back. I dropped into one of the open pedicure chairs and started asking about nail polish colors. Something with "Frolic" in the name.

There were a couple of shades, but none of the girls could recall using them on any clients in the last week.

The same was true at Lotus.

Orchid, however, was a different story.

A long-fingered woman with a trail of orchids tattooed up her left arm remembered a client.

"Who?" I asked.

The pedicurist's name was Linn, and she had a customer at her station. She waved me into a nearby chair. "You'll be next," she said.

"I don't need a pedicure," I said. "I just want some information."

Linn glanced over at Mrs. Chow and the store manager. They were sitting in comfortable chairs in the back of the store, chatting at six thousand words per hour. It looked like they would be at it for awhile.

"Soak first," Linn said. "And then we can talk."

Her customer, an elderly Chinese woman with pencil-thin eyebrows, was staring at me like I was the first strapping American lad she had ever seen up close. She asked Linn a question, and Linn merely smiled enigmatically and didn't reply. Which was all the woman needed as confirmation, apparently. She made a vaguely sexual gesture with her hands and laughed. She tapped me on the elbow and made the gesture again.

"She wants to know if you still do *sucky sucky*," Linn said.

I sighed. "I am all out of 'sucky sucky,'" I said. "Even for someone who is clearly refined in the finer arts as this lady."

Linn shrugged, and said something to her client, who laughed again.

My past—both parts of it—were no secret to the staff at the Chow salons. While my relationship with Mrs. Chow's dead husband afforded me a certain amount of deference, the more sordid parts of my history were an endless source of entertainment for the girls at the salons. Once, I had tried to explain that 'sucky sucky' was a horrible racist and gendered stereotype perpetuated by an ignorant male patriarchy. The woman I had been explaining this to had merely nodded until I was done talking, and then she made the universal hand and mouth gesture for blowjob and repeated her question about 'sucky sucky.'

Mrs. Chow had told them I did gay porn, which meant the girls at the salons thought of me in much they same way they thought of Baby Baby: as a cute pet to be pampered and coddled.

The dog and I both got our hair done more often than necessary. The dog enjoyed all the attention. I tolerated it. The alternate was to tell them the truth. In fact, Mrs. Chow might have done me a solid with her lie, but I wasn't going to tell her. It'd be another way in which I was indebted to her.

Meanwhile, I merely smiled and nodded along with Linn and her client until the woman was done. As Linn rinsed out the basin and refilled it, I slipped off my shoes and socks. I moved over a chair, and let the young woman put my feet in the hot bath. She scrubbed my skin with a pumice stone, making everything pink and shiny. She rinsed my feet off and refilled the basin with water that wasn't *as* scalding. "Soak now," she said.

Before I could say anything, she wandered off to help the cashier with some customers, and I was left to sit and soak. Baby Baby, bored because Mrs. Chow was talking and laughing with someone else and ignoring him, hopped into the seat next to me. "This water is nice and warm," I said. "Wanna go for a swim? I could hold you down."

His black nose quivered, and he stared at me with his adorable doggy eyes. I wasn't fooled. There was a deep well of animal cunning behind the limpid surface of those black eyes.

"Shoo," Linn said. She waved Baby Baby off the chair. The dog gave me a bit of side eye and then wandered off. Linn checked on my feet, and found them satisfactorily softened. She pulled over a tray of tools and started doing things to my toes that I didn't want to watch.

"Toenail polish," I said, getting back to what we were supposed to be talking about.

"What color you want?" she asked.

"I want to know about Iridescent Moonlight Frolic," I said.

"Good color." She glanced up and frowned. "But wrong for you. You need something like—"

"I don't care about my toes," I interrupted. "I want to know whose feet you put it on recently."

Linn frowned. "I do a lot of toes, Butch. I don't remember them all."

"You don't have to remember them all," I said. "Just this one. You said you did it for someone recently. You remember her, don't you? Tall. Dark hair. Expensive suits. Very well put together."

Linn frowned. "I do a lot of expensive ladies," she said.

Something clicked. "She's a regular, isn't she?"

Linn snipped something off the edge of my big toe, and for a second, I thought it was going to start bleeding. She picked up an emery board and started filing my nail. "Compassionate Crimson Alacrity," she said.

"Look, stop it. I don't give a shit about what color works for my toes," I said.

"She got Compassionate Crimson Alacrity the first time," Linn said patiently. "And then Turbulent Pearlescence. Last week, it was Iridescent Moonlight Frolic." She nodded at the expression on my face. "You must be patient when you are having a soak," she said. "Calms your chi."

I shut my mouth and kept it shut as Linn meticulously worked on my toes—first the left foot, and then the right. Satisfied with her handiwork, she rinsed my feet off again. "What color?" she asked as she toweled them dry.

I relented. "Something that'll impress the ladies," I said.

She nodded. "Of course.," she said. "I have a very impressive color." She went and retrieved two bottles from the rack. One caught the light like it was a flame trapped in the bottle. The other looked finely powdered black dust. "Hungarian Death Nun," she said.

"Which one is that?"

She shook the bottles. "Both," she said.

I didn't understand how that was going to work, but as I wasn't the professional, I let her do her magic. The flame went on in long streaks that made my feet look as though they had been dipped in lava. Linn dusted each toe with the contents of the second bottle, and the flames took on a more gothic flair. Like fire was coming out of the charred tips of my bones.

"Sit," Linn said when she was done. "It needs to dry. And then, sealer."

"All right," I said.

Linn dusted off her lap, and sat down in the chair next to me. She leaned close and spoke in a quiet voice. "Professional lady shows up in a black car. With a driver. She never has an appointment, but she never waits. You know?"

I nodded. "I know."

"Expensive shoes," Linn continued. "I do her toes. She pays cash. Tips well. Sometimes she talks on her phone. I pretend to not understand English."

"But she knows you do."

"She does," Linn acknowledged.

"And this last time? When she got Iridescent Moonlight Frolic?"

"She was talking about snakes."

"And?"

"She said something about NARC. Said it was happening soon."

"NARC?"

Linn shrugged. "I do not know what that word means."

"It means a lot of things," I said. "But none of them make sense in this context."

A tiny frown tugged at Linn's mouth. "That's all I heard," she said, dipping her head.

"You did great," I said. "Thank you."

Her head came up. "You are welcome, Butch." She gestured at my toes. "Sealer now. And then you'll be done."

"Excellent. Thank you."

As she got out of the chair and returned to her stool, I looked up and noticed Mrs. Chow was watching me. She met my gaze and nodded slightly before returning to her conversation with Orchid's manager.

We were done "running errands."

CHAPTER 10

ANGEL'S SUBARU WAS PARKED IN FRONT OF THE HOUSE WHEN we returned, and she was sitting on the patio bench out back. Baby Baby bounded out of the car as soon as Mrs. Chow opened the door. "Favorite daughter," she called as she followed the dog out of the car. "What a surprise."

Favorite daughter. Favorite husband. She only had one of each. I wondered if I was her "favorite pain in the ass" or if there were others. If so, we should start a club.

I set the parking brake and got out of the car. I eyed Angel over the BMW's roof. Her hair was a black wave about her shoulders, and she was wearing a grey jacket over a maroon blouse. Charcoal pants, and thick-heeled boots. A little color on her cheeks and lips.

"Favorite mother," Angel said, though the words didn't have the same ring to them. She stood as her mother approached and gave her a quick kiss on either cheek.

Mrs. Chow beamed, ignoring her daughter's tone. "Come inside," she said, her hand on Angel's elbow. "I'll make tea."

Angel didn't budge. "I need to talk to Butch," she said.

I shrugged off the piercing look the clan matriarch gave me. "You won't be long," Mrs. Chow said. "Tea will be ready soon." She clapped her hands for the dog. "Cookies," she called out to him. "Come along and have some cookies."

The dog knew that word. He dashed across the lawn, and went through the door the moment she opened it. Mrs. Chow didn't look at either of us as she followed the dog.

A tiny breeze toyed with Angel's hair, lifting it and making it dance across her neck.

"You look good," I said.

"We need to talk." Angel headed for the bungalow. I hustled around the car, but she got to the door before I did. I was surprised when she turned the knob and the door opened. I let her go in first, hanging back to examine the door. I had locked it when I had left, but there wasn't any indication the door had been forced.

"I know where the spare key is," Angel said.

"There's a spare key?"

Angel shrugged off my question. She walked over to the kitchen counter and pointed at two objects that weren't there when I had left. Stephanie's phone and a metal ring with some keys on it. "You want to tell me about this?" she asked.

"The phone belongs to one of the girls I drove to Tijuana," I said. "I told you about it—about them—last night."

"Not the phone," Angel said. "This." She pointed at the other item on the counter.

I wandered over. "It's a bunch of keys," I said. I recognized them, but I wasn't going to volunteer anything. She had come in and searched the bungalow while we had been running errands, and I was wondering if part of the reason we had been so long had been was to allow Angel time to do her little B & E. Two of the keys belonged to the station wagon I had left in the mall parking lot. There were three other keys—a house key, a garage key, and some sort of mailbox or locker key—and a key ring tchotchke from a franchise that was all over the Valley. It had some sort of chicken shack theme. It wasn't my kind of place.

"They're not yours." It wasn't a question.

"No," I said. "They're not."

"Where did you get them?"

"Why did you break in here—"

"I didn't break in. I used the spare key."

"Sorry, counselor. These semantic games always trip me up."

Angel flushed, but before she had a chance to say anything, Stephanie's phone squirmed on the counter. It made a noise that was supposed to be a church bell.

"It's been doing that a lot," Angel said. "Maybe you should answer it."

Glaring at Angel, I picked up the phone and flipped it open. "Hello?"

"Do you know how many times I've called?"

"I've been busy," I said.

"Uh-huh, whatever." I recognized Pen's voice. "Look, Steph's freaked out about her phone."

"Well, it's right here," I said. "In my hand."

"Really? And why is it there?"

"I, uh, look. I forgot I had it in my pocket last night. It was a long day. I was tired, and—"

"Too eager to dash off and get naked with your girlfriend?"

I glanced at Angel. Her arms were crossed and there was fire in her eyes. "She's not—never mind," I said. "It's none of your business."

"So you are fucking her."

"I'm—look, I'm starting to think I should toss this phone and—"

"Relax, big boy," Pen said, her voice softening. "I'm just teasing."

"Oh, well, that makes it all better."

"It's a woman's prerogative to be mysterious," she replied.

"Is that what you're doing?" I asked. "It feels more like you're being a pain in the ass."

Pen laughed. "Maybe you should spank me. Show me who's boss."

"You know, I think I have a piece of pine somewhere around here. It's not finished, so it might leave a splinter or two."

"Oooh," she cooed. "I won't be able to sit down for a week."

Angel cleared her throat.

I waved a finger—*this'll only take a minute, honest*—but the hand signal had no effect on her expression. "I can give it back," I said. "Just tell me where."

"I could come there," Pen said.

"No," I said. "That's not going to happen."

"Why not?" Pen pouted.

I sighed. I knew better than to answer that question, especially with Angel standing right there. "I'll drop the phone off at your parents' house. How about that?"

Pen was quiet for a moment. "Tomorrow," she said finally. "Six o' clock. And wear a nice shirt."

"What?"

"You can meet my parents."

"No, look. I'm just going to drop the phone off. That's it. I'm not staying—"

"No? Am I going to have to explain to Daddy what I found in the trunk of the car? All by myself?"

I couldn't figure out what she was talking about, and then I remembered. The gun. When I got back to the car, I had put it in the trunk.

"That's a bad idea," I said.

"Six o'clock," Pen said, and then she giggled. "Don't be late."

"Listen—" I started, but she had hung up already. I fumed, my hand tight around the phone. I wanted to throw it across the room. I wanted to swear loudly. If Baby Baby were in the yard, I would have gone out and punted him.

"Girlfriend problems?" Angel asked.

"She's not—" I snapped. I caught myself before I could go any farther, and I reeled in all the noise and anger. I tapped the phone against the counter as I counted in my head. Looking for my happy place. Breathing out my ears. Letting go. The knot in my chest dissolved, and I exhaled noisily.

"I'm going to have a beer," I said, turning toward the refrigerator. "You want one?"

"Sure," Angel said quietly.

I pulled a pair of bottles out of the nearly empty refrigerator. I opened them both and offered Angel one. I took a long pull from my bottle, enjoying the cold and bitter taste.

Angel took a polite sip from her bottle before putting it down on the counter. She looked at me steadily, waiting for me to say something. Waiting for me to start talking.

I took another swig. "It's a crap colored station wagon," I said, indicating the keys with the mouth of my bottle. "Maybe a decade old. I didn't like the setup, so I left it in a parking lot. When we were coming back from Tijuana, I couldn't let the girls drive themselves home, and so . . . " I finished with a shrug, as if the conclusion were self-evident.

"What lot?" Angel asked.

"That big outlet mall off the 5. Just before the border. The wagon is right outside the food court entrance."

"Where did you get the keys?"

"A woman gave them to me. She—well, her driver—drove me down there. She came along to make sure I knew what I was supposed to do."

"You were supposed to deliver a snake."

"Yeah. It was in the back of the station wagon."

"Convenient," Angel said. "Who's the woman?"

"I don't know who she is," I said. "She works for the feds, I think. Somehow. I don't know."

"But she knows you."

"Yeah, she does."

"And how does she know you?"

I thought about what Linn had told me, and the look Mrs. Chow had given me at the salon. "I'm not sure of that either," I said.

"Are they monitoring you?"

"Who?"

"The feds."

I shrugged. "I don't know."

"Do they have reason to be?"

I gave her a look as I took another drink from my bottle. Even though Mr. Chow had gone to prison for failing to pay taxes—sorry, his *alleged* taxes—the feds had only managed to seize a fraction of what they suspected he was moving around for other parties. A lot of pipelines had been altered because of his incarceration and death, but that didn't mean the feds had given up. The entire Chow family and its sprawling business empire in Southern California were still being monitored. I was only of incidental interest, unless they thought I knew something that would unlock all the family secrets, but I hadn't been his confidant in prison. I had just been his muscle.

"Yeah, okay," Angel said. She harbored the same suspicions I did about the state of affairs surrounding the family. "But it's a weird way to come at you."

"You think?" I drank from my beer. "I don't think they're after me," I said.

Angel didn't say anything, which told me I was on the right track.

"What am I supposed to do?" I asked. "If I keep wandering around in the dark, I might put my foot somewhere I shouldn't."

"More so than you already have?" She frowned as soon as the words left her mouth, and she tried to brush them off by reaching for her beer and taking a sip.

"Have I?" I wasn't going to let her off the hook.

She took a full swallow this time. "Nathan's firm has a client who is in the reptile business," she said. "Importing reptiles is, well, it's a grey area. For a long time, there weren't any laws outlining what could and couldn't be brought into the States. The government isn't in a rush to clear up the inconsistencies with the current laws. Endangered species are all protected, but there are a lot of other species that are in high demand at the zoos and with collectors. Where there's demand, there are people willing to supply that demand, especially when no one's quite sure what is legal and what isn't."

"Nathan is representing one of these suppliers?"

"The firm is," Angel corrected me. When I rolled my eyes, she relented. "Yeah, okay. Yes, he's Nathan's client."

"And he's in trouble with the feds."

"The Department of Fish and Wildlife," Angel said. "They're trying to curtail the import trade. They've been working some of these cases for nearly a decade. They have to get the illegal reptiles and the importer in the same room, you know? It's like any sting operation. They have to have clear evidence of a transaction occurring. Most of these guys are really good at using secondaries and blind deliveries."

"Like me, running that python down to Tijuana," I said.

"Like you."

"So it *was* a delivery."

Angel raised her shoulders. "Maybe?"

"You're not convincing me, counselor."

"I don't work for the firm," she reminded me. "It would be a breach of the firm's policies—as well as a breach of client-at-torney confidentiality—for me to know anything specific about Nathan's relationship with his client."

"But you're a smart lady," I said.

"I am," Angel said. "And when I told Nathan why you had called me this morning, he got very upset." She rapped her bottle against the counter. "Nathan has an investigator who serves papers and runs errands for him. I've never met him, but I was with Nathan once when they had a meeting. He drove a beat-up station wagon. I think his name is Rob or something. Nathan has a special ring tone on his phone for him. It sounds like a rooster crowing."

I glanced at the chain restaurant trinket on the key ring. Most of the paint had worn off, but there was still some red in the rooster's comb. "Cock Robin," I said.

"That sounds like a porn name," Angel said.

"It's not a very good one," I pointed out.

"Well"—Angel shrugged—"all of the good names were already taken." A smile tugged at her lips.

"So, you figure Cock of the Walk was supposed to be running an errand for Nathan," I said, keeping us on track. "But, for some reason, I get tapped to fill in for him."

"In his car." She tapped the counter again. "With his keys."

I considered possible scenarios. "Okay, so Cock of the Hour—"

Angel held up a hand. "Could you—"

"What?"

"Stop saying—just call him 'Rob,' okay?"

"Sure. 'Rob' has some kind of accident. Someone panics and thinks '*Oh shit, who do we know who can run an errand for us?*' But they don't call another investigator—the firm has to have more than one on retainer, right?—they go to an outside party. Someone they can coerce into doing the job. Someone who won't want to draw attention to themselves."

"Someone they have leverage over."

"They don't have any leverage," I said. "They might think they do, but there's nothing for them to yank."

"What about that trip you took over the summer?"

"I was visiting friends up in Oregon," I said.

"You don't have any friends in Oregon," she said.

"I made a new one," I said. "And I was visiting her."

Angel caught herself before she asked. She wandered toward the living room, her beer in her hand. "Rob isn't available, and this woman pulls you in to run a delivery. What was it? A tree python? Is it on the lists?"

I thought about what the pet store guy had told me. "I don't think so. It's rare, but not illegal."

"All you had to do was drop it off? They weren't supposed to pay you?"

I flashed back to the awkwardness in the warehouse. "Well,

maybe. I was told to get a receipt."

"A receipt?"

"Yeah, a receipt. But they were under the impression that I was supposed to be paid."

"How much?"

"We didn't get that far."

Her eyes flicked toward my arm. There had been blood on my sleeve last night. The shirt was in my bedroom. I should probably get rid of it, but nowhere near the house.

"Did you kill someone?" Angel asked quietly. Before I could respond, she countered with: "No. Don't answer that."

"They had guns and they seemed like the sort who knew how to use them," I said. "It didn't feel like a casual meet-up between reptile enthusiasts. It felt more like . . ."

"Like?" She prompted me when I trailed off.

"A drug buy." I said.

Her lips firmed into a tight line.

When she didn't offer any sort of cogent summary, I figured I might as well take a stab at it. "Nathan's firm is unaware of what's going on," I said. "A federal agency like, say, DEA or Fish & Wildlife scoops Rob up and replaces him with their own delivery boy. Everything else stays the same. Their new delivery boy is supposed to take the snake down to Mexico, pick up some package in return—probably a kilo of coke or something—and bring it back. Right? I wasn't supposed to get a 'receipt.' It was a euphemism for something else. They don't want to tell their delivery boy what he's really bringing back, because he'll tell them to go fuck themselves. He doesn't want to violate HS 11352."

California Health and Safety Code 11352 covered narcotics—possession, intent to distribute, and transportation. I was intimately familiar with this code. Sure, the coke had been in the car I had been driving, and so—technically—there was possession. And I had been driving the car, so that covered "transportation." But the rest? Intent to distribute and all that?

Well, it's old history at this point—and time served, thank you very much—but the State of California never forgets about these things. *Once a criminal, always a criminal* is how they like to call it. What other conclusion could they come to if they found a kilo of cocaine in my car, especially if I was coming across the border with it.

"Were they setting you up?" Angel asked.

"Maybe," I said. "Was giving me your number a nice way of making sure I had someone to call when I got picked up?"

She shivered slightly. "That's cold."

"That's the feds," I said.

Angel shook her head. "But you said they had no leverage on you. That they aren't watching you."

"That doesn't mean they don't have an ax to grind," I said.

"Do they?"

I finished my beer and went to the refrigerator for another. "There are easier ways to mess with me, if that's what they want to do," I said as I opened the second beer.

Angel didn't ask me to clarify that. "If they meant for this to work, then you were supposed to call me when you came back," she said. "You delivered the snake. You got the drugs. Why were you supposed to call me?"

"Because that would make a direct connection between me and you," I said.

"But we already have a connection," she said. "Why go to all that trouble?"

A thing that had been nagging me since Mrs. Chow and I had left Camellia suddenly came into focus. She had dragged me to the salons so I could discover the connection between the woman in the car and . . . *Not the family business*, I realized. *A connection between them and . . . someone in the family.*

Favorite daughter.

"Nathan's in trouble," I said.

Angel shook her head. "No. No, he isn't."

She answered too quickly. Her voice was a little too insistent. Trying to convince me.

"He is," I said. Suddenly, it all made sense. I knew who the asset was that Frolic was protecting. "I'm supposed to make sure *you* don't get hurt."

CHAPTER 11

ANGEL DIDN'T FOLLOW MY TRAIN OF THOUGHT, AND AFTER talking around it for a few more minutes, it was clear she wasn't in the same head space I was. I let it go. She was a Chow, and she would be obstinate until she decided otherwise. There was no point in banging my head against that wall. It was all too familiar. The disconnect left us at odds, though, and when Angel left, an awkward tension remained in the room.

How was I supposed to keep Angel safe if she didn't believe me?

There are only a few people who could change her mind, and one of them was in the main house. I put Stephanie's phone in my pocket, so someone else wouldn't wander off with it—Angel had taken Cock Robin's keys with her—and I wandered across the yard to the patio. Baby Baby heard me on the deck, and his yappy bark was better than a knock. I waited a polite second before going into the house.

Mrs. Chow was in the kitchen, sitting at the wooden table that afforded her a view of the driveway and the sidewalk. There was a teapot and a pair of tiny cups on a fancy tray in the middle of the table, and she was working on the crossword in the *LA Times*.

"Seven letter word for 'ill-mannered and rude,'" she said as I came into the room. "Starts with 'B.'"

"Baby Baby," I said. "No, wait. That's eight letters."

The dog was in one of the other chairs at the table. His gaze said he didn't find the joke funny. A ghost of a smile touched Mrs. Chow's lips. She tapped her pen on the table near the dog, and said something in Mandarin. The dog looked at her like he didn't understand Chinese. I helped him out by tipping the chair. His nails scrabbled on the wooden seat for a second and then he hopped off. He spun in a circle, like he was winding up for a barkathon. Mrs. Chow waggled her pen at him, and he swallowed all of his bluster. With a flick of his tail, he wandered off as if we were boring him.

"'Boorish,'" Mrs. Chow said as she wrote the word in the tiny boxes.

"It was on the tip of my tongue," I said.

She gave me an inscrutable look. I poured tea in both of the cups and put one near her hand.

"Your daughter doesn't like the idea of having a babysitter," I said after I tried the tea. It was hot and flush with the taste of jasmine and rose.

"No grown woman does," Mrs. Chow said.

"Who is the federal lady who gets her toes done at the salon?"

Mrs. Chow ignored my question. "'Not very bright,'" she said. "Three letters."

Back to the old game. "There are five letters in my last name," I said. "So that can't be it."

She wrote the answer down—*DIM*—and then picked up her tea and sipped it carefully.

"Your husband—may his spirit be forever at peace in a field of yellow flowers and baby bunnies—was just as manipulative as you," I said, "But he, at least, acknowledged it when I caught him doing it."

"My husband—may his spirit eternally nuzzle at the naked breast of my better self—wanted to turn a boy into a man. Now he is gone, and that boy is all grown." Her eyes flicked up and down. "Big and strong and full of wisdom, yes?"

"Your husband—may he always be upwind of the fields where the sacred cows shit—was . . . what was the word?" I nodded at the crossword. "Oh, yes. *BOORISH*," I said. "'Ill-mannered and rude.' That sounds about right."

Mrs. Chow wrapped both her hands around the tea cup. She pursed her lips and blew carefully on the hot tea. Her nails were immaculately done, as one would expect of the owner of half-dozen well known salons.

"I understand how it's part of the mystique that you're above it all, which probably works well for people who are born and raised in your culture, but I'm a local boy. Born up in those Rocky Mountains," I said. "Corn-fed, not terribly well-prepared by the public school system, and spat out by an industry that tends to eat its own. You can't be surprised that I blunder more than I walk in a straight line. But is that what you really want? Me blundering about? Surely, you want something a little better—a little more informed—when it comes to your daughter." I paused for effect. "Your *favorite* daughter."

"Only daughter," Mrs. Chow said. She put down her teacup and picked up the folded newspaper. She restored it to its full size, and flipped it over. Opposite the crossword puzzle, there was a half page advertisement for some event. It featured a large snake, coiled up in a dramatic pose. Across the top of the ad were the words: "North America Reptile Convention."

"NARC," I said, cleverly reducing the name to an acronym.

The convention was taking place this weekend. At the Los Angeles Convention Center. *Hundreds of dealers*, the copy read. *Thousands of snakes.* There was a long list of serpent celebrities who were going to be in attendance. *Every industry has its rock stars,* I thought.

"Lots of buyers and sellers," Mrs. Chow said, tapping a long nail against the ad. "All of it legal." Her finger drifted away from the page and tapped on the table. "But what happens over here?"

Conventions were like lightning rods. They drew all sorts. The dealers on the convention floor would be operating as legal entities, buying and selling their wares in plain view. Everything would be nice and tidy and well-documented. The part of the convention circuit that got advertised in the papers. However, when you had that many people in close proximity—especially when there were specialized interests in play—there was bound to be some back-room dealing. Transactions that would never be invoiced. Show up with a duffel bag and make a quick swap. No questions would be asked. No one would remember any faces.

You couldn't use a credit card for those purchases. You paid in cash, or with some equivalent. Something with street value. Like, say, a kilogram of cocaine.

I asked about boyfriend Nathan, and without too much drama, Mrs. Chow gave up his last name and the name of the law firm he worked for. Bracing the boyfriend wasn't going to make Angel happy, but the simplest way for a blundering oaf like myself to get some answers was to talk to Nathan directly.

I drove over to Century City—the land of chrome and steel in LA—and overpaid for an hour of parking in a lot. The law firm of Stepanish, Groiller, and Bernstein was on the sixteenth floor of a building that had all the personality of a brick. Someone had tried to do a nip and tuck job on the lobby, but you can only put so much chrome and glass over a concrete foundation before it starts to feel less like a habitable building and more like a first-year architectural student's design response to *What Would Happen If We Didn't Have Wood?*

The sixteenth floor, on the other hand, had been visited by an interior designer with an actual degree. The carpet was the color and texture of cute puppies and the wall sconces were a little too identical to be hard-carved, but man, they really tried to sell themselves as such. Past a pair of doors marked with the firm's initials, there was a lobby filled with potted orchids and ostentatious oil paintings. It felt like an abandoned Stanley Kubrick set.

SG&B rated two receptionists. They sat—trim and well-dressed—behind an imposing slab of marble. The firm's name was spelled out in big letters on the wall behind them. The receptionists, dark-haired beauties who had mastered the art of looking right through you—took turns answering the phone. They spoke softly, but precisely, into their respective headsets. It was a masterful illusion that gave the impression that this was a very important firm which had no time for anyone who hadn't made an appointment at least a decade ago.

There were three doors out of the lobby. None of them were marked, though they were filled with frosted glass. *There are things going on in here*, these doors said, *things which you will never be allowed to see, but you want to see them, don't you?* Up on the ceiling, near the corners of the room, there were several round globes of smoked glass. *Security cameras,* I thought.

The receptionist on the left finally deigned to acknowledge me. "Good afternoon," she said, looking through my midsection. She smiled, but there was nothing personable about her expression.

"I'm here to see Nathan Shackleton," I said.

Her eyes flicked down to something on the desk I couldn't see. "Mr. Shackleton doesn't have—"

"I'm not on his calendar," I said. "I don't have an appointment."

Her eyes flicked over me. If it were possible to be thrown out by a glance, I would have found myself in the hall. "Stepanish, Groiller, and Bernstein do not take"—she hesitated as she tried to remember the words she needed—"walk-in clients."

"That's okay," I said. "I don't want to see any of them. I'm just here to see Nathan Shackleton."

Beside her, the other receptionist paused between calls, as if she had never seen anyone so incapable of reading the vibe they were putting off.

"Mr. Shackleton is a very busy executive with this organization," the first receptionist said. "He does not have time—"

"He'll make time for me," I said. I gave the second receptionist a pleasant smile. The *I'm a professional and I do this all the time* smile.

She didn't seem convinced.

"I'm sorry," the first receptionist said, her tone telling me that she really wasn't. "I'm afraid you've made a mistake, Mr.—"

"Bliss," I supplied. "Butch Bliss." I waved a hand at the edifice of their conjoined desk. "Why don't you call him and ask. That's Bliss. B-L-I-S-S."

"Mr. Bliss, I'm not at liberty to interrupt any member of the firm when they might be in session with another client."

"Oh, I can wait," I said. I feigned interest in the oil painting hanging to my right. It depicted a grand ship, its sails full, racing across a fierce sea.

"Mr. Bliss, I can assure you that Mr. Shackleton has no openings this afternoon. Nor does he have any openings tomorrow, either. In fact, he's—"

"Booked all week?" I finished for her. "All those billable hours. He's quite the catch for SG&B, isn't he?"

She gave me a patronizing smile.

"I'll tell you what," I said. "Why don't you just write him a sticky note or something? Tell him that Butch Bliss came by to see him. I wanted to chat about a green tree python that he had me deliver, and—"

The leftmost door buzzed. Two men in dark blazers came through it. They had squared-off haircuts and chins that matched. One of them glanced at the receptionist, who gave him an almost imperceptible nod, and the other focused his attention on me. He had attended the same frosty seminar as the women at the desk, but he had gone back for an additional session of *Who wants to share a death glare with the class?*

The firm got what it paid for from these seminars.

I kept my hands in view as the goons approached. "All right," I said. "Mr. Shackleton would rather not talk about the kilo of coke he had me smuggle across the border. I get it. It's a little too personal. I'll go down to the *LA Times*. They can help me figure out what to do with it."

The second goon stopped in front of me. He was close—closer than two people should be unless it was a cocktail party and she was giving you all the right signals with her eyes and plunging neckline. He put his hands on his hips and flared his nostrils. He had three inches on me, and his neck was thicker than my thigh. His blazer could barely contain all his muscles.

I didn't move. I'd stood before guys even bigger than this dude—real murderous pieces of work. They were always trying to rule the room with this sort of monkey posturing. It was how everyone knew who was in charge. The only difference between prison and the lobby of SG&B was that, in prison, if you didn't back down, someone was going to get hurt. Maybe even killed. Here, in this posh Century City lobby with all these orchids and oil paintings? Nothing was going to happen. They wouldn't touch me. That was how lawsuits started. They were going to puff up and crowd in close, but that was it. They were going to wait for me to do something stupid. And then it was all defensible. *The nut job started it, Your Honor. I was just doing my job.*

The goon stared at me. Waiting for me to do something stupid. *I've gone to the seminar,* his stare said. *I can stand here all day.*

I could have waited him out, but yeah, I wouldn't get that time back. I'd had enough of that at Tehachapi.

I feinted to my left, and pivoted to my right as he moved in response. Without making contact, I flowed past him—*water around a stone*—and got two steps closer to the receptionists' desk. The other goon intercepted me, but he didn't touch me. The guy I had slipped around came up behind me.

I was in a sandwich. I couldn't move without making contact, and that would be all the excuse they'd need. *It looked like a threatening gesture, Your Honor.*

I raised up on my toes, trying to see around the brick with the Brillo haircut in front of me. "Tell Nathan I stopped by, would you?"

The receptionist didn't reply.

"Okay, okay," I said. "It was a *morelia viridis*—the snake I delivered for him. Do you need me to spell that for you?"

"It's time for you to leave," Brillo growled.

I lowered down, but stayed light on my feet. I gave him *my* stare—the one I learned on the state's dime. "You're in my space," I said. "As is your pal behind me. Where am I supposed to go?"

He shrugged. Spatial relations were above his paygrade, apparently.

"You've boxed me in," I said. "I'm sure you're well-practiced in all the hand-wringing and sad face-making that your bosses will need when the inevitable lawsuit lands, but that argument is going to be a tough sell with what's on the tape, isn't it? Unless, of course, SG&B has a habit of dropping tape."

He wasn't following my line of thinking. "Okay," I said with a sigh. "It's going to go one of two ways. One: I twitch, and you put your meaty paws on me. Shake me a few times and then march me downstairs. At which point, I go down to the *Times,* whip up a good tale for whoever is hungry for a Century City shit-stirrer of a story. I'll take the first ambulance chaser who calls after it hits print. We hit SG&B with enough paper to cover the desks of those gorgeous ladies—I mean, *witnesses*—over there. And we file for the tapes in the security cameras, which will show, fairly unequivocally, that there were two of you and one of me, and I never raised my hand. Or . . ."

"Or?" There was an actual hint of curiosity in his voice.

"Or I drop both of you in about twenty seconds and walk out of here without an escort. I'll still go to the *Times*, tell my story, find a good and sleazy personal injury lawyer—*bla bla bla*—but the bonus part is that you two get ambulance rides."

Brillo tilted his head from side to side. I heard his neck crack, which said more about his current state of chiropractic care than anything else.

"Really?"

Behind me, the other guy leaned in, shifting his weight.

I gave them one more chance. I raised my voice so the receptionist could hear me. "Are you sure Mr. Shackleton isn't available this afternoon?"

CHAPTER 12

I heard a gentle buzz from behind the desk. Brillo heard it too, and his eyes narrowed. He and I stood still, as if we were inside a soap bubble. One move—one breath is all it would take—and the bubble would pop. Who knew what would happen then?

A disembodied voice spoke. It came from the same place as the buzzing noise. "Ms. Cline: please show Mr. Bliss to conference room two."

It wasn't the voice of God, but it definitely came from somewhere on high. The guy behind me exhaled noisily before he stepped back. Brillo wasn't going to move, and so I stepped to the side. I didn't want to keep Ms. Cline waiting.

She was the one who had suffered my questions earlier, and she rose fluidly from her chair as I approached. She wore a blue dress that hugged her form. It had an artful scoop in the front that showed the base of her neck and a bit more, but not too much. Up close, I spotted a tiny charm nestled in the hollow of her throat. It was strung on a tiny silver necklace. A matching pair of charms hung off the bracelet on her wrist.

"This way," she said, indicating the door on the right of the desk. It magically unlocked as she approached it. I went through the door and turned, anticipating that she would be behind me. She wasn't.

Brillo dogged my heels, and when the door shut, he planted himself. Hands clasped in front of him. Face fixed in an unseeing gaze that missed nothing.

The carpet on this side of the door was gold and the walls were a richer brown—neutral colors that quietly whispered "money money money." The big canvases and potted orchids motif remained in play. The hallway went on for awhile before it made a right turn. There were doors on either side, and the second conference room was on my left.

I didn't dawdle.

The outside wall of the conference room was floor-to-ceiling windows, and the haze wasn't too bad. I could see as far as the Santa Monica Mountains. The room was filled with a long table and lots of chairs. There was a sidebar along the wall next to the door, and sitting on it were a water-filled decanter and a tray of fancy-looking glasses.

"Shut the door," the sole occupant of the room ordered. He was a rugged older man, the sort who looked like he had done action movies in his prime, but who couldn't be bothered with all the stunt work anymore. He wore a three-piece bespoke suit, unlike the off-the-rack jackets Brillo and his pal were wearing. His hands were large, and the silver ring on his right index finger would definitely leave a mark when he popped someone in the jaw.

"Have a seat, Mr. Bliss," he said. He was indifferent to my presence. His attention remained on the steno pad in front of him. He wrote with broad strokes, a fancy-looking pen held casually in his capable hands.

"I'll stand," I said. I was supposed to be cowed by this impressive display—the view, the table, the fancy suit and the fancy pen—but all of it missed its mark with me.

His hand hesitated for half a second before he continued to doodle on the pad.

I poured myself a glass of water. I drank it, refilled my glass, and poured water in a second glass. I carried it over and put it down on the table within his reach.

"It looks like thirsty work," I said. As I suspected, the pad was covered with illegible nonsense.

He stopped writing. His gaze went to the glass, and then to a tidy stack of wooden coasters near the center of the table.

"Oops," I said. "I'm more used to those formica tops they have at the police station."

He put his pen down and leaned back in his chair. "You are a pain in the ass, aren't you, Mr. Bliss?"

"Absolutely, sir."

He narrowed his eyes as he measured me. "You do any time?" he asked.

"In the armed services?" I shook my head. "No, sir. Did ten in the CDCR, though."

He gave that reveal a slight nod. "You met Frank," he said. It wasn't a question. "Green Beret. Special Forces."

"I'd be disappointed in SG&B if that weren't the case," I said.

"Do you know why I asked Ms. Cline to let you in, Bliss?" he asked.

"You're going to tell me, so I'd rather not embarrass myself by guessing incorrectly."

He had dropped the "Mister." I dropped the "sir." We'd be on a first-name basis in no time.

He lifted the steno pad. There was a picture underneath it, which he slid across the table. "You were making a lot of noises out there, Bliss. What were you hoping to accomplish by slandering Mr. Shackleton?"

I glanced at the picture. It was a glossy headshot of a man in a blue suit. He was sitting in a courtroom, the US flag hanging behind his right shoulder. He was wearing a well-rehearsed smile, the sort that doesn't come naturally on the human face. It takes practice.

"I was hoping to talk with Mr. Shackleton," I said. I tapped the picture. "This isn't him, by the way, but thanks for testing me."

He raised an eyebrow. "What makes you so sure?" he asked.

Angel would never date a dude who smiled like that, was the thought that ran through my head. I flipped the picture over. Contact info was printed on the back. "This is a headshot of a character actor who really wants to be hired for a courtroom drama one of the networks is pushing." I slung the picture back at him.

"You sound like a man who has done some work around here," he said.

"Back in the day, you and I were probably fighting for space on the dollar rental shelf," I said. "What was it? Sexy Euro-trash terrorists with dirty bombs or maniacal megalomaniacs with daddy issues?"

"Euro-trash terrorists were cheaper," he said. "You can do a lot of hair and wardrobe."

"I bet." I leaned forward. "You're not Nathan Shackleton," I said. I recalled last Thanksgiving. This dude was impressive enough I would have noticed him if he had gotten out of the car with Angel. Also, and I didn't want to be ageist, but yeah, he was too old for her. "I'm not sure why you're wasting your time with me."

"I'm not," he said. "Around here, they refer to me as *Mister* Shackleton. It alleviates confusion as to whether you're speaking of the father or the son."

"Oh," I said.

Mister Shackleton crossed his hands over the steno pad. "Let's start over, shall we? Why don't you tell me everything you can about my son, this snake, and this—alleged—kilogram of illegal narcotic."

I fetched two coasters from the tray and put one under each of our water glasses. "It starts with a hot dog," I began.

Shackleton took no notes, and his interruptions were short, pointed questions when I was vague on the details. As I talked, I refined my estimation of his background. He *had* done film work, but he had come up through the military. In an investigative capacity of some kind, I suspected, given the nature of his questions. I wondered what he did for SG&B. I suspected his job description didn't include filing briefs and taking depositions.

I finished my story, and Shackleton's only reaction was a slight tightening of his lips. "I've met Angel," he said. "Nathan's had her over for dinner a couple of times. A pleasant young woman. Bright. Good listener. She knows more about wine and French cooking than my son, in fact. Almost has her JD, if I recall."

"Almost," I said. "She's under the impression that SG&B might give her a call when she's done."

He made a vague gesture with his hands. "You like her," he said.

"We've known each other for awhile," I said.

That earned me a slight smile. "Has she turned you down?" he asked.

"For lunch?" I shook my head. "No, she usually shows up. Pays her half too."

"This isn't about you and her?"

"Well, I'm not here because I like your boy, Mr. Shackleton."

"You've never met him."

"I haven't," I said. Thanksgiving pass-by notwithstanding.

He cleared his throat and toyed with his pen for a moment. I had a vision of him stabbing me in the hand, and I kept them in my lap. Just in case. "You didn't actually see any drugs," he said.

"When I dropped off the snake?" I shook my head. "I did not."

"Cash?"

"My bag was the only one I saw."

"In a separate room, perhaps?"

"Sure. That's probably where the drugs were too." I raised my shoulders. "'Speculation, Your Honor,'" I said, trying for the pinched voice you'd expect to hear from an aggrieved lawyer on a prime time network drama.

He frowned. "Don't do that," he said.

"It works on TV."

"Lots of things work on TV." He picked up his pen again. "How much does a python go for, in the open market?"

"I dunno. What's the street value of a kilo of cocaine?"

"Don't conflate the two. That's not how it works."

"I don't know how any of it works," I said. "All I know is what a guy at a mall pet store told me. The snake's not that rare. Maybe two hundred bucks."

He uncapped his pen and wrote "200" on the pad. Fronted it with a dollar sign and then circled it a few times. So that it stood out from the doodling. "You know anything about a medieval scholar named William of Ockham?" he asked.

"Who?"

"He was a theorist and philosopher," Shackleton said. "Developed something called Ockham's Razor, which was a sentiment that you shouldn't over-complicate an explanation. The simplest solution is usually the right solution. KISS."

"Excuse me?"

"Keep it simple, stupid."

"Oh, sure," I said.

Mr. Chow used to say *Less is more* when we were doing tai chi. It was one of those koan sayings, the sort of pithy phrases that ancient monks used to spout at one another in an effort to show off their deep insight into whatever their spiritual hangup was. Mr. Chow had a saying that was similiar to "keep it simple, stupid." It was: "Don't be a moron." A good litmus check for doing tai chi and for surviving the day-to-day at Tehachapi. Outside, though, well, people have a tendency to over-think things. They wind themselves up into spectacular knots, trying to cover over inadequacies and things they feel guilty about.

For instance, Shackleton thought I was trying to shake down his son because that was the simplest answer in his world-view, but the flaw in that theory was that I gave a shit about his kid. Sure, I liked Angel, but did I like her enough to dream up some wild story about a drug run to Mexico in order to discredit her boyfriend? And if so, why had I come here? Wouldn't it have worked better if I had just gone to the paper?

"Well," I said. "Maybe we should ask your son."

Shackleton gave me a hard-eyed squint from his bag of intimidation tricks. It was a good glare—maybe he had been a special speaker at that seminar Frank and his pal had attended.

Keep your cool, Bliss, I thought.

"Why would I come here if I wanted to make him look like an ass in front of Angel?" I asked. "Do you think this is an extortion play? That might work—and I stress might—but only if he's done something that's worthy of the effort. And isn't asking him the easiest way to find that out? I mean, if you're keeping things simple, you shouldn't be talking to me. You should be talking to your son."

Shackleton blinked. The glare vanished, and it was like someone had switched off a spotlight. Without a word, he got up and went to the door. He opened it, spoke quietly to Frank who wasn't far away, and then closed the door again. He went to the sidebar, poured his own glass of water, and stood there with it in his hand. "Very well," he said. "Let's ask Nathan."

We waited, and I watched the shadow of a cloud wander across the white buildings of the Getty Museum. It had only been open for a year or so in its new Brentwood location, and it had already become one of those indelible landmarks of LA.

A few minutes later, when someone knocked at the door, it wasn't Nathan. It was Frank, and he whispered a few words to Shackleton and then withdrew.

Shackleton put his water glass down and wandered over to the windows. "My son is not in the building," he said. I had no sense whether he was surprised or angry by the news Frank had delivered.

"That's bad luck for me," I said. "Makes it hard to know whether I'm lying or not, doesn't it?"

"Apparently, he left shortly after you and I started talking," Shackleton added.

"That's terribly convenient," I said.

"It is," he said.

"Nicely played, though," I said. "You get me to spin out the whole story for you, giving your son time to wander off so when you play the 'keep it simple stupid' bullshit on me, it doesn't actually mean anything."

A grunt—it might have been a chuckle—escaped Shackleton's frame. "Did you think your performance out there was going to get you anywhere? I've seen better acting from extras who don't even speak English. This firm has a reputation in this city. We are discrete, and our clients value our discretion. If I asked Frank to make you disappear, you'd vanish so completely your own mother wouldn't remember having given birth to you."

"That's not as much of a trick as you think," I said. "But then, my mom has lost track of a lot of things over the years."

Shackleton didn't take the bait. He continued to stare out the window.

I thought about what hadn't happened. Frank was still outside the room. I was still inside. Nathan was quote *not in the building* unquote.

"You know he's involved in something," I said. "You don't know what it is, but my performance out there—worthy of a daytime soap opera or not—set off some alarms in your head, didn't it? You wanted to hear what I had to say. You wanted to see Nathan's face when you confronted him with it." I waved a hand. "But he's done a runner."

"I am in charge of security for Stepanish, Grollier, and Berstein," Shackleton said. "My directive is to maintain the firm's reputation and standing in the community. That includes the partners, junior lawyers, clerks, interns—Hell, I know more about the dumb fucks in the mailroom than their mothers do. I protect this firm and its clients. First and foremost."

"He's your son," I said.

Shackleton turned his head. "Yes, he is. And if I were merely his father, I'd come over there and knock your teeth out for what you're implying about my son."

"I wouldn't fault you for trying," I said.

His gaze bore into me. "Nathan drives a silver Porsche Boxster," he said. He rattled off the license plate. "I would like to know what he says when you ask him about the python. Frank will have Ms. Cline give you my direct line."

I stood up and headed for the door. Our little chat was over. "I'll be sure to call, sir," I said as I reached the conference room door.

"Oh, and Bliss?"

I stopped and looked back at him.

"Remember what I said about Frank. In case you're wrong."

CHAPTER 13

I WENT DOWN TO THE PARKING GARAGE UNDER THE BUILDING, and wandered around until I found the section reserved for SG&B. I didn't expect to find Nathan's Boxster, but strolling up and down the aisles gave me the opportunity to think about my meeting with Shackleton.

Who was he? Ex-military intelligence. In charge of the firm's security. Surrounds himself with other ex-military types. Has the big ring, but it's on his right hand. There's nothing on his left, which suggests there's no Mrs. Shackleton. Was he divorced? Widowed? Did it matter? Nathan's mother wasn't in the picture anymore. That was a conclusion that followed.

How had he come to work for a big Century City law firm? Had Nathan made introductions, or had Dad smoothed the way for his son when Nathan had graduated from law school? Regardless, I didn't think that Shackleton and his son hung out at the executive water cooler and talked about last night's ball game. Not because they weren't the sort who bonded over sports, but because Dad took his job seriously. Whispers of nepotism would not be tolerated. Plus, there was the fact he had thrown his boy under the bus without much hesitation.

Was it more than that? Was there estrangement between the two? Was Daddy wrestling with the realization that his boy wasn't a boy anymore? That he was out in the big world, making big boy decisions, and Daddy couldn't be there to protect him.

So many questions. I really did need to find Nathan.

My car was parked across the street in the lot used by the working class, and by the time I returned to it, I had no better sense of father and son. I felt like I was working on a puzzle without the box: I didn't know how many pieces it had, I didn't know what the picture looked like, and I certainly hadn't found all the edge pieces.

The smart thing to do was not think about the puzzle for a little while. You get frantic when you think you're supposed to figure something out, and the anxiety only increases when you think there is a time limit. *Less is more,* Mr. Chow used to say. *Keep it simple,* Shackleton had said.

A good workout works the brain as well the brute, Willie loved to say.

In another life, Willie would have been a poet. Not a very good one, but a poet nonetheless.

After returning to the bungalow and changing clothes, I walked to Willie's gym. The black sedan I had first spotted on Wilshire was parked at the end of the block, almost as if it knew my routine. I mixed things up and went the other way, just to see if it would follow me. I had a few blocks to second-guess my suspicions; it wasn't quite the same make and model as Frolic's, but it loomed, regardless. A foreboding presence at the edge of my awareness.

It was after five by the time I finally made it to the gym (without any visible tail), and the place was buzzing with office drones looking for an endorphin rush. It didn't matter what the latest exercise craze was, Willie made sure there were a couple of energetic and perky instructors who would shout and cajole a room full of sweaty and flabby office workers. Most of the regulars were across the street at O'Douligan's, killing brain cells until the dilettantes were done admiring themselves in the mirrors and leaving the dumbbells out of order.

I was buzzing myself—a little wired around the edges—and I didn't mind the noise. I found a corner where I could skip rope without whacking anyone, and once I was good and loose, I lost myself in a few tai chi forms. Pushing all the tension of the day out through my palms and the bottoms of my feet. Extending my spine. Filling my spirit basin back up again.

The place was still busy by the time I was ready for the shower, and because crowded showers make my back and shoulders itch, I opted for the steam room. There were two men in the hot box: Stevie—Willie's muscular nephew—and Willie.

"Missed you this morning," Willie said. He was angular and lean, like a coyote. He eyed you like one too.

"Late night," I said as I climbed up to the top bench. I had nothing on but a towel, much like the other two men. Stevie was sprawled on the opposite bench, and while the steam obscured a lot of him, it didn't obscure enough. His towel looked like a washcloth on his muscular body. He was working on a power-lifting program—some kind of training for a reality TV show. Contestants had to dead lift a car or something like that. Stevie trained a lot. He also sweated a lot.

Moderation was hard for Stevie.

"Huh huh," Stevie chuckled at my comment.

"It wasn't like that," I said.

"Shoulda been, dude," Stevie chortled. "Shoulda been."

"I heard you got plucked out of line at Horatio's," Willie said.

I cracked an eye and looked at him through the haze. "Horatio tell you?" I asked.

"Nah," Willie said. "Word got around. There was a pool."

"A what?"

"A betting pool as to why you got snatched," Willie said.

"I put twenty down," Stevie said. "Parole violation."

"You don't get parole if you've served your time," I said.

"Oh," Stevie said. He shifted on his bench. "Anyway, you owe me twenty bucks."

"How do you figure that?"

Stevie shrugged. "*Pah-role*, dude. That's what it is: you're not in jail, but you still screwed up. It ain't my fault, therefore you owe me."

"Occasionally, I regret saving him as a kid at my brother's house," Willie said. "That one time when he was sucking water in the wading pool."

"Nothing says you can't fix that oversight," I said.

"I'd need a couple of elephants to hold him down now," Willie said.

"I like elephants," Stevie pointed out.

Talking with Stevie was a lost cause, and so I told Willie about the exchange in Tijauna and the subsequent encounter with Angel. I skipped some bits—mostly the parts where the girls got naked—and wound up with the meeting at SG&B over in Century City.

"I've heard of this Shackleton dude," he said when I finished.

"Yeah? What have you heard?"

"Army Intelligence. Maybe military police. Or a private contractor in Iraq during Desert Storm? Something like that."

"Well, he's running security out in Century City now."

"How about the son's license plate?" Willie asked. "You get anything on that?"

"You think they just give that info over the phone to ex-cons?"

"Don't tell them you're an ex-con when you ask."

I smacked my forehead. "Is that what I did wrong? Man, I knew it was something."

"You don't have someone you can call?"

"I don't have a lot of need to check out license plates," I said.

"You must be a pretty shitty private detective, then."

"I'm not," I said. "I'm just a guy who—"

"A guy who likes a girl who likes some other guy who is messed up with illegal snakes and coke?"

I wiped the sweat off my face. "Something like that," I said.

"Relax," Willie said. He leaned over and slapped me on the shoulder. "I have a friend who's got a second cousin who knows someone who lives in the same apartment complex as—"

"Yeah, I get it," I said. "Six million steps removed."

"Write it down," Willie said. "I'll see what I can do."

"Okay. Thanks, Willie."

Stevie had been watching us talk. "Is there going to be a fight?" he asked.

"A—what?" I asked.

"For the girl. You gonna go punch this dude in the nut sack?"

"I—I hadn't thought about it that much," I said.

"You should," Stevie said. He made a fist and sucker-punched the steam rising from the pit in the center of the room. "*Boom*. Make him talk funny for a week."

"I'm not sure that's going to solve anything," I pointed out.

That didn't seem to faze Stevie. He gave me a *If a dude takes your girl, you should punch him in the balls* sort of shrug.

I looked at Willie. "I'll write it down," I said.

"Leave it with Lorraine at the front desk," he said. "I should know something in a day or two."

"I'll try to stay out of trouble until then," I said.

Willie snorted like he didn't believe that was possible. Stevie sucker-punched the column of steam again. "Right in the nuts," he said. In case I wasn't sure.

"In the nuts," I echoed.

To be fair, it would make me feel better about everything. And that satisfaction shouldn't be dismissed outright.

The sun had set by the time I left Willie's, which made it easier for the black sedan to hide. It took me a few blocks to notice it, even with the streetlights. When I reached the end of the next block, I figured it was time to see how dedicated they were.

I turned right, and as soon as I was out of sight, I broke into a sprint. I didn't take the alley—that felt obvious—but there was a sports car and a panel van parked near the end of the block. I darted behind the panel van and crouched down by its rear tires. There was no streetlight overhead. I was in the shadows.

I didn't have to wait long.

The black car nosed through the intersection and turned in my direction. It cruised slowly down the street, and as it passed the van, I crept behind it. I peered out from behind the bumper, watching the sedan as it reached the next intersection.

There was no stop sign, but the car slowed. The driver was looking for me, and he let the sedan glide through the intersection. It kept going after that, picking up speed. I watched it go, and it didn't make any effort to circle back. They weren't interested in playing games.

It wasn't like they didn't know where I was going.

However, their cavalier surveillance suggested they were merely keeping an eye on me. What I was up to wasn't as much a concern as whether I was bumbling around.

I bumbled on home. Was screwing up the delivery of the snake part of their plan? If so, I had done my part. Now it was someone else's turn. But who? Nathan? The person who was supposed to get the snake in the first place? Or was the person next to panic supposed to be . . . Angel?

I didn't like that line of thinking, and I tried calling Angel when I got back to the bungalow. She didn't answer.

Stephanie's phone wanted my attention. There was an icon saying there was voice mail waiting. As I stared at the tiny phone, it chirped at me. A batter indicator was flashing. If I was going to listen to the messages, I needed to do so soon.

I sighed and punched buttons. As I suspected, the messages were from Pen.

The first one: *I'm lonely. Do I have to wait until tomorrow?*

The second: *Play with me?*

I didn't get to hear the third one. The phone gave one final beep before it shut off.

☆

I had trouble falling asleep. Every time I closed my eyes, I fell into a dream where I was in the car, driving back from Tijuana. Every time I looked over, there was a different woman in the seat next to me. First it was Stephanie; then, it was Pen; finally, it was Angel. They were all fiddling with the buttons on their blouses. Stephanie laughed about the awkwardness of the situation. Pen had no trouble with her buttons. Every time she inhaled, they all popped their button holes, which is a simple trick that every wardrobe person knows how to do. The first time you see it happen on set, it's like movie magic, but after the hundredth time or so, it's just part of the job. And . . . *Action! Inhale. Blouse pops open. Try to look surprised.*

Angel wasn't in any rush, but when she reached for the second button, Mr. Chow would pop up in the back seat, rising like a demonic jack-in-the-box

Masturbation, he would crow, *is submission.*

He liked to remind me—and anyone else who would put up with his diatribe on this topic—that masturbation in prison, where the guards were always watching us, was an act of hidden shame and submission. You were a victim of your desires, and when you jerked it, there was a good chance someone was watching. And when you abandoned yourself to your most secret desires like that, you were submitting to their watchfulness. *If you let them see you,* he would say, *they will know you are weak. Do you know what happens to the weak ones?*

It was a rhetorical question. We all knew, and so we did our best to not be weak. Though, all it did was make us tense and cranky.

Mr. Chow was of the opinion that being slightly cranky made for better situational awareness. A man on edge is a man more likely to sense danger before it showed up. He'd be more likely to react swiftly and aggressively when the time came.

A man on edge was more likely to do something, instead of waiting for something to happen to him.

Eventually, I got up, put on my black tracksuit with the hoodie, and slipped out of the bungalow through the spare bedroom window. That bedroom faced the back fence, and I went over it easily. The alley was dark and empty, and I went to the end of the block where I checked the street.

No black sedan.

I stayed close to hedges and shrubbery, and worked my way toward the street in front of Mrs. Chow's house.

The black sedan was parked at the curb, about halfway between Mrs. Chow's house and the intersection. The house at the corner had a decorative brick wall around the front yard. It was meant to be a deterrent against passive-aggressive neighbors who walked their dogs past other people's houses so that the beasts could shit in yards other than theirs. On the yard side of the wall, there were enough shadows to make for a good hiding place. After about twenty minutes of pretending to be a shadow within a shadow, I was rewarded with a slight rocking motion as whoever was in the car shifted in their seat.

I had been picking at the bricks during my surveillance, and I didn't think the mortar was very good. Slowly, I rocked a few bricks along the top row until I found one that was looser then the others. It didn't take long to yank it off the wall. It wasn't as heavy as I would have liked, but it would do.

I stood up and threw the brick. It went through the back window of the sedan with a satisfying crash.

Derek came out of the car like he'd been stung by a wasp. He had his gun out and he looked around wildly, trying to figure out where the brick had come from.

He quickly realized the gun was the wrong thing to be waving in a residential neighborhood, and he tucked it away. He came around to the back of the car and examined the damage the brick had done to his window.

I waited. He looked around again. For a moment, I thought he was going to come down to the street corner, but he turned and went back to the driver's side door. He opened it, leaned in, and pulled the trunk release lever. When he returned to the trunk of the car, I knew that was my opportunity.

I tried to be quiet, but he heard me when I got close. He started to turn, but I caught him low on the back and shoved him against the car. His head bounced off the edge of the trunk, and I felt his legs wobble. I gave him a quick one-two in the kidneys. While he was still off-balance, I banged his head against the car once more, and then shoved him into the trunk. His legs hung out, but I scooped them up and shoved him all the way in.

I slammed the trunk shut.

Either there was a in-trunk release lever or there wasn't. If there was, I only had a minute or two before he found it. There wasn't any time to waste.

I went around to the driver's side door and yanked it open. The dome light didn't come on—he wasn't a total loss for a spook—but the lack of light meant I had to stick my head into the car to order to see anything. A bulky phone was plugged into the cigarette lighter. There was a cardboard box of sodas and packaged snacks on the passenger's seat. A manila folder was tucked behind the box.

Derek started banging on the lid of the trunk. He gave up after a moment and then the car rocked as he slithered around in the dark trunk.

I was out of time. I leaned farther in and grabbed the folder. I grabbed the keys from the ignition for good measure.

I locked the doors on the car. The manila folder tucked under my arm, I walked away. I tossed the keys down the storm drain in front of Mrs. Chow's house, and then I went back to the bungalow as if nothing had happened. Back in through the spare bedroom window.

Only then did I open the folder and look at what it contained.

CHAPTER 14

THERE WERE TWO PIECES OF PAPER IN THE FOLDER. ONE WAS a criminal summary: my mug shot, highlights of my incarceration, and an interesting paragraph summarizing the state's assessment of my psychological health. Lots of pop psychology that speculated on my relationship with my father and what my mother's death meant to me, but for the most part, it was the sort of multi-syllabic word salad that looks good on the page, but which doesn't really say shit when you parse it.

The other piece of paper was a surveillance summary of my daily routine: where I lived, where I went when I left the house, what kind of car I drove, and who I might run into during my perambulations. There was a medium-sized photo clipped to the page. It was a profile shot with lots of sun and an out-of-focus background. Something taken with a telephoto lens. I didn't recognize anything in the background, but the picture looked like it was taken in the last six months or so.

I thought about what Willie had said about me being a shitty PI. All I had on Nathan was his last name, where he worked, and a description of his car. Compared to the summary judgement and character assassination that Derek was working from, I was a toddler who couldn't even draw a picture with wax crayons. I wasn't a private investigator—the state of California has some laws about licensing and bonding and all that, and most of it boils down to "no" for ex-cons—but all that meant was I couldn't get my name in the phone book or have it stenciled on the door of some office.

The more I thought about it, the angrier I got. I had done my time—time that hadn't even been mine to serve. The drugs

I had allegedly been transporting hadn't been mine. The car I had been transporting them in wasn't mine either. Turk—the dude who had come to shiv me in the prison shower—hadn't been my doing either. And yet, I had given ten years of my life to the state of California for all that. And now? I was a convicted felon. I couldn't vote. I couldn't own a gun. And I had to check that very special box—*why yes, I do have a record*—on every job application, ensuring that no respectable business would hire me.

If I hoped to be a part of normal society again, I was supposed to take whatever grief anyone wanted to give me, because I was a criminal. We don't want them living in our neighborhoods, but we're monsters if we ship them all off to a tiny island, aren't we? *Oh, I guess they can stay, but let's keep a close eye on them. Be vigilant and ready to throw them back into jail at the slightest sign that they're doing bad things again.*

Most of the time, I didn't let the societal stigma of being an ex-con get under my skin, but this bullshit with Frolic was tipping the scale. *No more,* I thought, as I went to the closet where I kept the toolbox. *I'm done being everyone's punching bag.*

I settled on a clawhammer. That would do.

I threw some clothes into an overnight bag. I grabbed a wad of cash from my safe, and as an afterthought, I grabbed Stephanie's phone from the counter. I threw the bag into the trunk of the Mercedes, and let it roll into the street before I started it up. I parked it across the street from Derek's car, pointing in the opposite direction.

The street was quiet. The only house with any lights on was farther up the block. The trunk of Derek's car was still closed, and briefly, I wished I hadn't tossed the keys into the storm drain, but better safe than sorry, right? Grabbing the claw hammer, I got out of my car and approached the black sedan.

Standing by the back wheel on the driver's side, I rapped lightly on the trunk lid.

The car rocked as Derek twitched in the trunk.

"Can you hear me, Derek?" I called out.

"Fuck you," came a muffled reply.

"I want to talk."

"Suck my dick, Bliss," was his reply.

"The way you're folded up in there, you can probably suck it yourself," I said. "Might be a nice way to pass the time until some old lady out walking her dog finds you."

Derek squirmed again, and I waited for him to stop. "Before you try to shoot me through the trunk, think about what that's going to sound like in there," I said. "You'll be deaf, and then you won't be able to hear the awesome deal I have for you." I waited a second. "Plus, you'll probably miss."

He was quiet for awhile. "What do you want, Bliss?"

"I want to know who you're working for."

"Fuck off," was his reply.

I nodded. I had expected that. He wasn't going to play nice. Not at first. "Who was the woman in the car yesterday?"

"Eat shit," he said.

Well, so much for asking nicely. I banged the clawhammer against the trunk a few times, and then I backed off. Just in case he decided the chance of putting a bullet in me was worth the hearing loss.

He didn't shoot. I circled the car so I was on the passenger side. "You ready to try this again?" I asked.

"I'm going to shoot you in the balls when I get out of this trunk," he shouted.

I nodded. Also predictable, but we were getting somewhere.

The gas tank was on the passenger side, and I worked the claw end of the hammer against the metal door of the gas tank until it popped open. "You know what I just did?" I asked. "I've got the gas tank door open. You know what I'm going to do next?"

"You're a psychopath, Bliss," Derek snarled.

I rapped the clawhammer against the trunk lid. "That's not what it said on my psych profile," I pointed out. "Don't get overly dramatic, Derek."

"Fuck you, Bliss."

I twisted the gas cap the wrong way, and it made a clicking noise. "Come on, Derek. You're boring me."

Between my banging around with the clawhammer and his shouting from the trunk, we had made enough noise to rouse someone in the neighborhood. A light had gone on in a hallway inside a nearby house, but it had clicked off shortly thereafter. I leaned against the car and stared at the house. Sure enough, the curtain in the front window twitched. We had an audience.

"Who are you working for?" I asked again.

"I can't tell you that," he said.

"Can't or won't?" I asked.

"What difference does it make?" he asked.

"Tell me her name," I said.

"Who?" he replied.

I tapped the clawhammer against the side panel of the car. Near the gas tank. "Jesus, Derek. Who do you think?"

He was quiet for a minute, and when he spoke, I almost missed what he said. "Fitzroy."

"What's that?"

"Her name's Fitzroy," he said. "Emmanuelle Fitzroy."

"You're kidding me," I said. I stepped back from the car. In doing so, I caught my heel on the curb and nearly fell, but the sudden scramble to keep from spilling on my ass saved my life. A muffled gunshot echoed in the trunk, and a hole appeared in the side panel of the car. Not far from the gas tank. If I had been standing there, leaning forward to hear Derek's confession, I would have taken a bullet in the chest.

I stayed low. My heart was pounding. Was he going to shoot again? Had he heard me stumbling around? *No, he couldn't have,* I thought. He couldn't hear anything right now.

Fitzroy. Was that really her name, or had he fed me some bullshit, hoping it would lure me close?

A police siren wailed in the distance. The neighbor across the street had called the cops. I was out of time.

I scrambled to my feet and darted off for my car. I needed to vanish.

Derek could tell his story to the cops. They'd get a kick out of it, especially the part where Fitzroy—if that was really her name—showed up and shut everything down.

I drove north until I hit Sunset, and then I went east until I was in West Hollywood. I found a payphone in the parking lot of a Ralph's, and I called Angel's number. She didn't pick up, and this time, I left her a message. "Call me back" I said, reading off the number on the pay phone. "I'll be here for ten—maybe fifteen—minutes."

I waited a half hour, trying not to let my heart rate jack up every time I heard a siren. I heard more than one—it was West Hollywood, after all—but none of them came anywhere near the grocery store lot.

I tried Angel again. She still didn't answer. I left another message. It was starting to feel like a bad stand-up routine.

I didn't have anyone else to call, and so I went into Ralph's for beer and a vegetable platter. I paid cash for one night at the cheap hotel across the street, put my car in the back, and ate my dinner in the shabby room. Thinking and drinking time.

After a couple of beers, Emmanuelle Fitzroy still seemed like a made-up name, but I was coming around to the idea that Derek had told me the truth. It was the name she told him, but it wasn't actually her name. That seemed like something she'd do. *I'm smarter than you, Bliss,* was what that name said. *You are so out of your league. I know more about you than you know about yourself.*

One of the films that made a lasting impression on young Robert Bliss—corn-fed drifter from Colorado—was *Emmanuelle*, one of the great X-rated films from the 1970s. It starred a Dutch actress named Sylvia, and she opened the door for a lot of young men and women who wanted to get naked on film. Emmanuelle might have been a classic name for girls during the early part of the century, but after that film? No one named their kid Emmanuelle. It had to be an alias.

Another film that made an impression—it came out around the same time—was *Jaws*. Part of what lured me to Hollywood was the naive idea of landing roles like the one Robert Shaw had in that film. But younger and sexier, and without getting eaten by the monster at the end of the second act. You know what I mean.

It turned out there weren't a lot of opportunities to play roles like that—characters like Quint were rare. But there were a lot more chances to play unnamed studs who looked good from the waist down, and well, loosing one's innocence was all part of the Hollywood story.

I finally fell into a beer-fogged dream. It was like someone had pitched a sexy horror movie—a mashup of *Jaws* and *Emmanuelle*—but the monster was a giant snake and not a shark. Pen played the female lead, and her top was wet for most of the film. I got to play that younger version of Quint, all the way through the second act, which ended with lots of screaming. Some of it was mine.

CHAPTER 15

In the morning, after washing away the remnants of the dream with a cup of something closer to steamed sock water than coffee, I drove over to the restaurant Tony managed in Santa Monica. It wasn't open for breakfast, but Angel's younger brother would be there, prepping for the lunch shift.

Of the four Chow siblings, Anthony was the one who got out from under his dad's influence. He went off to culinary school and spent most of the last decade of his father's life in New York, working for a series of successful restaurants. There was some press which said these successes were due, in large part, to Tony's incredible palette and eye for detail. However, when his father was diagnosed with colon cancer, Tony came back to the West Coast. Family mattered more, in the end.

After Mr. Chow passed, Tony stayed in LA. He opened up a bistro a few blocks from the Santa Monica Promenade. It had about two dozen tables and it served lunch. That was it. He didn't advertise, which immediately made the restaurant one of those secret spots the locals won't even admit to knowing about. Not surprisingly, this turned it into a hot spot—like that place on Sunset that was always in the trades—but at Three Hares, it wasn't about been seen by the paparazzi. It was about good food and deal-making.

I parked in back and wandered into the restaurant. The smell of freshly roasted coffee and fresh baked goods was enough to make my mouth water. Maria, his pastry chef, was painstakingly assembling a tray of tiny parfait cups with two types of chocolate cake, caramel fudge, and a profusion of leaves and berries. Each cup looked like a miniature forest.

I watched her work for a few minutes. Her focus was absolute. It was only when she finished the tray did I speak up. "Hey, Maria," I said gently, so as not to spook her.

She looked up and her eyes twinkled. She was a petite Latino woman, with a slender face and a little extra around the middle. She had a tattoo of roses running up her left arm. "Hey, Butch. I wondered how long you were going to stand there."

"I didn't want to disturb the artist at work."

She waved a hand. "I've been making these little bastards every day for three weeks now. This ain't art. This is work." She flashed me a grin.

I pretended not to notice the dig. "Tony around?"

"Went to the bank," she said. "Should be back in a half hour or so."

I nodded. "I could wait, I suppose."

She shrugged. "You could."

I glanced toward the front of the house. "Any chance I could get an espresso or something?"

"That depends on whether or not you're qualified to run the machine."

"I have raw talent."

"You know what that'll get you."

"I do," I said. "I certainly do."

She waved a hand toward the espresso machine on the far side of the kitchen. "Make me one too, would you? I have two more trays of this to build."

I wandered over and put that raw talent to work. I nearly burned myself on the steam wand before I decided that straight shots would work best. I filled up two tiny cups and brought them back to Maria. She finished the row she was working on—all those tiny trees, arranged in neat rows—before she picked up the espresso shot and downed it.

"You going to stand there and watch me the whole time?" she asked.

"Actually, I'm looking for Angel," I said. "You wouldn't happen to know her address, would you?"

Maria cocked an eyebrow. "Why are you looking for her?" she asked.

"She's not returning my calls," I said.

"Maybe it's not a good idea that you see her right now, you know?"

"It's not like that."

"Like what?"

"We're not—look, she's been with . . . what's his name?"

"Who?"

"The dude she's seeing."

"Oh, him. Yeah. Whatshisname."

"He's made an impression on you too, I see."

She shrugged. "It's none of my business." She pointed a gloved finger at me. "And it's none of yours either, Butch."

"I'm not trying to break them up or anything. I just need to talk to her."

"So why don't you ask her mother?"

I gave her a look. "Would you?"

Maria held up her hands. "Okay, okay."

"Besides, Mrs. Chow doesn't like the idea of me and her daughter being in the same room together."

"And why is that?"

I sighed. "Look. I'm not stalking Angel. There's nothing going on."

"So why are you looking for her so hard?"

"I just—look, do you know where she lives or not?"

Maria let out a short laugh. "I've got no idea," she said.

"What? Why didn't you say that to begin with?"

Maria shrugged again. "I don't know. Look, I'm sorry. I guess. I should have said something."

It was my turn to shrug. Maria watched me for a minute and then went back to working on her desserts. I didn't say anything. I just leaned against the wall and waited. After about ten minutes, Maria exhaled noisily. "Are you going to stand there until Tony comes back?" she asked, a note of exasperation in her voice.

"I guess so," I said. "Seems like the best choice right now."

"Jesus Christ, Butch. Go look in the office. I think Angel's address is on the board in there. She orders food a couple of times a week."

"In the office?"

"Yeah," she said. "Right in plain sight. You don't even have to touch anything."

"I won't," I said.

"Good."

"Thanks, Maria." I kissed the back of her head as I scooted past.

"Hey, Butch," she called out. I stopped and looked back at her. She smoothed a lock of hair out of the way with the back of her hand. "Don't be an asshole and make me regret this," she said.

"Never," I said.

She stared at me for a few seconds, assessing whether I was feeding her a line, and then she nodded and went back to work.

I didn't even have to step into the office. I could see the bulletin board on the wall from the door. There was a notecard pinned to the board with Angel's address on it, as well as the gate code. Brentwood. North of San Vicente.

The community where Angel lived was new. A developer had bought up a chunk of a hillside—maybe a half dozen ranch homes—and carved up all the lots into narrow rectangles and long triangles. Lots of little condominiums, stacked and squeezed together. Three floors: single car garage, main floor, and an upper floor with a couple of bedrooms. There was a small balcony perched on the front of the each condo, like a forward observation deck on a sailing ship. The house numbers were painted in white on the curb, making it easy for everyone from police officers to delivery people.

What made Angel's place even easier to find was the silver Porsche parked in the driveway. There was an unbecoming scratch on the driver's side that went nearly the entire length of the car. Someone had been distracted while driving.

I parked along the street, but blocked enough of the driveway that Nathan couldn't get away without damaging two expensive European cars. I ran the bell and put my thumb over the peephole. I heard someone come down the stairs, but they didn't open the door right away. I felt pretty clever about my thumb over the peephole until the curtain of the small window next to the front door was jerked aside. Angel glared at me. I smiled and gave her a friendly wave. Her face disappeared, and for a moment, I thought she wasn't going to unlock the door.

She did, though she stood in the doorway, a very frosty glare on her face.

"I know that look," I said. "I get it from your mother often."

"This isn't a good time, Butch," she said.

"New car?" I asked, hooking a thumb toward the Boxster in the driveway.

"It's not mine," she said.

"Really?"

"You know whose it is," she said.

"You haven't been returning my calls."

"This isn't a good time, Butch."

"Well, if you had returned my calls, maybe we could have scheduled something."

She continued to glare at me. I was immune to it. You can only be exposed to something for so long before it no longer has any effect on you.

"We need to talk," I said. "You, me, and him. This thing is starting to get out of hand."

"This *thing* is not a thing," she said.

"It is most definitely a *thing*, and if your boyfriend is telling you otherwise, he's lying to you."

"He's not lying to me," Angel said defensively.

"Uh huh," I said. I showed her the paperwork I had gotten from Derek's car. "I got these from the driver who took me down to San Diego. He's been following me since I got back."

"What are—" She stopped as she started to read. "Holy shit, Butch," she breathed when she finished. "This is intense."

"Tell me about it. Now where does one get this sort of profile?" I asked. "And why?"

"I . . . I don't know," Angel admitted.

I nodded toward the stairs. "Maybe Nathan knows," I said. "We should ask him." Before she could stop me, I started up the stairs.

The main floor had an office/spare bedroom, an open kitchen, and a broad living area. Not many places to hide. I went up another flight of stairs where I found an open area, which Angel had turned into a reading area with a small table. There were four doors off the hall. Two more bedrooms, a bathroom, and the master bedroom, which looked out over the front of the house.

Nathan was sitting at a table near the window, hunched over a laptop. He looked up when I entered the room, and his expression went from concerned to barely contained panic. He quickly recovered and slapped on his lawyer face. Slack mouth. Empty gaze. *Dead fish face*, we called it on the inside. It was meant to show nothing, not even a spark of life.

Nathan Shackleton looked like a child's drawing of his father—kids have a terrible understanding of anatomy, but they do soft shapes pretty well. Where his father sported a steel bar up his ass, Nathan slumped. His legs were crammed under the small table, and somehow he made the Harvard sweatshirt he was wearing seem too large. His hair was a mess and his stubble was a couple of days past hot and sexy. His eyes were blue, though more cornflower than royal on that spectrum. He cleaned up well—as best as I could be bothered to recall—but this wasn't it.

"Hey, Nathan," I said. I sat down on the chest at the foot of the bed and put my hands between my knees. Trying to not appear too confrontational. "How's it going?"

"Oh, ah, it's . . . okay, I guess."

"That's a nice car out front," I said, nodding toward the French doors at the end of the room. "Yours?"

He nodded gingerly, as if he wasn't sure how I was going to react to his answer.

In truth, I wasn't sure. I squeezed my knees together. "Nasty scratch on it," I said. "I know a guy. Has a shop off Wilshire. He can probably buff that out."

Nathan tried to focus, but his face remained empty. "Oh," he said. "Yeah. Guy on Wilshire."

Angel stood in the doorway, her arms crossed. She looked like she was holding in all the tension for both of them.

"Angel hasn't been returning my calls," I said. "Figured I'd drop by."

"Oh, well, I"—Nathan's eyes slid towards Angel—"I thought—Didn't we have . . . "

"Butch isn't staying long," Angel said.

"Long enough to hear a good story or two."

"A good story?" Nathan echoed. His eyes watered, and he started to pick at the top of the table.

Could he look any more guilty? It was almost embarrassing to watch. It was almost like he was—

"What's he on?" I asked Angel.

"I'm not sure. Xanax, maybe. He's been drinking too."

A tiny giggle slipped from Nathan's lips. He tried to force it back in, but all he managed to do was give himself the hiccups.

"Kind of early in the day for that, isn't it?"

Angel sighed and shook her head. "We got into an argument the other night. After we met at the restaurant. He stormed out. I had classes and so I was gone all day. He wasn't here last night when I got home. I tried calling him a few times but"—she paused and looked at the floor—"this wasn't the first time . . ."

I waited. Nathan hiccuped.

"This wasn't the first time we had had a fight," she said. "He always ignored my calls for a few days. It was his way of punishing me, I guess. It's—whatever. It's . . ."

"It's not that important," I said.

"Yeah," Angel rocked her foot back and forth against the floor. "Anyway, he called late last night. Said he needed my help. There'd been an accident. He was—I finally managed to get him to tell me where he was, and it wasn't far from here. I walked down, and found his car half off the road with that scratch on it. Nathan was okay, but he was clearly out of it. I drove the car back here, dragged him inside, and put him on the couch. I checked on him a few times during the night, just to make sure he hadn't . . . you know . . . and now, he's . . ." She trailed off and pointed at Nathan.

"Yeah," I said. "He's at the top of his game, isn't he?"

She fought to keep the corners of her mouth from twisting.

"Can I shake him a few times?" I asked.

She shook her head.

"How about taking him out back and turning the hose on him?"

"The HOA frowns on that sort of thing," she said.

"That's waterboarding," I said. "This would just be water sports. Everyone likes water sports."

Angel shook her head again. "You're so—" She didn't finish.

"Yeah, I am your favorite," I said.

She pushed off from the doorframe. "I'm going to make some coffee," she said. "For all of us." She went downstairs to the kitchen.

I sat and watched Nathan for a few minutes. He hiccuped and scratched the table and wouldn't meet my gaze. His eyes tracked me well enough though when I stood up, and there was a brief glimmer of something in them. Fear? Anger? It was hard to tell. Regardless it was something.

Lawyer Boy was trying to act.

I've seen heavy Xanax use, and I've seen decent acting. Nathan Strickland wasn't good at either.

While Angel fussed with the electric coffee maker in the kitchen, I sat on one of the bar chairs on the other side of the granite-topped island. "Nice place," I said. "Expensive?"

She lifted her shoulders, but didn't say anything. The coffee maker was one of those do-everything-but-wipe-your-chin machines. It didn't require that much fussing. She wasn't in a rush to talk.

Ah, we were playing the waiting game. Even though she was a Chow, she should know better. I knew the Tehachapi Stillness technique. She wasn't going to win this.

Something bumped against the house. A long object dangled past the living room window. As I started to get up, a human body pinwheeled past. There was a loud crash, followed by the Boxster's car alarm.

Angel beat me to the stairs. We rushed outside and found a figure sprawled on the hood of the Porsche. He was clutching his leg, and between tones of the car alarm, we could hear his shrieks of pain.

Nathan had jumped off the third floor balcony. He was an even worse stuntman than he was an actor or a lawyer. The fall had broken his leg.

CHAPTER 16

It got crowded in the driveway when the paramedics arrived, and I went back into the house. I could watch all the fuss from the living room window, and so I made myself a cup of coffee and waited. A police cruiser showed up, and the officer talked with Angel while the paramedics put Nathan on a stretcher and loaded him into the ambulance. The ambulance drove off, flashing its lights but not running its sirens. The officer passed Angel something which she tucked into her back pocket, and then he went back to his car. He put his lights on and did a sloppy u-turn in the street, turning around in the same direction the ambulance had gone.

The top of the Porsche was creased and dented. I had to give Nathan some credit. He was doing a fine job of messing up his car.

Angel came up the stairs. She had a dazed look on her face, and she got as far as the kitchen before she came to a stop. She leaned against the edge of the counter.

"I made coffee," I said.

Her head came up slowly. "What?"

I raised my cup. "We were making coffee before . . ."

Her eyebrows scrunched together. "He . . . he jumped . . ."

"He did," I acknowledged. "From the third floor, no less."

"Why—why would he do that?"

"Didn't want to talk to me, I guess."

"But I thought he was . . . in the state—oh God, I never should have left him alone."

I shook my head. "Whatever he was on—if he was on anything—peaked hours ago. He was strung out, sure, but he wasn't as doped up as he wanted us to think."

"But . . . why?"

I shrugged and took a sip from my cup.

"This is all so bizarre," Angel said. "Nathan is—has been— he's not like this. He's usually very calm. But . . ."

Of course there was a 'but.'

"Since you called the other night," Angel continued, "he's been . . . stressed. Is this because of that snake?"

"I would assume so."

"What did you call it?"

"The snake?"

"Yes, what kind of snake was it?"

"A green tree python."

"No, you called it something else. Something like 'mortadella' . . ."

"*Morelia viridis*," I said.

"Yes, that's it." She thought for a minute. "But that's not it," she said quietly, talking to herself. "That's not what he said."

"What who said?"

"Nathan." Her shoulders squared and her voice became more animated. "He didn't want to talk about it—about any of it— but I caught him mumbling a few times when I first brought him here. I didn't pay much attention because it seemed like he was off in his own world, but there was something he kept coming back to. What was it? Coral? Corallus?" She snapped her fingers. "*Corallus caninus*," she said. "That's what it was."

She gave me a triumphant smile.

"I'm afraid the punchline is eluding me," I said.

"*Corallus caninus*, Butch. It's a different snake."

I tried to piece together why this was important. "So I had the wrong snake?"

Some of her triumph faded. "It's a different snake," she repeated.

"Yes, I get that, but so what?"

Her shoulders slumped. "I . . . I don't know, I guess."

"We could go to the hospital and ask Nathan, but I'm worried he'll try to jump out another window."

She blinked at that idea. "Let's not do that," she said.

"You told me the firm has a client who is in the reptile business. Do you know who it is?"

She shook her head. "No."

I glanced toward the stairs, remembering the laptop I had seen on the table upstairs. "What about his laptop?" I asked.

"Butch!"

"What?"

"We can't—that's his."

"I know it is. That's why I want to look at it."

"I can't—that would be a violation of his rights."

I stared at her. "Really?"

She cocked her head at me. "What don't you understand about a person's right to—"

"No, I'm well aware of the rights protecting a private individual from unreasonable search," I said. "I'm just surprised you think that's going to stop me."

"Anything on that laptop—anything you find there—is inadmissible in a court of law," she protested.

"Ah, I'm sorry, counselor, but I'm trying to stay out of the courtroom." I tapped my chest. "Ex-con, remember? If we end up in court, then I'm fucked."

"But—"

"But what?" I said, a note of exasperation creeping into my voice.

"It's password protected," she said. "His laptop. It's got a password on it."

"Oh," I said. "That'll—that changes things."

Angel covered her face with her hands. "You're—I can't be a party to this," she said when she uncovered her face. "I'm not—I'm not . . . I'm not like you. I have to respect the law. I have to respect people's rights."

"Sure," I said. "I'm sorry I suggested otherwise."

She held up a hand to stop me from saying any more. When I closed my mouth, she dug into the back pocket of her jeans and pulled out a ring of keys. She put them on the counter. "I'm going to take a shower," she said. "We can talk about other options when I'm done."

She wouldn't look me in the eye as she left. I waited until I heard water rumbling in the pipes upstairs before I walked over to the counter and grabbed the keys. The plastic security fob had the Porsche logo stamped on it.

There was nothing in the trunk of Nathan's car but the spare tire and the kit to change the tire. The glove box had the car's user manual, one of those maps which showed where all the famous people lived in LA, a box of wet wipes, and a narrow rectangular box with a bunch of his business cards. I took several. Just in case. In the center console, I found his vehicle registration—which included his home address—a partially used roll of quarters, an old ball point pen, and a half a pack of cinnamon gum.

Behind the passenger seat, I found a bag from a drive-thru burger place on Sunset. There was a receipt in the bag that said Nathan had had the munchies around midnight last night, and that he had paid cash.

Other than that, the car was spotless. Like he had it detailed and vacuumed once a week.

I wrote his home address down on the back of the receipt. Just in case.

I felt like I was missing something, and when I searched the car again, I realized there was no bag. Nathan had his laptop, but where was his bag? Or briefcase. Or whatever it was that lawyers carried around. I went back into the house and carefully snooped around the upstairs rooms.

I found a leather briefcase in the spare bedroom. It was closed and locked. I cocked an ear toward the master bathroom, listening for the shower. Still running.

I closed the bedroom door. Just to give myself a few more seconds.

The briefcase had a three-digit combination lock, and the dials weren't set to '0-0-0.' I ran my thumb lightly across the ridged edges of the dials and thought about what the combination might be. The rightmost number was halfway between a five and a six, while the other two numbers were centered. I shifted the rightmost digit up one value and tried the lock. No luck. I shifted it down. That didn't work either.

The shower turned off in the other room. I didn't have much time.

Okay, so we're naturally lazy, and when things get repetitive, we do as little as possible, even when it comes to keeping our shit secure. We try to remember to lock our doors at night and when we leave, but who hasn't forgotten once or twice? And locks like that—and like the one on this briefcase—won't stop anyone who really wants to get in. They're merely a deterrent for the curious—the idle degenerate, like myself, who was being nosy where they shouldn't. It doesn't really matter if you have four or eight or fifteen locks, one will do. One is enough.

Most people don't change the combination of a lock when they get it. Most don't even think to wonder if they could. It's a lock. It keeps the casual thief from getting frisky and nosy. Ninety-nine out of a hundred times, that's all it takes. But that one person who thinks their shit is valuable? They figure out how to change the combination. They set it to something they can remember, because they don't want to have to think about it. They want security, but they don't want to have to worry about it. They've got a lock; they're safer than everyone else. But man, setting that all the time is a pain in the ass. And so they pick a combination they can remember. Something they think of without thinking too hard. Something easy. Something personal.

I dug out the receipt where I had written down Nathan's address. His street address has four digits: 1-5-2-3.

The combination on the safe was 3-3-6.

Something easy to remember. Something that didn't take much effort.

I changed the dials to 3-2-5—the last three digits of his house address, but backwards—and thumbed the release on the briefcase.

It opened.

The briefcase was tidy, like his car. There was a stack of unmarked file folders and a plastic case with a flap that snapped shut. Inside the plastic case were a bunch of receipts, and I wasted a few seconds glancing through them. Lunches, lunches, and more lunches. Nathan hadn't scribbled any notes on any of them. The file folders contained loose pages of handwritten notes, and I tried to make sense of Nathan's handwriting.

God, he was a terrible note-taker. They were filled with cryptic references, one-word questions, and half-finished doodles.

"Butch?" Angel was in the hall outside.

I started shoving the stack of file folders back into the briefcase. There were only two I hadn't looked through. The first one had a letter from a financial advisor. I didn't even bother pulling it out of the envelope. The other folder was . . . empty.

I was still staring at it when Angel knocked at the door. "Butch?"

"Just a sec," I said. I tossed the last folder onto the stack, threw in the receipt box as well, and closed the briefcase. I thumbed the combination dials, changing one or two of the numbers—just like Nathan had—and then stood up. The case was on the bed, but at least I wasn't fawning over it. "Yeah," I called. "I'm in here."

Angel opened the bedroom door. She was wearing a heavy robe. A towel was wrapped around her head. Her gaze went to the briefcase on the bed, lingered a second, then then she looked at me. "I'm hungry," she said. "You?"

I swallowed quickly. "Yeah," I said. "I am."

She looked at the briefcase again. "I'll get dressed," she said, making eye contact.

"I can drive," I said. "My car is—I'm out at the curb."

She nodded. Her gaze dropped to the floor and then she left, shutting the door behind her. Only after she was gone did I let out the breath I had been holding.

There was something on the floor, next to my foot. It had fallen out of one of the folders. I bent down and picked it up. It was a business card.

REPTILE WORLD
Jack Trevellian
Chief Herpetologist

CHAPTER 17

After an awkward lunch with Angel, I dropped her off at the hospital. She promised to let me know if Nathan wanted to talk, but I wasn't going to wait by the phone. The man jumped out a window to avoid talking to me. I got the hint.

It was going to be tough for him to scamper off and hide. The leg would slow him down, and his father was going to assign one of the law firm's large ex-Special Forces dudes to be his new best friend. Not because I was that persistent of a pain in the ass, but because there were other people that Nathan was keen on avoiding.

Just a guess. There was something about that guy. I didn't understand what Angel saw in him, but maybe this was just a stressful time or something. Or maybe I was biased. Whatever.

While I drove up into the hills above Bel Air, I thought about something else. Like that I had stumbled onto a global, multi-tentacled conspiracy. The sort responsible for cattle mutilations, or crop circles, or non-pasteurized milk.

Nathan's place was on a twisty road off North Beverly Glen, and when I spotted the house, I drove past. The road dead-ended a mile farther on, and I was forced to turn around and head back.

The white panel van advertising a local HVAC company was still at the curb at the house past Nathan's. There were two smoked glass windows set in the back doors of the van, and there were extra antenna sprouting from the roof. It was the "Subtle as Fuck Fed Surveillance Van."

So much for peeking in the windows at Nathan's place. If I did, I'd end up as a guest star on a very special episode of *America's Favorite Dumbass Criminals*.

Unlike most of this town, I didn't need to be on TV that badly.

The light at the bottom of North Beverly Glen took a long time. I got bored and dug out the business card I had found in Nathan's briefcase. *Redondo Beach*, I read. *That was what? Off the 405, somewhere south of LAX?*

Someone out that way would be able to give me better directions. When the light finally changed, I turned right on to Santa Monica Blvd, and headed for the 405 interchange.

Reptile World was the building with the giant snake painted on it. Otherwise, it looked like all the industrial warehousing along this stretch of Redondo Beach. The rest of the buildings had neat little type and logos that suggested a lot of science was being done. As I parked my car in the nearly empty lot and wandered toward Reptile World, I wondered if the science guys ever came across the street and borrowed lizards to test their simulated Martian landscapes.

The interior of the Reptile World was, in fact, like being transported to another planet. Little effort had been made to transform the interior of the warehouse, and the ceiling was a maze of ducts and heavy fans. Rows of metal cages were stacked four and five deep, and the rows disappeared into the hazy vanishing point of the warehouse. On my right were a series of walled habitats with raised platforms and chest-high railings. On my left were habitats enclosed in wire mesh, and a misty fog hovered over these cages like a petulant micro-climate.

And it smelled . . . dusty. You might think snakes and lizards don't have a smell, and individually, they probably don't smell like anything in particular. But when you put thousands of reptiles in the same room, all that "don't smell nothing" turns into something, like old leather that been drying out under a desert rock for a year or two. It wasn't a bad smell; it was merely one that made my skin itch.

It reminded me of the Box at Tehachapi—the hole where the guards put the especially violent inmates when they needed some time to chill. As a policy, Tehachapi didn't have solitary confinement, but that didn't mean they didn't believe in 'taking a time-out.' I had gone to the Box twice, and both times, I had only been there for an hour or so.

It was larger than a coffin, but smaller than a coat closet. You could turn around, but just barely. I didn't lose my shit—lots of inmates did—and the only reason I kept it together was all the stupid mindful meditation Mr. Chow had drilled into the heads of the handful of *grasshoppers* he had gathered.

The Box was down in the basement of the main building, back behind the heavy boilers. It was always hot and dry in there. Sweat, piss, spit: it all dried instantly. All that remained was a residual tang to the air—a not-so-delicate reminder that you weren't the first to spend time in the Box. Your fear was just another greasy layer quick to cook off.

"Can I help you?"

I blinked heavily, my chest tight. I could feel a trickle of sweat running down my back.

A shaggy-haired young man was standing in front of me. He wore a yellow shirt, marked with that same snake that was on the outside of the building. He had a name tag that read "Shawn." In the corner of the tag, there was a small cartoon lizard.

"Huh, uh, yeah," I started. I licked my lips and shoved all the memories of Tehachapi back into the darkness where they belonged. "Hi, uh, yeah. Hi, Shawn. I'm, um, I'm looking for a snake."

He smirked and spread his hands to encompass the warehouse. "Snakes? We got 'em," he said.

"Yeah, of course you do," I said. The lights were still too bright, but the walls were far away, so I was going to be all right. "I'm looking for a green one. A python. It likes trees."

"The *Morelia viridis*?" Shawn asked. "That's the Latin name for the green tree python. Is that the snake you're looking for?"

"Yeah, the tree python. That's the one."

"I got some of those," he said. He gave me that half-smirk again, like I was some rube who didn't understand where I was. *God-dammed Reptile World, man. Of course we have the stupid snake you're looking for.*

"How many?" I asked, playing the game.

He laughed. "A lot."

"More than six?"

"A lot more."

"Gosh," I said. "How much?"

"How much do you want to spend?" He asked.

"It's a fucking snake, Shawn. It's not a high performance sports car."

His smirk faded, and honest to God, I didn't feel bad about it.

"Look," I said. "It's a present. I need to—you know—look smart about snakes and stuff. I'm trying to impress this person, right?"

His smirk came back as something harder, more of a sneer. "And you think the *Morelia viridis* will do that?"

"I don't know, Shawn. Will giving a lady a big green tree python get me laid?"

He flushed. His eyes flicked left and right. "Dude, I wouldn't give a—a woman a snake like that."

"Too subtle?"

"What? No. It's not subtle at all. It's totally a—" He made a vague gesture toward his waist.

"Maybe I want her to be—" I made a similar gesture.

His eyes followed my hands, and when he realized what he had done, he got even more embarrassed.

You know? Not being ashamed of male anatomy is probably a superpower.

"Look, Shawn, this gift? It's not for a lady." It was time to rescue him. "You're right. It's totally the wrong message to send.

But, if I was giving this to a dude, that's okay, right? Not because I want to have sex with him—no, it's not that. It's more that I want to impress him. I want him to think I'm a badass. You know? And I think he's a badass too. You get what I'm saying, Shawn? What kind of snake is going to give me cred?"

"Well, we have some hooded cobras—"

"No, Shawn. Nothing dangerous. Jesus, this guy has kids. I want something cuddly and big, and . . . I don't know, but this green tree python sounds like it's not all that exotic. You get what I'm saying?"

Shawn rubbed his chin. We were back in his treehouse, so to speak. "Something like the python, but rarer, perhaps?"

"Yeah, rarer," I said. "But not super expensive. I want to make a good impression, but I don't want to overdo it. What about—oh, what was it? I heard about this other snake. A clingus camus? No, that wasn't it. *Colossus capri*—no . . . Wait! *Collapsus canus*. That's it."

His face had been scrunching up as I invented words, but with the last, his eyes brightened. "*Corallus caninus*," he said.

I snapped my fingers. "That's it. That one."

He nodded, pleased with having saved me from butchering any more scientific names. "Yeah, okay. The *Corallus* is sorta like the *Mordelia*, but it's not all that rare."

'You got any?"

"Sure," he said. "Right over here."

He headed for the mesh-enclosed habitats along the lefthand side of the warehouse. I fell in behind him. "So," I started casually as we walked. "I hear your boss is a pretty major herpestologist."

"A what?"

"Snake guy. Herpestology."

"Her-PET-ology," he said. "No 's.'"

"No what?"

"You said it like 'her-PEST-logy.'"

"My mistake," I said. "Her-PET-ology."

Shawn wagged his head at my cluelessness about the lingo.

We stopped at a cage with a pair of short trees growing out of large pots. The tree's limbs grew straight out of the trunk, and the branches were covered with loops of scaly green snakes. Metal basins at the base of the tree contained more snakes. *Lazy slackers,* I thought. They couldn'tz be bothered to climb back up the tree when they fell off.

"*Corallus caninus,*" Shawn said. "The emerald tree boa."

At first glance, they looked like the one I taken to Mexico: long, green, with a white pattern along its back.

No, wait. Had the tree python had those markings?

"And over here is the green tree python," Shawn said, sensing my confusion. He led me to another mesh-covered cage with the same set-up: stunted trees, snakes looped on bare branches, snakes in bins.

"Naturally, one is a boa and one is a python," Shawn said. As if the difference was as obvious as the difference between, say, an orange and an orangutan.

"Naturally," I said. I peered into the cage with the pythons. These snakes had markings on their backs too, but the pattern was smaller. I pointed at the snakes in the cage. "The markings aren't the same," I said.

"That's right," he said. "Pythons are Old World snakes. Asia, Africa. Even though you can find them all over Florida."

"Why is that?"

"Because they get big and people freak out. They don't know what to do with them, and so they dump 'em."

"Like cats and baby goats," I said.

He stared at me. "Yeah," he said slowly. "I guess."

"What else?" I said. "There's got to be something more than one is native to that side of the world and one isn't."

"Well, the big difference is that pythons lay eggs and boas don't. They give birth to live baby snakes."

I went back and forth between the two cages, gauging the difference between the two species. If you didn't know better, and if you didn't have one of each on hand, it could be hard to tell them apart. "What else?" I asked. "I mean, if I don't have eggs and baby snakes to compare."

"Pythons have an extra set of bones in their jaws," Shawn said, warming to the idea of showing off his snake knowledge. "And on their bellies, their scales are paired. In boas, that's not the case."

"Like pythons were zippered up, once upon a time," I said.

"Sure," Shawn said with a shrug. "Like zippers."

"Okay, let me see if I have this straight." I hooked a thumb at the python cage. "More jaw bones, zippered, and lays eggs." I pointed at the other cage. "Boas have fewer bones, they're not zippered, and they make miniature snakes."

"Yeah," Shawn said.

"But other than that, they're identical."

"Well . . ." Shawn wasn't quite ready to go on record with that conclusion.

"So who gives a shit about one over the other?"

Shawn frowned. "They're—they're different snakes," he said. He was struggling to not be offended by my crass ignorance about herpetological nuances.

"Look, Pythons come from the other side of the world— or Florida, which is the same thing, frankly. Are they more expensive?"

"Than the boas?" Shawn shook his head. "No, they cost about the same."

"Are they finicky eaters? Like cats?"

"Cats aren't"—he wrinkled his nose—"both species of snake eats mice and rats. Lizards, too. And bats."

"Bats? That's cool."

"Yeah. It's pretty cool."

I didn't say anything. Shawn didn't either. After a minute of both of us trying to figure out how snakes could catch bats,

Shawn started to fidget. I had confused him enough he didn't know which snake he should be trying to sell me.

"These aren't all that exotic," I said.

He looked crestfallen, thinking that he had blown the sale, but he realized I wasn't walking away. I was still on the hook.

"Come here," he said. "Let me show you something."

We walked deeper into the warehouse, where mesh cages gave way to smaller and more secure cages. Wooden shelves were filled with rows of glass aquariums, each of which looked like they were single or double occupancy. I saw colored snakes, snakes with hoods, snakes that looked like rocks, snakes that looked perpetually pissed off, and black snakes that would be invisible at night.

Shawn stopped and pointed at a cage on the middle shelf. The cage contained a heat lamp, a rock, and a pale yellow snake that was half-coiled on the rock. It looked like the ones we had been looking at before, except its markings were tiny circles with dots.

"*Corallus caninus*," he said.

"What?" I looked again. "That's one of those boas? But it isn't green."

"It isn't," he said. "But—technically—it's still a *Corallus caninus*, an emerald tree boa."

I put my face close to the glass and peered carefully at the snake.

"It's an albino," he said. "It's very rare."

"How rare?"

The smirk came back. "Very," he repeated.

A tag on the cage agreed with Shawn. *Corallus caninus.* The price of the snake wasn't quite the same as a high performance sports car, but it was only missing a zero or two.

"Now that's exotic," I said. I tapped the glass, and Shawn made a motion to stop me, but caught himself before he actually grabbed my hand. "Is it a one-in-a-million thing or can you—I don't know—can you breed them?"

"It's possible," Shawn said. "But it takes a—"

I nodded. "A herpetologist. I glanced at some of the other cages and realized they were empty. "This the only one you got?"

He shook his head. "Some of our stock is over at the LA Convention Center," he said. "NARC."

"Oh, right," I said. "The reptile convention. That's this weekend, isn't it?"

"Yeah, it is."

"You going to be there?"

His face lit up. "Yeah. It's going to be awesome."

"How about Jack?"

"Who?"

"Your boss. The head herpetologist."

"Oh, Mr. Trevellian. Yeah. Yeah, of course."

I tapped the glass on the cage again. An idea was starting to come together in my head. "Can he hook me up?"

"Hook you up?"

"Can he help me breed these?"

Shawn glanced at his watch, and then rubbed the back of his neck. His eyes strayed toward the front of the store. "You'll—you'll have to ask him," he said.

"I will," I said happily.

He gave me that *Thanks for wasting my time, asshole* smile that salespeople do so very well. "We'll have a booth in the main hall," he said. "You should check it out."

"I plan to," I said. "You've been really helpful, Shawn."

"Yeah, no problem," he mumbled. He darted off before I could murder any more snake names.

I leaned over and looked at the albino boa one more time. "You're a pretty one," I said quietly.

It's the pretty ones that always get us into trouble.

☆

I grabbed a flyer on the way out. Reptile World was offering special pricing on all sorts of critters in conjunction with the North American Reptile Convention. I was distracted by the variety of lizards they were selling, and I was surprised to hear someone call out my name.

I looked up, squinting in the afternoon sun. I had parked close to the road, and the only car near mine was a black sedan. The back window was down, and I recognized the woman sitting in the car.

"Hey Frolic," I said. I walked over to the sedan and showed her the flyer. "Need any lizards?" I shaded my eyes and peered at the person in the front seat. "Derek still mad at me?"

"Derek is taking some time off," Frolic said. She leaned forward and rested her arm on the window sill.

"That's a good idea," I said. "Rotating a crew during a surveillance keeps them fresh."

Her fingers rose and fell on the window. Her hair was loose today, hanging about her face like a wave. Her lipstick was darker, in keeping with the severity of her jacket. "Shopping for a friend?" She raised a finger toward the warehouse behind me.

"Nah. I've been learning stuff," I said. "Did you know that pythons aren't indigenous to North America?"

"I didn't," she said.

"Yeah, they're Old World snakes."

She raised an eyebrow. "Are they?"

"They're similar to boas—which are native to this part of the world—and some of these species are nearly identical."

She raised an eyebrow. "Really?"

"Absolutely." I rolled up the flyer and tapped it against my palm. "For instance, say you had a snake in a sack—hypothetically speaking, of course."

She acknowledged this with a wave of her fingers.

"And say this snake is an emerald tree boa—one of those that is common around here—and, say, you put the sack down for a minute and left the room. While you're gone, someone sneaks in and swaps that snake out with one of those Old World versions—you know, the green tree pythons."

"Who would do that?" She asked, feigning outrage at the idea.

"I know. Who would do that?"

She shrugged.

"And unless you knew to check whether the snake had a zipper on it, you probably wouldn't notice."

"A zipper?"

"Sure," I said, indicating my front. "Along the belly."

"That's a fascinating story, Mr. Bliss," she said.

I tapped the flyer against my palm. "Do you know what I can't figure out, though?"

"What?" she asked.

"Did *you* switch snakes or had they already been swapped when you pinched Cock Robin?"

She gave me a sly smile. The sort that probably made junior agents get all squirmy and think inappropriate workplace thoughts. "I like you, Butch," she said. "You ask interesting questions."

It wasn't lost on me that we were suddenly on a first-name basis, which lead right into my next question. "Let me ask you another one, then," I said. "Did your parents have a thing for French porn, or do you not trust the men you hire to shadow me, Emmanuelle?"

Her mask was solidly in place, and I only caught a tiny glint of annoyance in her eyes. Her smile gave her away though. It wasn't quite as alluring the second time around. It was the one she wore in public when she was thinking murderous thoughts. "Stick to the plan," she said.

"There's a plan?"

She laughed, the hard lines vanishing from her face. "Don't be too curious," she cautioned me as the window started up. "Some snakes aren't as docile as your tree snakes. You don't want to find an *unfriendly* one in your underwear drawer, do you?"

I flashed on the black snakes I had seen in the store, and I recalled the name on their cage: *black mamba*. Frolic made eye contact one last time as she powered up the window, and she acknowledged we were thinking the same thing with a tilt of her head.

Operation Trouser Snake suddenly became much more ominous.

CHAPTER 18

By late afternoon, I was tried of trying to figure out Frolic's angle in this whole affair. I took a shower in the cheap hotel room's bathroom—ran it full blast until my skin was furious and pink. I shaved, put on a decent shirt, and threw all my bags into the car.

By meeting me at Reptile World, Frolic had been letting me know that she knew where I was. I hadn't gone as dark as I had thought. In which case, I might as well sleep in my own bed instead of this cheap motel.

Before that, though, I had a date: dinner with Pen at her parent's house.

The Beverly Hills neighborhood wasn't much different during the day. Every house was still hedged and gated, and there were few signs that any of the houses were occupied. Here and there, I spotted men doing landscape work, but they all had the sun-darkened, baggy-clothing look of hired help.

The house where I had dropped Pen and her friends off the other day had been built during the post-war years when ostentation hadn't yet eclipsed a dedication to classical forms. Planted square to the street, it looked like someone had swiped a French country house and tried to obscure its origins with a lot of bric-a-brac and ornamentation. You know how some churches take several generations to build, and each spire and door reflect a different era of architectural aesthetics? It was like that, but in quintessential Hollywood fashion, it veered into tacky kitsch in its efforts to impress. The only people who think this sort of thing is a good idea are the people who have enough money to not care what the neighbors think.

I had stopped at a wine shop on Wilshire where I knew a guy who wouldn't upsell me too badly. He had recommended a couple of whites, and I had picked one of the pricier ones. I wasn't sure why. I wasn't hoping to make a good impression. I merely wanted to give Pen Stephanie's phone and get the gun. If the cost of that was a two hundred dollar bottle of wine, that'd be the cost of my earlier error in judgment.

But now, seeing the house, I was glad I had bothered.

I pulled my car up to the intercom and pressed the button.

The intercom crackled. "Hello?"

"Oh, hello," I said. "I'm, uh, I 'm here to see Pen . . ." I didn't know her last name. "Yeah, Pen. She invited me over for dinner." I grabbed the bottle of wine and held it up.

No one can see it, you idiot, I thought.

"Okay," the voice on the intercom said. I felt like I had stumbled on the secret password.

The gate buzzed. When it opened enough for my car, I eased through and followed the driveway as it curved around the front of the sprawling porch.

There was a stone fountain of leaping fish in a grassy plot nestled in the curve of the driveway. There was water in the base of the fountain, but nothing flowed out of the open mouths of the fish. I wondered if they were saving water or if they had gotten tired of watching the water go round and round and round.

I joined a blue Ferrari and a silver Mercedes in the driveway. The Mercedes was the same model as the one Pen had been driving the other night, but there was no sign of her car.

The front doors of the house were immense, in keeping with the whole "Welcome to our house of worship!" motif. Another stone fish was attached to the righthand door, and its curled tail was actually a knocker. I rapped it against the heavy door, and it sounded like I was tapping a block of marble with a fork.

I heard something like a stone block being shoved across a brick floor, and one of the doors slowly swung open. Inside stood a small Latina woman in a grey uniform. She wore white shoes with thick soles, and her gaze said she hoped I was worth all the trouble it had taken to open this heavy door.

"I brought wine," I said, showing her the bottle.

She lifted her chin, indicating that I needed to bring the offering closer if she was going to be bothered to look at it. I did, presenting it so she could read the label.

"Wine," she said. Her voice sounded like it was coming out of a kid's squeaky toy. Her gaze remained resolute, as if she remained unconvinced about the reason for my presence.

I gestured toward the cars behind me. "I left my ice pick and ax in the car," I said. "I was going to get them later, unless you want to see them now . . . ?"

The corner of her mouth twitched. "I'll put out more towels," she breathed. She moved out of the way, allowing me access to the house.

I went into the house and turned around to help her with the door, but I needn't have bothered. For all the imposing architecture, the door moved like it had been hung by a master carpenter. Without a word, she started off toward the back of the house, her shoes whispering on the polished marble floor.

The rooms I passed were arranged like museum sets, as if *Sunset Magazine* were going to be here any minute to do a six-page spread on decorative styles of the mid twentieth century. Flowers gleamed under recessed lights that were mathematically precise in location and wattage. Napkins on the immense oak table in the inordinately large dining room looked like they had been shellacked into their perfect accordion shape. The crystal decanters on the side bar were luminous, and the levels of booze in each were exactly the same.

The kitchen was larger than the one at Three Hares. A marble-topped island dominated the room, and someone had tried their best to cover it with a spread that wouldn't have been out of place on a big-budget Hollywood production. Broad picture windows let a lot of light in, and outside, there was an Olympic-sized swimming pool. Off to the right was a small bar, with fully stocked shelves and a curved marble countertop.

The woman who had met me at the door took my wine. "Eat something," she said, indicating the food on the island. She put the wine in one of the stainless steel refrigerators and wandered out of the kitchen, leaving me to navigate the hors d'oeuvres on my own.

There were a half-dozen varieties of cheese, each with its own implement for slicing, spreading, or cutting; a variety of olives, some pitted and some not; loaves of bread, pre-sliced into small, bite sizes, along with a variety of spreads to go on the bread; in the meat department, there was salami, prosciutto, and a thinly sliced meat I didn't recognize; and several dozen deviled eggs nestled together on a silver tray.

How was I supposed to have an appetite for dinner if I grazed this spread?

Additionally, there were bottles of fizzy water, two pitchers of some kind of punch, and an open bottle of red wine. Because this was a classy house, a variety of glasses were already laid out in neat rows. I counted eight sets, which gave me an idea of how many were expected for dinner.

I sampled the olives, and was debating whether the pinkish spread or the white spread with flecks of green was appropriate for sourdough bread when a tall woman in a yellow and orange cocktail dress swept into the room.

"Lucia," she was saying, "can you move—" She stopped when she spotted me. "Oh, I didn't realize . . ."

"I'm either early or at the wrong house," I said.

"It's quite all right," she said. She offered her hand. "Natasha Verlaine. So glad you could join us for dinner."

"Robert Bliss," I said, taking her hand.

We sized each other up. In heels, she could look me in the eye, and she had the toned body of a professional actress. Her skin was flawless, and a good make-up artist could change her to a half-dozen different ethnicities without any trouble. Her long brown hair had a touch of blonde highlights. Her eyes were dark, her lashes were long, and there was an artful symmetry to her face. The sort of art one paid for. She wore diamond studs in her ears, and a string of diamonds hung around her neck. Her dress fit her well, and her legs were firm and long. Her pumps and watch strap were orange, accessorizing nicely with her dress.

"Have we met before?" she asked. Her hand remained in mine, and her eyes examined my face closely.

"It's been a long time since I did any studio work," I said.

"But you used to," she said. "Which studio?"

"Oh, I'm sure it's not around any more," I said.

She laughed and slipped her hand free of mine. "Few are," she said. "But I've been in this business for a long time. Mr. Bliss. Maybe I've heard of it."

"Please call me 'Butch,'" I said.

"Butch," she said. Her expression cooled as she stared at me. I could almost see the thought forming in her head. "Butch Bliss," she said. "Why does that name sound familiar?"

"It's the alliteration," I said. "It makes everything seem familiar."

"Now I am curious. Which studio did you work with?"

"It wasn't even a real studio," I said, trying to change the subject. "They had offices out in Pasadena . . ."

"Please," she scoffed. "Film is film. It doesn't matter where it is shot. Hollywood is a small town, in many ways. I'm sure we know the same people: actors, directors, producers. People we've—"

"It was a long time ago," I said. "And I haven't kept up with any of them."

The maid—Lucia—wandered back into the kitchen. I took advantage of her presence to grab a tray and follow her as she took a tray into another room. It was off to the left of the kitchen, and it was a modestly decorated sitting room. There were two couches, a handful of overstuffed chairs, a sidebar that was long and wide, and a pool table at the back of the room. Lucia put the plate she was carrying on the sidebar and took mine before I could put it down. She waved me off before I could make a further nuisance of myself.

"Would you care for a cocktail, Mr. Bliss?" Natasha stood in the doorway, blocking any chance of flight from the room.

"Only if it means you'll stop being so formal with me, Ms. Verlaine," I said.

"Bourbon," she said. Before I could say anything, she disappeared in a swirl of yellow and orange.

Lucia came in from the kitchen, carrying more trays. I got out of her way as she approached the sidebar.

"Is it obvious?" I asked as she fussed with the arrangement of the hors d'oeuvres.

"Is what obvious, sir?"

"That I'm a bourbon drinker."

Lucia regarded me for a second. "Ms. Verlaine is a very perceptive lady," she said.

"I bet I can guess what she drinks," I said.

Lucia was a pro. She gave no indication she had any opinion—pro or con—about what I had just said. Nor did she give any hint she was annoyed that I was keeping her from her job.

"Gin and tonic," I said.

"Gimlet," Lucia replied. Having played the game, she bustled around me, heading for the kitchen.

"I was close," I called after her.

"Close to what?"

A man dressed in a blue sports coat, blue-striped shirt, and slacks came into the room. His hair was short and curly—the sort of curl that only a lot of product can achieve—and his teeth were whiter than white. His skin glowed from a liberal application of Tan in a Box, and he was one of those who unbuttoned their shirts enough to give the ladies a hint of chest hair and whatever silver jewelry hip men wore these days. An expensive watch peeked out of the sleeve of his sports coat when he thrust his hand at me. He had a leading man's jaw and the energy of a hunting dog, eager to please.

"Tom Verlaine," he said, squeezing my hand in a calculated manner. "Man of the house."

He said it like he was telling me the role he was playing in this family drama. It was how movie stars introduced themselves the first day on set.

"Robert Bliss," I said. "Guest of the family."

"Nice to meet you, Bob." He gave my hand an extra squeeze, in case I wasn't sure how friendly he was. "Fancy a drink?"

"Ms"—I caught myself and corrected—"Mrs. Verlaine was kind enough to guess my cocktail of choice."

"Ah, I know." Tom smiled broadly. "Beer."

"Actually, no," I said.

He made a face suggesting I was incorrect about my own personal preferences. "You struck me as a beer man."

"Well, in a pinch," I confessed, not wanting to be a jerk about his assumptions. I was a guest, after all.

He slapped my arm like he had just earned a point. He moved to the sidebar and grabbed a handful of olives. "What keeps you busy, Bob?" he asked, timing the words around olives going into his mouth.

"This and that," I said.

"That a full time gig?"

"It tends to be seasonal," I said. "As you can imagine."

He laughed, spraying a bit of masticated olive. I was contemplating diving behind a couch when his wife returned, carrying two glasses. One was a very full martini glass, and the other was a lowball glass filled with bourbon. A solitary cherry floated in the amber liquid.

"Here you are, Butch," she said. "A Manhattan."

"Thank you." I took the offered glass. We lightly tapped the rims of our glasses before raising them to our lips. I watched her sip from her martini, and she watched me watch her.

"Darling," Tom said, stretching the word into a three-syllable whine.

"Mmm?" she asked, raising an eyebrow and looking sidelong in his direction.

He spread his hands, showing us how empty they were. "Nothing for me? I'm dry over here."

"I was attending to our guest," she said. She fluttered her eyelashes, pretending to be the demure wife.

He wasn't fooled. He dropped his arms with a noisy huff. "Excuse me a sec," he said, giving me a pained expression, as if it hurt him to break off from the incredibly rewarding conversation we had been having. He went to the door of the sitting room. "Lucia," he called. "Where's the beer?"

"Coming, Mr. Verlaine," came the reply.

He clapped his hands in delight. "You golf, Bobby?" he asked as he returned to where his wife and I were engaged in our staring contest.

"Butch," I said absently, still watching the way Natasha's lips touched her glass.

"What's butch? Golf?" He glanced at his wife. "Since when?"

"No, I prefer 'Butch' to 'Bob' or 'Bobby,'" I said.

"Sounds like a stage name. Is 'Butch' your stage name, Bobby?" Tom made a big deal of moving between Natasha and I to get at the olives.

"No, it's just the name I prefer people use when they talk to me," I said.

Tom shrugged as if he didn't understand what the fuss was all about. He popped more olives in his mouth.

"You mind if I call you 'Tommy'?" I asked.

"Most people call me 'Dr. Tom,'" he said. "But whatever. It doesn't matter to me."

"Right," I said. I took a long pull from my drink. I had already been here too long.

Natasha had been staring at me during this whole exchange. I thought it was because we had been doing a bit of light flirting over cocktails, but now I wasn't so sure. There was something brewing behind her eyes, like she was trying to remember something important. She had a piece to a puzzle, one she hadn't been aware that she had been trying to put together. As I watched, a terrible realization crept across her face.

"Ah, Lucia," Tom said, clapping his hands as the maid returned with a tray laden with microbrews. "What do you have there?" He met her by the door, forcing her to stand awkwardly as he examined the label of each bottle.

Natasha mouthed a single word. *Bobby.* She started to form a second word—one that started with a 'B' as well—and then she covered her mouth. Trying to keep the word from coming out.

I took another drink from my cocktail. Yes, I had definitely overstayed.

She lowered her hand. "Bobby," she whispered. "That's why you prefer 'Butch.' Because of Bobby Banger."

"Yeah," I said. "Good old Bobby Banger."

Yeah, Hollywood's a small town. You do, eventually, run into someone who's worked with someone you know. Or slept with someone you know.

CHAPTER 19

Natasha and I were spared further reminiscences about mutual friends by the arrival of two more guests. The young man had more than a passing resemblance to his father—brought on, no doubt, by visits to a Beverly Hills specialist. The young woman was everything you'd expect from a trophy girlfriend in this zip code: tan, blonde, dripping with precious stones, and sporting a sleepy-eyed expression that had been a cliche back when I was working. Dr. Tom smiled broadly at the sight of the pair. "Junior!" he exclaimed, and the two men slapped into a handshake that doubled as a photo op. Tom—Senior—then embraced his son's companion, and while she showed an admirable display of expensive cosmetic dental work, she couldn't hide the tension riding her shoulders from Dr. Tom's familiarity.

"Dad, you remember Cassandra," Junior said. There was a confused squint in the corner of the younger man's eye. Things were happening in the wrong order.

"Of course," Dr. Tom gushed. "How could I forget a woman like this?" He took her hand, and for a second, I thought he was going to stroke it. "It's a pleasure to see you again," he said.

Out of the corner of my eye, I saw Natasha tip back her martini glass.

"Can I get you another?" I asked as she ruefully eyed her now empty glass. "Gimlet?"

She looked at me, her eyes unfocused, her thoughts elsewhere. "Why, yes," she said thickly. "That would be lovely." She found her poise. The charm came back.

"A double?" I took her empty glass.

"Of course," she said. Her smile slipped a fraction as she tried to grab her glass back. "Let me help you," she said.

"I can handle making a gimlet," I said, keeping the glass out of her reach.

She followed me as I headed for the door. "Shaken or stirred?" she quizzed me.

"Shaken," I said.

"Savage," she snapped briskly, and then, all smile and charm for the new guests. "Darlings!" She gave her son a quick one-two air kiss, and then offered Cassandra a more refined and polite society hug. "Tom and Cassandra, this is Butch," she said, forcing me to stop and be polite. "Butch: Tom and Cassandra."

"Hi," I said. I didn't offer to shake hands or go for a hug. My excuse was that my hands were full.

"I am going to educate Butch here on the proper making of a gimlet," Natasha said. "Would you like one too, dear?"

"I'm going to have a beer," Tom Jr. said, and there was an awkward pause when he realized that his mother hadn't been asking him.

"That would be lovely," Cassandra said, filling the conversational void.

"Come along then," Natasha said, linking her arm in Cassandra's and directing me with her head.

We left the Verlaine men in the sitting room. I walked over to the bar and went behind the marble countertop. It was all very tidy: shakers and mixers on the top shelf, ice maker on the right, small refrigerator on the left. I opened the refrigerator and checked for gin.

"Butch is Penelope's guest this evening," Natasha explained to Cassandra. "My daughter is—as usual—late."

I had put Natasha's glass and my Manhattan on the counter, and because she was nervous or because she didn't want a perfectly good drink to spoil, Natasha picked up the lowball glass and took a large gulp.

"She does this on purpose," Natasha continued. "Mostly to embarrass whoever it is she has invited."

Cassandra had a sympathetic look on her face.

"I'm not embarrassed," I said. "How could I be? I'm enjoying the company of two fantastic ladies."

Natasha took another large gulp from my drink. "You're too good for her," she said. Her eyes were bright and there was more color in her cheeks. She pointed at me with the hand holding the glass. "Does my son say nice things like this about you?" she asked Cassandra.

I grabbed the bottle of gin in the refrigerator and put it on the counter. "Since you think I'm going to do this wrong," I said, "perhaps you should remind me how to make a gimlet." I grabbed a pair of glasses and put them on the counter too.

"Two ounces of gin," Natasha said. "Three quarters of an ounce of lime juice and not quite as much simple sugar."

I grabbed a shaker, put a handful of ice in it from the ice maker, and found the lime juice and simple sugar in the refrigerator. "Sounds easy enough."

Natasha stared at the shaker in my hand. "A gentleman does not shake his gin," she said. "A gentleman stirs."

I put gin, lime juice, and simple syrup in the shaker. Slipping the metal lid on, I made eye contact with Natasha as I gripped the shaker in both hands. "I never claimed to be a gentleman," I said, and I shook the shaker vigorously.

Both ladies watched me intently, and when I finished and started to pour the gimlet into the two glasses, Natasha cleared her throat. She realized she was still holding the lowball glass and she hurriedly put it down on the counter.

Cassandra made a noise like a balloon farting. "There's this bartender at Lawton—down on the Promenade—his name's Terry. He wears these white t-shirts, and they always get damp from the water and ice behind the bar. I always tell him I want my martini shaken, not stirred."

"I bet you do, dear," Natasha said dryly. The expression on her face said she would have done the same. She picked up one of the glasses and handed it to the young woman. She picked up the second one and, her eyes on my face, raised it to her lips. "It'll do," she said after she had taken a small slip.

Cassandra laughed again. "Like that movie," she said. "'It'll do, pig,'" she said in a mock accent. "'It'll do.' Wouldn't it be so groovy if you could teach a pig to mix cocktails?"

Natasha opened her eyes wide and made a large 'O' shape with her mouth. "Get out of here," she said, lightly slapping the other woman on the arm. "Wouldn't that be the cutest thing?"

"I know, right?" Cassandra squealed a little, and some of her gimlet spilled from her glass as she shook with excitement.

"You should totally get Junior to buy you a pig," Natasha said.

"I should?"

"You should."

"Oh my god. Right now?"

"Yes, do it right now. It'll be so cute. You can get a little outfit for it."

Cassandra squealed again, and darted off toward the sitting room as fast as she could on her six-inch heels. I watched her go. Distantly, ice shifted in the cocktail shaker and it sounded like the single tick of a grandfather clock. Time slowing to a standstill.

Natasha drained her glass. "Shoot me now," she said as she put the glass down. There was none of the faux levity in her voice now, and all of the mock enthusiasm was gone from her face.

"You were acting," I said.

"I'm a professional," Natasha sighed. "It's what we do." She waved a hand at the bottle of gin. "Make me another one, please, and be a gentleman about it this time, would you?"

☆

Penelope showed up a lifetime later (though it was only about an hour). She swept into the sitting room and was greeted with a chorus of "Darling!" and "Sweetie!" They descended on her like locusts, and when she managed to extricate herself from her brother's clinch, she came over and threw herself against me. "I see you've met everyone," she whispered in my ear.

"They're a handsy bunch," I said.

"Like this?" Her hands slithered down and cupped my ass.

"There you go," I said, moving away from her hands. "Lowering already low standards."

She wore a red blouse that flowed around her like it was nothing. She tucked it into her black pants, which made it cling to her in a distracting way. Her black pants disappeared into thigh-high boots, and her hair was pulled back into a severe ponytail that whipped around when she turned her head. She looked good, and I dutifully murmured as much as her father strutted over.

"How long have you two known each other?" Dr. Tom asked.

"Since Tuesday," I said, trying to think of a way to avoid the Father of the Daughter speech I knew was coming.

"This Tuesday?" He paused, and if he was thinking about how many days it had been since Tuesday, there was no sign on his wrinkle-free forehead. Science wasn't going to allow such pliability.

"Isn't this . . ." He turned to Pen. "Tuesday?"

"Family dinners are so dull," Pen said quickly. "Butch is great fun."

Dr. Tom's eyes flicked in my direction.

"I'm great fun," I repeated.

"No, no," he said, shaking his head. His eyes weren't all that focused, and I couldn't blame him, really. He had been drinking beer this last hour like it was bottled water. "Family dinners are dull?"

"Oh, Daddy," Pen said. She put her hand on his arm and he leaned forward, expectantly. She patted him, and then darted off to talk to her mother, leaving me to deal with her befuddled father. The whole thing happened so quickly that it felt practiced. I wasn't the first date to be stuck in an awkward conversation with her father.

Dr. Tom blearily focused his attention on me. "Well, I'm having a good time," I said.

Across the room, Cassandra laughed noisily at something Tom Junior had said. I pointed her out to Dr. Tom. "See? She's having fun too."

Dr. Tom swayed as he focused on the lithe form of his son's date. His face brightened. "We're all having fun," he said. A sloppy smile creased his face. "That girl . . . " His smile slipped a bit, and he didn't finish his thought. "You interested in having kids, Butch?"

"I try not to think about it all that much," I said.

"Don't," he said firmly. He jabbed a stiff finger at me. "Don't do it." Jab. Jab. "They turn into their mothers and . . ."

I was spared any further illumination on the matter of mothers and daughters by Lucia. The maid appeared in the doorway to the kitchen and announced that dinner was ready in the main dining room. There was a stampede, as if people were afraid there weren't enough seats. I had seen the main dining room, and I didn't see the need to rush. Neither did Pen, and in short order, it was just she and I in the sitting room.

She beat me to the door, where she leaned against the frame and gave me a scorching look meant to light my loins. "My mom make a pass at you?" she asked

It wasn't what I expected her to say.

"No," I said. "She hasn't."

"Well, it's early yet," she replied. With a wink, she rolled off the doorframe and disappeared.

I hesitated, wondering if I should put a barstool through one of the big windows in the kitchen and escape while there was still time.

☆

Natasha was in charge of who sat where, which is how I ended up at her end of the table. Lucia had taken a leaf out of the table at some point, changing the Sunset Magazine ready set-up into a more intimate setting. Pen sat next to me. Across from me was Tom Junior, and Casandra sat next to him. Dr. Tom sat at the far end of the table, opposite his wife, which meant when she kicked off her shoe and started exploring with her foot, it was my leg she found and not her husband's. Pen found excuses to put her hand on my leg, and by the end of the salad course, I was well squeezed and tickled.

Not looking at either woman meant I got to watch Tom Junior noisily eat with his mouth open.

As Lucia cleared the salad plates, Dr. Tom applied a monstrous piece of equipment to the bottle of wine I had brought. The device looked like it could de-core an apple or de-bone a rabbit as readily as it could extract a cork. Maybe all three at once. Even with the assistance of the machine, he fussed a lot. I wondered how much fine detail work he was doing in his practice.

Eventually, the cork popped out with a satisfactory noise. Dr. Tom poured a generous amount into his glass, and then proceeded to give Cassandra an impromptu lesson in wine-tasting.

Bored with her husband's fawning, Natasha filled the time by wiggling her foot up my pant leg.

"Pretty good for an '85," Dr. Tom pronounced after he was done with the theatrics of swishing and spitting.

"What is it, dear?" Natasha asked.

"Oh, didn't I say?" He laughed a little too loudly, his eyes sliding toward Cassandra. Checking to see if she had noticed his fine-dining gaffe. Fortunately, she was staring at the wine and spit he had deposited back in his glass. Lucia, well practiced in the family foibles, whisked the glass away.

Dr. Tom peered at the bottle. "It's a Domaine Leflaive. From Les Combettes. Let's see . . . Ah, yes. The Puligny-Montrachet Premier Cru."

Natasha looked at me and raised an eyebrow.

"It was on sale," I said.

Dr. Tom filled a new glass (adroitly provided by Lucia) and then filled Cassandra's. Almost as an afterthought, he filled Pen's, though he only gave her half as much. "A toast," he said, standing up and raising his glass. While he stared off into space like he was thinking of something incredibly moving to say, Lucia grabbed the bottle and hurried to pour wine in the remaining glasses. "To new faces," Dr. Tom said, glancing at me and then Cassandra. He hesitated as if he was going to say more, and then he nodded abruptly and drank from his glass.

"Way to make it about you, Dad," Pen said.

A red flush started up Dr. Tom's neck, but before he could say anything, Natasha loudly commented on the bright flavor of the wine. "Have you been to Burgundy, Butch?" she asked. "That's where this wine comes from." She glanced at her daughter. "Am I getting that right, dear? Isn't Les Combettes in Burgundy?"

"Sure, whatever, Mom."

Lucia had left the bottle at this end of the table, and Natasha picked it up. "Reading French wine labels can be difficult," she said as she examined the label. "You have the name of the winery." She touched the label with a finger. "And then the name of the actual vineyard where these grapes were grown, and then the designation of the quality of those grapes." Her finger traced along the complicated name of the wine. "A Chardonnay from the Puligny-Montrachet vineyard. Premier Cru. Do you see?"

I nodded. "That's what I told the guy. 'These are special friends, and so I need a special wine. Something really nice—exotic, even.'"

Natasha made a bit of a face. "Oh, that's very sweet," she said. "But I hope you didn't pay too much." She paused, just long enough for me to open my mouth. "This is a Premier Cru," she said. "Not a Grand Cru."

"Son of a bitch," I breathed. "That guy told me it was tops."

Natasha patted me on the hand. "It's a good thing he's cute," she said to Pen.

Pen raised her glass to that.

CHAPTER 20

WHILE LUCIA CLEARED PLATES AFTER THE MAIN COURSE, I excused myself and went in search of a bathroom. Mostly, I wanted to put some distance between me and the two Toms, whose volume increased in direct correlation with the amount of alcohol they had consumed. Eventually, I found a small closet with a toilet and a mirror next to a laundry room that was larger than most high school locker rooms. After I was done doing my business, I sat down on the closed toilet and closed my eyes. I imagined doing some exercises—*Repulsing Monkey, Plucking a Sparrow's Tail Feathers, Petting the Wild Horse, Carrying the Fucking Tiger Over the Fucking Mountain . . .*

The tiny room wavered slightly—not quite spinning and not quite closing in on me, but definitely two Manhattans past rock solid position in time and space.

I dug out Stephanie's phone from my back pocket. I could leave it here in the bathroom. Make a break for the front door. Find a window and do that thing that Paul Simon always sang about. Let this family drama play on without me. In fact, as primetime dramas went, this one felt like it was on the fourth or fifth season already. The cast was tired, numb to the typecasting they had been saddled with; the writers hadn't come up with a decent storyline for at least a season and a half; and the cost of the endless parade of guest stars was making the producers twitchy. The only way to save this show was cancer or an unexpected pregnancy. Those were always worth an extra season or two. Hell, maybe I should go back out there and say I was both pregnant and had cancer. That would be excuse enough, wouldn't it?

I sighed and shoved the phone back in my pocket. I was being uncharitable. Lucia had cooked an amazing meal, and it didn't look like anyone was going to notice but me. I should show gratitude to the help, at least.

When I came out of the bathroom, I found Natasha leaning against the wall. She stirred as the door opened, and before I could get around her, she lurched forward. I backed up into the tiny room, and she followed. There was enough room for her to shut the door behind her.

"Natasha—" I started, but she shushed me with her hand. I had turned off the light as I had left, and we were in the dark. I got caught between the sink and the toilet, and having found me, Natasha leaned her full weight against me. Her hands roamed over my body, and I got a mouthful of hair as she tried to find my lips with hers.

"I don't think—" The sound of my voice was all she needed, and her mouth locked on mine. She had a handful of my shirt in one hand, hanging on to me, and her other hand started fumbling with my pants.

She broke off from sucking on my lips—partly to breathe and partly to move her mouth near my ear. "You think too much," she whispered. Her teeth bit down on my earlobe and I tensed, my hands falling instinctively to her hips. She responded by grinding harder against me. When she found something pressing back against her, she let out a throaty groan.

"Natasha," I said, moving my hands up from her hips, but all I managed to do was cup one of her breasts. She made more noises.

Naughty sex in a closet before the dessert course always did wonders for ratings. Given my previous thoughts about the state of this TV show, I shouldn't be surprised, right?

With some effort, I pried her off. "Natasha," I said firmly. "This isn't a good idea."

"Why not?" she asked.

An obvious answer presented itself in my head. It was followed by the inevitable response on her part, which led to a circular conversation that wasn't going to resolve itself readily. "We should go back to the table and have dessert," I said.

She leaned against my arms, and her fingers tugged at my waist. "You said you were fun." I could feel the pout coming off her. "That doesn't sound like fun."

"Dessert is always fun," I countered.

"So's a quick fuck in the closet," she said.

"Natasha," I said. Then, opting to be less familiar: "Mrs. Verlaine—"

A shudder ran through her. "Fuck him," she hissed.

"Excuse me?"

"*Mrs. Verlaine.*" There was venom in her voice, and she jerked herself out of my grasp. "That asshole was nothing before he met me. *Mrs. Verlaine.* I had a career before I married him. *Carmel.* That's what it says on my SAG card. *Natasha Carmel.* I'm nobody's pet wife."

She heard my quick intake of breath, and she laughed quietly in the dark. "You remember me now, don't you, Robert 'call me Butch' Bliss?"

I sagged against the wall. She moved around in the dark, and I felt a fleeting brush of her body as she leaned against the sink. I didn't react to her proximity. I was caught in the past.

Back in the day, Bobby Banger and I had been the talk of our corner of the town. Two young studs, on the rise. Bobby had a few more films in the can than I, and he was getting more offers and attention than he could handle—not that he wasn't trying. I was getting a handful of offers, and at least one studio was pitching an imaginary conflict between the two of us—a marketing department's wet dream. The tabloids were attaching Bobby to every actress in town who could survive the association with a porn star (and with a few who couldn't, but had been spotted in the wild with him anyway). But the persistent rumor within the industry was that he was seeing a married actress, a household name that was a fixture in a daytime drama. A name everyone knew. People were saying Bobby was going to propel her to a new stage in her career, in the byzantine way that Hollywood raised your social standing in light of what would been seen as self-destructive behavior in any other industry. But then I had gotten popped for a truckload of coke and had gone upstate for a few years, where I had lost track of all the gossip. The California Department of Corrections and Rehabilitation didn't include *Variety* and *People* in its lists of approved magazine subscriptions.

"I was in the middle of re-negotiating my contract with the studio," Natasha said. "The studio was pushing back, fighting with my agent over the amount he said I was worth. The show's numbers were consistently high, year over year. It had won Daytime Emmys, and there was a lot of press backing up the argument that I was the reason housewives were tuning in every day. Me. Natasha Carmel." She sighed. "My agent threatened to walk away from the table. The studio came back with pictures. Pictures of Tom and some of his clients. Ugly pictures they were going to leak to the tabloids. What would middle America think when they saw those?"

I could imagine. There was a reason I fell out of touch with my mother after I went west. "I'm sorry," I said.

She turned and moved closer to me. Her thigh pressed against mine. Her hand traced along my shoulder. "Oh, it gets better," she said quietly.

I let my hand fall against her hip. She nestled in tighter.

"I was at a party one night. Out in Malibu. That's where I met Bobby. It had been a really shitty week and I drank too much. He came on to me"—she shrugged and turned, pressing her hip against mine—"He came on to all the girls, so it wasn't that flattering. Plus, who hadn't hit on me in Hollywood? Anyway, I let him make eyes at me and tell me all sorts of things that he could do. It was fun. It was distracting. And then he came up with this idea. Are you ready for this?"

I didn't say anything, but I squeezed her hip with my hand to let her know I was listening.

"'You should get caught fucking someone,' he said. Do it in the back of Mr. Verlaine's car. At Mr. Verlaine's office. In Mr. Verlaine's bed. It didn't matter. The headline would be the same. Wholesome soap queen gets revenge on her titty-fucking husband by screwing a porn star on his desk. 'Think about the scandal,' he said. 'Think about the look on his face when he finds out . . .'"

I cleared my throat when she didn't finish the sentence. "Bobby was never very good at thinking things through," I said.

She shook her head. "No, he wasn't."

"But you told your agent about this, didn't you?"

"I did," she sighed. Her hand slid down onto my chest and I tensed, but she stopped halfway and left it there. "Honestly, I hadn't thought much about it, except as something he and I could laugh about, but when he called me a couple days after we had talked, I knew he had told the studio. He was so excited. The threat of revenge against my husband with a well-known porn star had been an incredible bargaining chip. The studio had agreed to all of his terms, including giving me time off every year to shoot a major." She shook her head. "But until the deal was signed, I had to be seen with Bobby, just enough to keep the illusion alive. To make sure the studio followed through."

"So . . . you and he never . . "

She let out a genuine laugh. "Oh, I fucked him, Butch. Several times, and I would have kept fucking him, except—"

"Except what?"

"You went to jail," she said softly.

"What does that have to do with anything?"

She shifted, and I felt her breasts press against me. Her face was close to mine. "He was obsessed with you," she said. "He was always talking about you. How you were going to knock him off the top. How he was going to wake up one day and find that no one would pay him to take his pants off. 'We got Bliss; we don't need you any more, Bobby.' That's what he was terrified of hearing, and when you went to prison, well, he didn't have to worry any more, did he?"

"No," I said. My throat was dry. "No, he didn't."

"He turned into an asshole," Natasha said. "Even more so than Mr. Verlaine, who—all his faults aside—really does love me."

Something splashed on my shirt. When her shoulders started to shake, I put my arms around her and held her.

Eventually, she sniffed. We both became aware of how tightly pressed together we were. I started to squirm away from her, but she wasn't going to let me get away from her. "Be a gentleman and give the lady the room, would you?" she whispered.

I stopped moving, surprised by her question. "Sure," I said. It took a little effort, but I extricated myself from our embrace and found the door in the dark. The light from outside the bathroom made me squint as I opened the door far enough to squeeze out. Suddenly, Natasha was close behind me. She put her mouth next to my ear, and she snaked one arm around my waist. "Bobby also said you had a bigger cock," she crooned in my ear. She bit my earlobe again, and then shoved me out of the bathroom before I could react.

The door shut firmly behind me, the lock clicking.

I stood in the hallway, dazed and light-stunned. My belt was half undone. My shirt was untucked. It wasn't hard to imagine what was going through Cassandra's head as she stood there, not five feet from me.

"Oh," is all she said.

"Thank God," I said. "If you had been anyone else, this would have been really awkward."

☆

I managed to escape after dessert, which was suprisingly stellar—it almost made up for the rest of the evening. Natasha pouted theatrically when I made my excuses, but there was a glimmer of relief in her eyes that I was leaving. Cassandra's wide-eyed expression dimmed, and I felt bad for a moment, very much aware that I was abandoning her to the family, but you can't save everyone, right? Neither Dr. Tom nor Tom Junior noticed my departure, and in an hour, they'd not remember my name.

Pen followed me out, and when I was clear of the house, I pressed Stephanie's phone into her hand. "That's quite the family you have there, Penelope," I said.

She frowned slightly at my use of her full name, but she had lived with it long enough to develop all sorts of armor against it. There was enough of an evening breeze that her silk shirt kept clinging to the shape of her breasts. "So my mom did make a pass at you," she said.

I gave her a hard stare. "You know what I used to do for a living, don't you?"

She tried to brush off the question, but when I didn't stop with the glare, she wrapped her arms around herself and stared at the fountain. "It wasn't hard," she said. "There's this thing called the Internet, you know."

"Who did you think would figure it out first? Your mom or your dad?"

"Please." She snorted. "Dad's fucking clueless."

"And if Natasha hadn't figured it out before she fucked me in the bathroom, would you have told her later?"

She wouldn't look at me.

"Jesus, Pen, you are a piece a work."

"Look at my role models," she said bitterly.

I shook my head. "Where's the gun?" I asked.

"I don't have it," she said.

"That wasn't the deal," I said. I didn't even bother trying to feign surprise.

She shrugged. There were goosebumps on her arms.

"Okay," I said. "Keep it. What the fuck do I care?" I started to walk away.

She came after me, grabbing my arm. "Butch," she pleaded.

I stopped, but didn't look at her. After a moment, she let go of my arm. "You gave me back Stephanie's phone," she said softly. "How can I call you now?"

"You can't," I said.

"Butch," she whined. "I'm lonely. Please . . ."

I looked up at the darkening sky, thought about how turning around was a terrible idea. I shouldn't do it.

"Give me another chance," she whispered.

I exhaled loudly. "One," I said. "And only one. On my terms this time. And I get the gun back. That's the first thing that happens."

She didn't say anything. *Don't turn around,* Mr. Chow said in my head. *This isn't how you win this. Don't turn—*

I turned around. She had her arms behind her back, and was looking very downcast. When she realized I was looking at her, she squirmed a bit and then inhaled deeply. "And then . . . ?"

"One chance," I said, holding up a finger. "And if you are good, and if you don't do something outrageous, and—"

She was already nodding.

"—and you get some fucking therapy," I said. "Then, maybe. We'll see, okay?"

In my head, Mr. Chow threw up his hands. *One,* he said. *One thing. That was all you had to do.*

I've had a couple of drinks, I snapped at him. *It's been a trying couple of days.*

"Okay," Pen said. There was a bright light in her eyes. Before I could stop her, she darted forward and kissed me briefly—but fiercely—on the mouth. "Okay," she said again. "When?" Her face was filled with such eagerness.

You've done this to yourself, haven't you? I thought. *You should have walked away. You should*—and then an idea occurred to me.

"What—what did you say you were studying?" I asked. "Biology?"

"Yes," she said. "Well, biodiversity, but—"

"You know something about reptiles."

"I do," she said. "And birds and mammals and . . ."

"Good," I said, cutting her off. "Then here's what I need from you: we're going to the LA Convention Center tomorrow, where you're going to help me figure out the difference between boas and pythons."

CHAPTER 21

I don't like crowds. Nor do I like public spaces. It's a prison thing, and I own it, but too much open space and too many people make me nervous. It's hard to keep an eye on everyone within twenty feet, especially when they were all moving like spastic beagles.

In the yard, you felt it when someone moved differently. There was a rhythm, and when it broke, everyone knew. You learned to pay attention without staring wide-eyed at everything all at once. The ones who got shanked were the ones who weren't paying attention. The ones who were thinking about private time in their beds after lights out. We were one big centipede in the system—all uniform segments with uniform legs. But when one set broke the shuffle, all the other legs noticed. There was a ripple that went up and down the rest of the body.

In the yard, your best friend was the wall. That poorly painted concrete cooled your backside. Inside the house, you kept your distance from the bars of the cells. Who knew what was going to pass through those narrow gaps? In the common room and cafeteria, you paid attention to who was looking where, and for how long. *One left, two left, three right, four back of head, five eyes front, six left . . .* When you were done counting, you started again, tracking what had changed. *Was five still looking at you? Who was six talking to? Was he, in fact, still talking?*

You couldn't control your environment, but you could know it. You could read it, feel it, anticipate it.

The main hall at the LA Conference Center was the size of two football fields, and it was crammed full of bodies in motion. It was a convict's worst nightmare.

Well, okay, second worst nightmare. The first being three dudes coming at you with sharpened spoons in the shower, but that's a specific issue with prison. On the outside, the nightmare was people. In the case of NARC, there were also snakes.

Pen met me at the registration table. She cut a path through the crowd, heads turning as she walked toward me. She was wearing black—pants, boots, and short leather jacket. Underneath the jacket, she was wearing a tight t-shirt with an iridescent lizard decal on it. Her hair was looped into an easy knot at the back of her head, and she wore a shade of lipstick that looked like she had careened through an orchard of plum trees. She had a dark purse slung over her shoulder.

I had bought day passes that included access to the dealer's area, and they came with bright green lanyards. I felt like a tourist wearing mine; Pen made it seem like the staff at NARC had picked the color because it went so well with her eyes. We didn't bother with programs; we were only here for the immense hall where hundreds of thousands of reptiles were on display to a rapturous and raucous audience of kids begging their parents for some kind of lizard. *Dad, all the other kids have snakes! Dad, get me something pretty. Dad, I'm going to die if I don't have a pet turtle. Please, Dad, please? I've been so good. If you love me, you'll get me a lizard.*

It was always Dads who got stuck taking the kids to the reptile shows. Moms knew better. They didn't want one of those fucking things in the house.

Moving through this squirming chaos of scales and squealers were the wrinkled, slit-eyed speculators. The ones who were there to talk about what wasn't on display. The ones who spoke in coded phrases. *Got a Black Sally? I need a pale GTP for a lady friend, you know what I mean?* Making esoteric hand gestures that said "frilled" or "forked" or "bearded." Paying cash, and leaving no trace behind. Who needs a receipt when everyone knows everyone anyway, right?

There was a crackling energy in the room that reminded me of industry parties where everyone was looking to score. It didn't matter what it was. Drugs. Gossip. Agency introductions. Here, it was satchels and suitcases, fumbling handshakes and nervous laughter, along with furtive glances being passed back and forth.

Jesus Christ, they weren't very good at it, but they didn't have to be, did they? Who was watching? Just an ex-con who was trying his best not to hyperventilate, and his sexy sidekick who didn't understand the definition of "low profile." Nor would she ever learn.

Reptile World's booth was, as the guy at the store had said, front and center. There were more than a dozen guys working as many long tables. They were hawking lizards, turtles, snakes—hell, they could be selling mini dinosaurs for all I could tell. Behind the bustle and boom of the salesmen, there were a coterie of managers, who were busy with specialty cases and what passed for celebrities in the snake world. I was trying to figure out which one was Trevellian when Pen bumped into me.

"I'm bored," she said. She pressed herself against my arm.

"We haven't seen every booth yet," I said.

"We haven't seen any of them," she said. She nodded at Reptile World's gigantic booth. "You look like you're trying to talk yourself out of asking a girl to dance or something."

"Girls make me nervous," I said, flushing at her noticing my interest in Trevellian's operation.

She leaned closer, her breasts rubbing against my arm. "How nervous?" she asked.

A fat dude in a blue t-shirt with a picture of a long snake and a really terrible pun about length versus girth stopped in front of us. "Look at that gecko," he said loudly to his friend, pointing at Pen's chest.

"Shiny," his friend said. He was just as a fat, and the attention-grabbing text on his shirt was even more banal.

Pen gave them a hard stare, and like many boys who think t-shirts sporting double entendres are clever, they misread her glare as an invitation to interact with her. "We like snakes," the first one said. He pointed at his shirt, in case we hadn't seen it already. "Cause they—"

"Because they make a funny noise when you step on them," I said, trying to save him the embarrassment of finishing his sentence.

"No," the fat snake fan said. "That's not why." He screwed up his face like he couldn't believe I was so misinformed about how snakes work. He pointed at his shirt. "It's because—"

"Because they have brains larger than your testicles?" I guessed, still not getting the joke.

"No," the fat guy said. "What's wrong with you, dude?"

"Come on, Gary," the first guy said. He was starting to figure out that I was trying to save them. "This guy's an asshole."

"This asshole isn't staring at my tits like a couple of knuckle -dragging snake-lickers," Pen said sharply. She stepped in front of me, as if I needed rescuing from these two morons. "And by *snake-lickers*, I mean . . ."

Nope. She was never going to understand the concept of low-profile.

"Fuck you, bitch," Gary said. He gave Pen the finger. "I'm not gay." He darted off as she edged toward him, moving more quickly than I would have thought possible for a guy with ankles as thick as his. His friend lingered for a second, trying to decide if he was brave enough for the finger too, but his flight of fantasy fled, and he scuttled after his friend.

"Jesus," she muttered after they were gone.

"Sorry about that," I said.

"Why?" she asked. "Because you didn't steal them from their cribs and abandon them in the woods when they were babies?"

"It was a busy week," I said. "Lots of cribs. I must have missed a few."

"You're such a slacker," she said. She smiled when she said it, and a lot of the annoyance and disgust left her face.

I caught sight of a man in a dark brown cowboy hat shaking hands with fans at the Reptile World booth. He wore a fringed leather vest with jeans and a t-shirt. He had an enormous belt buckle—like the kind you saw on rodeo champions—and it had a raised picture of a coiled rattlesnake on it. Something halfway between an outlaw biker handlebar mustache and a full-on braided Viking beard was stuck to the front of his face. He laughed at something, putting his hands on his hips and making a show of his amusement, and I caught sight of his t-shirt.

It said "King of the Road," and there was another coiled rattler on it.

That was Jack Trevellian. I had no doubt.

He was working the crowd. Shaking hands. Hugging the ladies. Telling stories. Laughing like he was trying out for a Douglas Fairbanks revival. You didn't approach Jack directly. You queued in one of the many lines that went serpentine-like around the Reptile World booth. You waited until Jack found you.

I eyed the lines, thinking that Jack was more likely to notice Pen and her sparkly gecko than me. I wasn't sure I was ready to go queue like all the rubes if that was going to be the end result.

Pen watched me fidget. "Why are we here?" she asked.

"I want to look at some snakes," I said.

She put her hands on her hips and looked around. "Well, there's a bunch of them here," she said. "You should get to looking."

I pulled her toward a nearby booth, where there was a open-top cage with several tree pythons in it. "What are those?" I asked, pointing at the snakes.

She wrinkled her nose. "Python," she said.

"How can you tell?" I asked.

"Because it says so on the sign."

"Okay, so if there wasn't a sign, how could you tell?"

She shrugged. "No idea."

"I thought you said you knew something about reptiles."

"I'm studying biodiversity," she said. "I'm not memorizing the Peterson Field Guides."

The guy working the booth had overheard us, and he came over to be helpful. "Boas have a more defined pattern on their bodies," he said. He reached into the cage and gathered up one of the snakes. It slithered and curled around his arm, annoyed at having been disturbed. "See here?" he said, pointing to the white pattern along its back. "Small dots. Also, look at this." He grabbed the snake at the back of its head. When he squeezed it with two fingers, the snake's mouth popped open.

"What the fuck—" Pen stumbled into me as she backed up.

There were multiple rows of sharp, nearly translucent, fangs.

"Pythons have an extra upper jaw bone," the snake handler said. "That's where you get the extra teeth."

The fangs were extended, but even so, they still curved inward. Once the snake got those in you, you weren't going to get them out without tearing the snake's head apart.

The snake guy realized he was scaring the lady, and he backed up. He put the snake back in the cage, letting go of the head last. It snapped at him, but he was already out of reach. "They, uh, they aren't poisonous," he said nervously. Not because of the snake, but because he might lose a sale. "They don't eat anything larger than rats. Plus, you should see their young. Some real beautiful colors. Reds and oranges."

"Baby snakes?" Pen didn't like what she was hearing.

"Yeah, they lay eggs," the man said. "They are so pretty when they hatch."

"But with teeth," I said.

"Oh, no, man. Not 'till they're older." He fumbled for one of his brochures. "Here. Look at this. See? See how pretty they are?"

He gave me a knowing smile. "Pretty girl like her needs a pretty snake, don't you think?" He flapped the brochure at me.

"Pretty girl will put a foot in your balls if you try to surprise her with a snake," Pen said.

"Ah, pretty girl has spoken," I said to the snake guy. "And I like my balls, so no thanks."

"Aw, man, come on." The snake dude either didn't think Pen was serious or had been without his own balls for so long that he didn't remember what it was like to have them. I gave him a sad smile and backed away. Pen was right in step with me.

"What is up with you and these snakes?" Pen asked when we were far enough away from the booth that we were clear of any final guilt the guy was going to throw at us.

"I had one in the car when we went down to Tijuana," I said.

"What?"

"It was in my duffel bag," I said. "I was delivering it to someone down there."

She frowned, and I could tell she was trying to recall the parts of that evening where she wasn't mad at me or trying to seduce me. "You—you didn't have it when we came back," she said.

"I didn't."

"So you delivered it."

"Sorta."

"Sorta?"

I spotted a display of snakes that were pale yellow. They had a very distinct diamond pattern along their lengths. "Those are tree boas," I said, dragging her toward the booth. "They're usually green, but you can breed them so they get all pale like that. See how they look like the tree pythons?"

"But they're not," she said. "Boas are ovoviviparous."

"What's that mean?"

"They give birth to live young. They don't lay eggs."

"They probably have less teeth, too."

She shuddered. "Yes, they have less teeth. Jesus, Butch." She rubbed at her arms. "What's the big deal with these snakes? Were you supposed to deliver a boa or a python? Is that it? Which was it?"

"I don't remember," I said. "Things got a little excitable."

"What does that mean? How excitable?"

I was about to answer when convict brain spotted a familiar face. A face that shouldn't be here.

I turned away before the guy could spot me. "Well," I said, keeping my voice calm. "See that guy over there with the tape on his face?" I asked.

She looked around and I felt her tense when she spotted who I was talking about. "Yeah, I see him," she said. "It looks like he broke his nose or something."

"Or something," I said.

She looked at me. "Let me guess. That 'something' was you, right?"

"It was," I said. "Right after that, one of his pals shot the snake that was in the duffel bag."

What was Droopy doing here? I scanned the crowd. Was anyone else looking at Pen and me? Droopy didn't strike me as the type who would run off and do something solo. He was part of a crew, which meant Twitch and Julio were probably here too. Twitch might be hanging back, what with having been shot in the foot, but Julio would be on the prowl.

An itch started in the middle of my back. It was the sort of itch you get when you know there is a snake in the grass somewhere, but you can't see it.

CHAPTER 22

IN AN ATTEMPT TO GET AWAY FROM DROOPY, I NUDGED PEN toward one of the side halls, where it was all about frogs. "They're not even reptiles," Pen said as passed a pair of young girls try to count all the brightly colored frogs in a twenty-gallon aquarium.

"Nobody likes a know-it-all," I said.

"Oh, come on, Butch," she said. "I thought you wanted me for my brains. Are you just like all the other boys?"

I caught sight of a familiar face: Gary, the annoying dude from earlier. He was a rock in a sea of bodies, staring at me with what he imagined was a gunslinger's squint. He lit warning lights in my head. We saw the things that were out of place. Camouflage was all about blending in, and Gary was not a blender.

I touched Pen on the arm, directing her away from Gary. I spotted his pal at a nearby booth. He hadn't seen what Gary was doing, but it was only going to be a matter of time. As we headed farther away from the main floor, I almost missed the third guy who was watching us.

This guy was doing a better job of being invisible. He wasn't tall and he was wearing an Army surplus jacket and camouflage pants—the sort of outfit that wasn't out of place at a convention like this. The thing that gave him away was his hair. His blond hair swept up from his forehead in a tall crest that made me think of a rooster strutting around the barn yard.

"Cock Robin," I muttered, putting a name to the hair. His presence complicated things. I didn't know who he was working for. Was he reporting to Shackleton at the firm? Had Frolic turned him? Was he operating on his own?

He realized I had spotted him, and a shaggy smile broke across his face. He raised two fingers, pointed them at his eyes, and then forked them in my direction. Letting me know that he knew that I knew.

I put my hand on Pen's elbow, steering her again, but I kept my grip this time. "Time to go," I said.

"We just got here," she complained.

"Too many people," I said. "It was a bad idea."

She pulled her elbow free of my grip. "This is bullshit," she said. "You're trying to cut this sort. You're trying to get out of our deal."

"No," I said. "That's not what I'm doing."

"You bring me downtown," she said. "Where a bunch of dorks stare at my chest and some dude gets all hot and creepy about pythons. If I wanted to be around this sort of stupidity, I would have stayed on campus."

"Pen, I'm sorry. I made a bad choice. Let's go somewhere else and talk, okay?"

"No, it's not okay," she snapped. "And you know what? Fuck you for what you said to me last night. I deserve better than that."

"No, damnit—" I had looked away for a second and now I couldn't find Cock Robin.

"Oooh. You're not even paying attention to me now."

"No, wait—"

That's when she slapped me.

I was surprised more than I was hurt, and for a moment, I lost track of everyone around me. All I could see was Pen's backside—she was storming off after having smacked me. I felt like I was juggling a pair of chainsaws and a live alligator, and I had almost lost a couple of fingers to the gator in the last toss. "Pen—" I started after her.

A guy in a bright yellow shirt stepped in front of me.

"Is there a problem?" he asked. The word 'security' was screen-printed on his shirt, nice and tidy across his left pectoral. He had a wide belt with pouches and a walkie talkie with a mike on a long cord.

"No," I said. "There's no problem."

I made to go around him, but he stepped to the side, forcing me to stop again.

"Excuse me," I said, trying to keep my temper in check. "Do you mind?"

"I do," he said. "It's time for you to leave." He nodded behind me." "Turn around and walk straight to the exit back there."

"That's him," a voice said off to my right. "He threatened me."

Gary and his friend had come over to watch convention security throw me out.

I tried to find Pen, but there was no sign of her. There were, I noticed, more yellow-shirted dudes heading in my direction.

I held up my hands so the security guard could see they were empty. "There's been a misunderstanding of some kind. I don't know what you think is going on, but—"

"Throw his ass out!"

The security guard turned toward Gary and his eager-to-see violence pal. "Please, sir," the guard said. "There's no need—"

I slid past him as he tried to keep the riffraff from working themselves into a frenzy. I finally caught sight of Pen—*how had she gotten so far ahead?*—and I let everything else around me become nothing more than the shifting walls of an obstacle course I had to navigate to reach her. *Move like water,* I heard Mr. Chow say in my head. *Be like the wind. There is no straight path. There is only motion that takes you from where you are to where you want to be. If you have to move—if you have to break free—then go directly. Go, with purpose and intention.*

It was a dance, weaving and darting between bodies that seemed frozen. You glided through gaps. You slipped between couples as they momentarily drifted apart. You rolled around the tangled clusters that were too dense to slip through. When you faced a wall of people, you headed for them with such focus and intensity that they felt the wave of your approach and scattered before you could hurl yourself on them.

A flash of yellow signaled in my peripheral vision. I didn't stop, but I changed direction abruptly. The security guy was surprised at my course correction, and I grabbed his outstretched arm. Using his own momentum, I spun him into a display of lizard literature.

Another guard was in close pursuit. He was chunky around the middle, and all the excitement had left him wheezing and huffing. When he realized I wasn't going to run, he slowed down and tried to catch his breath. When I came at him, he couldn't reverse his air flow fast enough to yell. I tapped him in the gut, enough to get him to double forward, and then I slung him along, helping him collide with the first guy who had recovered from his encounter with the literature rack.

The crowd was reacting to the excitement. Everyone was moving. It was impossible to find a single face. *Flow like water across stones,* Mr. Chow said. I nodded in agreement, and kept moving in the direction I had been going. I would find her eventually.

And then I did. She was over by a pair of doors. Not the exit. Internal doors that led into the maintenance areas of the convention center. There was someone standing next to her. It was—

Twitch. The guy I had shot in the foot.

I gave up any polite pretext in my movement through the crowd. "Pen," I shouted as I started to bull toward her. People kept getting in my way, and I would lose sight of her and then find her again. "Pen!" Twitch had his hand on her arm. He was pulling her toward the doors. I shouted her name a third time, and this time she heard me. She wrenched her arm free of Twitch's grip. She turned and made eye contact with me, and then Droopy came out of the crowd. He and Twitch hustled her through the doors.

I wasn't that far behind them, and when I burst through the same door, I found myself in an empty hall that bent around the convention center public areas. I heard Pen's voice, echoing from around the corner, and no longer encumbered by the crowd, I ran after her.

I came around the corner at a sprint, and ran into a serving cart that had been left in the middle of the hall. I bounced off it, careened off the wall, and turned right into Droopy's fist. The floor came up and hit me too.

"You like that?" Droopy shouted at me. My face and shoulder hurt. I was seeing spots. A hot bloom of pain shot through my chest—Droopy had kicked me in the ribs. I curled up, trying to breathe. Trying to figure out what was happening. I caught a flicker of movement—Droopy was coming at me again—and I ducked my shoulder. His kick hurt, but at least it wasn't against my ribs this time.

I pushed against the floor, sliding back from Droopy's feet. He hesitated, and it was enough of a pause for me to get my feet under me. I stumbled back, bumping into the wall, and I looked around wildly, trying to figure out who the players were. Droopy was in the middle of the hall, his fists clenched and raised. Off to my left, I spotted Twitch and Pen. He had his hand tangled in her hair, using his grip to keep her under control.

"Let the girl go," I wheezed. "She's got nothing to do with this."

"*Imbécil*," Droopy spat. "You're not giving the orders here."

I nodded as I wiped at my lip. There was blood on my hand. "That so?"

My brain was fuzzy and my movements felt off, but Droopy moved even more stiffly than I. I shuffled out of the way of his first swing, punched him once in the ribs, and backed away. He snarled and whirled, dropping his guard.

I was next to the stupid cart. It had the remnants of a coffee service on it, and I snatched up one of the coffee pots. It was plastic, but it would do. Droopy swung at me again, and I batted his hand aside with the coffee pot. Whipping it by the handle, I smacked him right across the tape on his nose. He shrieked, and staggered back, blood coursing down his face.

Down the hall, Pen twisted in Twitch's grip. She brought her heel down sharply on his foot—whether she knew it was the foot I had shot in the warehouse or not, she chose well. Twitch howled and let go of her hair. She backed away from him, clawing at her purse. What the hell was she—

The gun. She had the gun in her purse.

It was big and ugly in her hands and everyone froze as she started waving it around.

"Careful," I said, putting up my hands.

She edged along the wall toward me, waving the gun back and forth at the pair of Mexicans. "Don't move," she snapped. Droopy was hunched forward, breathing heavily through his mouth. His face was an ugly mess of fury and pain. Twitch was vibrating with rage too.

I eased toward her, and when I got close, I said her name lightly. She didn't respond, and I touched her shoulder. She flinched, and everyone tensed. "Let's put the gun away," I said. I touched her shoulder again, more firmly this time. "This isn't what any of us want, okay?"

"Who are these assholes?" she demanded. "What do they want?"

"It doesn't matter," I said. "But let's not make it worse by shooting someone." I slid my hand down to her elbow. "Why don't you give me that, okay?"

She shook her head, but there wasn't a lot of urgency in the movement. The gun wavered, but it didn't drop. I kept moving my hand until I was touching her wrist. "Let me have it," I said. "Let me have the gun."

"They were hurting you," she said, almost in tears.

"It's okay," I said. "I'm fine. Really. Just give me the gun, and then you can check. You can take care of me."

"P . . . Promise?"

"Yeah, I promise."

My hand was on her hand now, my fingers touching the metal slide of the gun. Slowly, the barrel of the gun dipped and her grip loosened. I got my hand on the gun, and quickly slipped it out of her grasp. Droopy and Twitch started to move forward, but once I had the gun in my hand, I pointed it at them again. "Don't—" I said.

Droopy's eyes widened. "That's—that's my gun," he said thickly.

"Yeah, it is," I said. "And—"

The gun's weight was off. It felt too light. Without letting my apprehension show, I brought up my other hand and cupped the base of the weapon. There was an empty space there, a hollowness where I expected to feel the bottom of the magazine.

"Pen," I said quietly. "Where's the—you got the gun out of the trunk, didn't you?"

She nodded. "That's where you left it."

I cleared my throat lightly. I kept my two-handed grip. "And did you—was there anything else in the trunk . . . ?"

She looked at me, her brows furrowing. "Was I—"

Twitch reached under his jacket and produced a pistol of his own. It looked a lot like the one I held. "I have one too," he said. He ducked his head slightly, as if he was trying to look under my hands. "Mine has bullets," he said. "Does yours?" He laughed at the expression on Pen's face. "Uh-oh, *problema*?"

Droopy figured out what Twitch had already guessed. Pen had found the gun in the trunk of her car, but she hadn't found the magazine. I had unloaded the weapon when I had put it in the trunk. I was pointing an empty gun at these two.

I stepped forward, pushing Pen behind me. I pointed my gun at Twitch. Did I have a round in the chamber? I couldn't remember if I had ejected it. "*No problema*," I said. "I shot you once; I'll do it again."

Droopy decided he wanted to risk it. With a roar, he charged. I didn't bother pulling the trigger. There wasn't time to recover if I was wrong. I threw the gun at him. It hit him in the face.

A loud noise echoed in the hall. Something punched me in the shoulder. I was knocked off-balance, and then Droopy plowed into me. I slammed against the wall, banging my head against the hard concrete. All of a sudden, I felt like I was drowning, and then everything went dark.

CHAPTER 23

I LOST SOME TIME, AND WHEN I OPENED MY EYES AGAIN, MY first reaction to my surroundings was that I was in the infirmary at Tehachapi. *Trouble with the Double-Z,* I thought. They were an Aryan Nation gang—white dudes who were keen on being white and being dudes. After the incident in the shower with Lando Turk, I was told I had the balls to be a Double-Z. My cellmate at the time, a skinny kid named Ralph who was doing a nickel for grand theft, nagged me relentlessly about asking to join. He figured if I got in, he might have a chance too.

Mr. Chow's thoughts on the matter were that if I wasn't willing to shank someone for the Double-Z, they were going to turn me into a sex pet. I'd spend most of my sentence on my knees.

Aren't you going to protect me? I had asked Mr. Chow. After all, he had killed Turk. Wasn't there some sort of responsibility owed?

No, he said. *You're going to protect yourself. If you don't, then people might wonder how a soft white boy like you did Turk. Once they start thinking that, they're going to think about other things, and I don't want that.*

So, this is about you, then.

Of course, he said. *You're going to be someone's bitch. Whose bitch might be the only choice you actually get to make in here.*

They don't like people who don't pick sides. They're going to hate me.

They already hate you. You had the best job in the world and you got caught doing something stupid. They don't respect stupid.

What do they respect?

Strength. He made a fist and hit me in the face. *See? Soft. Slow.*

When he went to hit me again, I blocked his fist. Clumsily, like I was waving my arms to scare off a bear.

Mr. Chow nodded. *You have made a choice,* he said. *Good. We will start your training tomorrow.*

Three weeks later, Ralph tried to smother me with my pillow. I was to have been his initiation into the Double-Z. When he botched the job, he went with plan B, which was a stiffened piece of bedspring taped to a couple of popsicle sticks. He got me twice before I broke his arm and cracked his skull on the bars of our cell.

Stupid kid. He had been in and out of juvie most of his life, stealing anything not nailed down to pay for a life-long drug habit. The only reason he was in Tehachapi was because they charged him with stealing the car *when* they caught him, which was two days after his eighteenth birthday.

The Double-Z would have broken him for failing to smother me, but he developed a stutter while recovering from his injuries. It was enough to get him transferred down to Lancaster. They had head doctors in Lancaster who could figure out if his newfound verbal tic was trauma-based or if it was a psychological manifestation of other issues.

Ralph's wire shank had put a hole in my lower intestine and grazed my gall bladder. It wasn't good enough for a transfer, and so I stayed in bed until the prison doc thought I wouldn't rupture something while shuffling around the cafeteria.

As I focused on my surroundings, I realized I wasn't in the prison infirmary. There was no wire mesh covering the overhead light fixture. There was a door on the closet where the toilet was, and there were drapes along one side of the room. Light bled around the edges, as if there were windows behind the curtains. There were no windows in the prison infirmary.

There was a hospital-issued bracelet around my left wrist, and a finger monitor attached to my left index finger. The cord trailed back to a machine that was cheerfully recording my vital signs, and next to the bed, there was a tray with a plastic cup and straw on it. I was wearing a pair of boxers that weren't a brand I wore, and when I moved my legs, I didn't feel encumbered in any way. I wasn't chained to the bed. I could leave if I wanted to.

There was a dressing on my shoulder, and when I sat up—slowly, mind you—I felt gauze and tape stretch across my back. There were dark bruises along my right side, and I dimly remembered being kicked. Before . . . before I got shot.

I couldn't recall how I had gotten here. My brain was confusing what had happened recently with events from my past. *It's the way your mind processes trauma,* Willie had told me once. We had been talking about sports injuries and the like. *Your brain tucks all that shit away,* he said. *Rolls you back to another time when you were hurt. Reminds you that you survived that experience, and that you're going to survive this one too.*

There was no reason to rush things. I wasn't in prison. I wasn't being held against my will. My ribs ached. My shoulder hurt, and judging by the bandages, the bullet had either gone through my shoulder or the doctors had taken it out. I was going to make it. Everything was going to be fine.

But then I thought about Pen, and when I tried to get out of bed, the headache lurking in the back of my head reared up and squeezed. The room got bright and I lost track of time again.

The second sign I wasn't in the prison infirmary was my nurse. She made eye contact and smiled when she checked on my bandages. Even asked me if I wanted some Jell-O.

"You don't get Jell-O in prison," I muttered.

"What's that, honey?" She paused at the foot of the bed.

"Nothing," I said. "I like what you've done with—with—"

"Save the flattery for when you get home," she said, patting me on the foot. "You'll need it then."

Shortly after she left, I had a visitor. I didn't recognize him, but the gold shield clipped to the pocket of his suit jacket was identification enough. He was a well-put together man in his mid-forties. Neatly clipped mustache. Lines on his forehead and around his eyes that said he spent time outside. Hands that said he could do the outside work too.

"How you feeling, Mr. Bliss?" he asked. He didn't wait for an answer. "Detective Green," he said. "Robbery-Homicide." That's what it said on the business card he flashed before putting it on the tray beside my bed.

"Who died?" I asked. My mouth was dry, and I eyed the plastic cup with the straw that was also on the bedside table.

"No one has died," Green said. He had a little black notebook, and he started thumbing through it.

"Did someone steal my wallet?" I asked.

"I wouldn't know anything about that," he said. He found what he was looking for and he peered at his notes for a second. "Do you feel well enough to answer some questions?" he asked.

"Will you go away if I say no?"

He shook his head.

I reached for the cup. "Knock yourself out," I said.

"You served some time, didn't you, Mr. Bliss?"

I sucked on the straw, enjoying the cool taste of water.

"Drugs?" he asked.

I kept drinking, but I was polite about it and looked at him as I did. Letting him know I was hearing his questions, that they weren't worthy of my time.

He shrugged. I wasn't the first hard case he had ever interviewed. He flipped a page in his notebook. "Were you at the Los Angeles Convention Center yesterday?"

I took the straw out of my mouth. "What day is it?" I asked.

"Saturday," he said.

I thought hard about my calendar. "Yeah," I said. "Friday. I was at the convention center. At the reptile show."

"Did you attend the show by yourself?"

I shook my head. "I was there with someone."

"Personal friend? Business associate?"

"Personal friend."

"This personal friend have a name?"

"Penelope Verlaine," I said.

Green liked that answer. He made a notation in his book. "You two arrive together?" he asked.

"Separately," I said. "But we met at the registration desk. I bought day passes for us."

He reached inside his jacket and produced a badge and lanyard. "Like this?" The lanyard was that same green color and the badge had the word 'FRIDAY' on it.

"Yeah," I said. "Like that."

He tossed it on the bed. "That one is yours," he said.

"Oh, I'm glad I passed that quiz," I said.

He reached into his pants pocket and brought out the clip I used to carry my cards and cash. "And here's your wallet." It joined the badge on the bed.

"Look at that. Case closed," I said. "You guys are good."

"Did you and Ms. Verlaine argue about anything while you were at the convention center?" he asked.

"I don't recall any argument," I said.

"She didn't slap you?" He watched me closely. "That strikes me as 'argumentative.'"

"I see how you could think that," I said.

"You think she might have deserved the same in return?"

"No," I said. "That's not what happened."

He raised an eyebrow, but didn't say anything.

"Is she okay?" I asked.

"We're not talking about her," Green said. "We're talking about you. What did you do after she slapped you?"

"I didn't hit her," I said firmly.

"Did you hit someone else?"

I almost said 'no,' but the word got caught in my throat. I struggled to recall the events at the convention center. Who were the guys in yellow shirts?

"Take your time," Green said.

The door opened, and a man in a wheelchair rolled into the room. The door banged off the wall and would have smacked the guy's chair, but the woman following him caught the door before it could. I recognized her, and my pulse sped up at the sight of Angel Chow. It went even faster when I realized the guy in the chair—wearing a heavy cast on his right leg—was Nathan Shackleton. He didn't look the part in his designer sweatsuit, but he knew the routine. "Good afternoon, Detective. This interview is over." He waved a hand at me. "This man is a client of Stephanish, Groiller, and Bernstein. He will not be answering any more questions for you at this time. Thank you, and have a good day."

Green sized up Nathan in his sweatsuit and cast. Then he looked at Angel, who, even though she wasn't dressed like a TV lawyer, looked better than Nathan did.

Which wasn't hard, frankly. He was pale and hadn't shaved. And the wheelchair and cast would only work if this was an *Ironside* reboot.

"You have any ID?" Green asked.

Angel held out a business card. "I'm going to call the firm," Green said after reading the card.

"Of course you are," Nathan said. "Be sure to ask for Mason Shackleton. He's in charge of client relations." He sat up in his chair. "He's my father," he added, in case Green hadn't figured it out.

"Okay," Green said. He dropped the firm's card in his notebook and closed it. "What were you saying, Mr. Bliss?" he asked.

"Detective—" Nathan cut him off.

"Okay, okay." Green put up his hands. He navigated past Nathan and Angel. He paused, considering something, and then he nodded at Angel and left. No one said anything—no one moved—until the door had fully closed.

I cleared my throat. "So, how long have I been a client?"

"Since I got this phone call," Nathan said. He dug his phone out of his pocket and handed it to Angel. It was a fancy phone, with a lot more buttons than necessary to make calls. She pulled up the voice mail and hit play.

"Hey, Nate, it's me. I don't know what the fuck is going on, but I don't like it. Not one fucking bit. Call me ASAP. I got this vibe that you're working for them, and—yeah—I can't have that, Nate. That's no good for anyone. They're going to fuck you, Nate. You're not going to like it. They're going to take over the world, and we're all going to end up having baby snakes shoved up our—just, just, goddamn it, Nate. Whatever they promised you is bullshit. That's what they do. Call me, asshole. Oh, and I've got the girlfriend, so don't do anything stupid."

I looked at Angel and then I looked at Nathan. "And that was?" I asked, even though I had a pretty good idea.

"Jack," Nathan said. "Jack Trevellian."

I looked at Angel again. "I'm a little confused," I said. "Maybe it's whatever pain meds they've got me on, but aren't—aren't *you* his girlfriend?"

Angel's mouth firmed into a tight line. Nathan looked away. His hands fluttered in his lap. I felt like I had missed something.

"Wait. Who does Jack have?"

"He's not very good with names," Nathan said. "Angel. Pen. They're sound sort of the same . . ."

"Sort of? They're not even close."

"He's got *your* girlfriend," Angel said, cutting to the quick.

"She's not—" I started, but then her words sank in. "Oh, what?"

CHAPTER 24

"WE SHOULD—" I STARTED, BUT NATHAN WAVED AT ME TO shut up.

"We're not talking about this here," he said.

"You brought it up!"

He tried to turn the wheelchair and ran his foot into the end of the bed. He yelped in pain, and Angel gave him a look that wasn't entirely sympathetic. I rolled my eyes, which didn't hurt, and started to get out of bed, which did. I paused, one leg off the bed. "I'm not staying here," I managed.

Angel examined my lack of attire. "You're not dressed for running around," she said.

"No shit," I replied. "Help me find my pants." I flapped a hand at Nathan. "Go distract the nurse or something," I said.

Nathan got his chair turned, but there was no way he could manage the door by himself. Shaking her head, Angel went to help him. I worked on getting both feet on the floor. It was more complicated than I remember it being.

The machine next to the bed started beeping when I took the finger monitor off. I scooped up the NARC lanyard and my money clip, and then I yanked the top sheet off the bed, wrapping it around my waist. It would have to do.

Angel got the door open for Nathan, and he nearly ran over the nurse as he rolled out of the room. She bustled in as soon as he was clear. "Mr. Bliss, what are you doing?"

"I'm getting out of bed," I said.

"You shouldn't be—you'll aggravate your injuries."

"It's a shoulder wound," I said. "I'm just going to be walking and standing. I'm not going to be throwing free throws or driving for the basket." I leaned heavily against the bed. The room was starting to spin counter-clockwise. "Unless you and yours did a really bad job of patching me up."

The nurse glared at me, and then she frowned at Angel. She didn't contradict me.

"That's what I thought," I said. I shuffled a step away from the bed. "I appreciate your care and attention, but I going to walk out of here."

"You can't walk out of here," the nurse tried. "It's against hospital policy."

"Lady, I spent a decade at the California Correctional Institute up at Tehachapi, and let me tell you something: that was a place you couldn't walk out of. This place? Short of you hitting me over the head with a bedpan, I'm walking."

She exhaled noisily. "All patients—even the stubborn ones—must leave the hospital in a wheelchair. That's the policy."

"Oh," I said, wobbling. "That's, uh, you know? I'm okay with that policy."

She crossed her arms. "Sit down," she said. "I'll get you a chair."

"I've made it this far," I said. "I think I'll keep standing."

The nurse looked at Angel, who shrugged apologetically. "He really is that stubborn."

The nurse shook her head and walked toward the door.

"Hey," I called after her. "Could I get some pants?"

She stopped and looked back at me. "Garments are to be administered at the discretion of the nursing staff," she said. There was a flicker of a satisfied smile on her lips.

"I'm not getting any pants," I said to Angel after she was gone.

"You did force her hand," Angel pointed out.

"Isn't there some oath they're supposed to uphold?"

"That one is about not doing harm. Personal embarrassment, including the self-inflicted kind, isn't covered."

"I'm not embarrassed," I said. "What if it is cold out there?"

"It's LA," Angel said. "It's never cold." Her gaze went up and down my form. "So your nipples might get hard," she said. "It's not like that hasn't happened before."

Nathan and I were a pair: two idiots sitting in wheelchairs outside the hospital entrance, waiting for Angel to bring the car around. And when she did, there was lots of clumsy dancing about who got to sit where, but we finally managed to get everyone loaded up. Angel wheeled out of the turnabout and headed for the street. She was of the opinion that we should go to her place.

"No," Nathan countered. "Take us to the office."

"My place will be more comfortable," she argued. "Plus we can get Butch some clothes there."

"My father is at the office," Nathan said. "We can talk privately there."

"There are clothes that will fit me at your place?" I asked Angel.

"I'm sure something will fit," Angel said.

I was in the back seat, and she wouldn't meet my gaze in the rearview mirror. I looked at the back of Nathan's head and tried to imagine myself in his designer sweatsuit. "We're not the same size," I said.

"Take us to SG&B," Nathan said. His voice was loud for the enclosed space of the car, like he was trying to drown out the conversation Angel and I were having.

"Whose clothes are they?" I asked.

Angel changed lanes and sped up. Her hands were tight on the wheel. "They're just some extra clothes," she said. "Don't worry about where they came from."

"I'm not worried," I said. "I'm just curious."

"Who gives a fuck about the clothes," Nathan shouted. "Go to the office!"

Nathan's outburst pushed us all to silence, and we kept our thoughts to ourselves as Angel navigated toward a highway interchange. I kept my mouth shut until she had taken the turn and merged onto the 10.

"Can I say something about—" I started.

"No." Nathan barked the word.

I decided to shift the topic slightly. "I saw Detective Green in the waiting area when we left," I said. "Did you see him?"

"I saw him," Nathan said.

"Do you think he's following us?"

Angel swerved slightly as she checked her mirrors. Nathan waited until she got the car back in the center of the lane before he spoke. "I'm sure he is."

"That might be a problem. Nathan—"

"We're not talking about it in the car," Nathan said.

Angel had found a blanket in her trunk and I had thrown it across my lap. The ache in my shoulder was getting stronger, and the headache at the back of my neck was an ever-tightening vise. I should have swiped a pillow from the hospital. "Can I—can I ask something unrelated to all of this?" I asked.

"What?" Nathan snapped.

"Could you turn down the A/C? It's a bit chilly in here."

Angel finally made eye contact in the rearview mirror. Her eyes weren't wide with panic, but there was little humor in them.

"Do you need proof?" I asked.

That got me a smile. "I'll take your word for it," she said. She fiddled with the settings on the console, adjusting the air flow in the back of the car. It blew on my toes, which made me think of tiny goats and—

"I'm going to need some aspirin soon," I said. "Or maybe something stronger . . . " I leaned against the window as best I could without disturbing my shoulder and watched the city flash by. After awhile, it smeared, getting all fuzzy and hypnotic.

I started to have a thought about getting some rest, worrying about my endurance, and then I was gone from the world again.

Frank met us in the parking garage. He had a pair of metal crutches for Nathan. For me, he had a terrycloth bathrobe and fuzzy slippers. Both were stamped with the logo of the Beverly Hilton, but I wasn't going to quibble. "No pants?" I asked. Frank gave me a look that said he'd survived for weeks in the desert without pants during the Gulf War, fighting for God and country and oil futures so that I could have light and heat and sex anytime I wanted with anyone I wanted.

I was getting pretty good at reading Frank's expressions. Or, my mind had slipped its lease and was galloping away from me. I was going to imagine it was the former, but it was probably the latter.

Frank used his keycard on the executive elevator, and we rode non-stop to the sixteenth floor. Both of the ladies behind the desks in the lobby of SG&B pretended they didn't see us as we shuffled through. I was impressed by their resolve. Nathan looked like a penguin as he humped along on his crutches.

We were directed into the same conference room where Mr. Shackleton and I had talked the other day. He wasn't there, but there was an assortment of sandwiches from a nearby deli on the sidebar, along with cold sodas and fizzy water. Nathan grabbed a grinder and a Coke, and managed to make it down to the far end of the table without falling. He tackled his sandwich like a man who had been lost in an indoor shopping mall overnight. I stared at him as he ate. *I've seen that face,* I thought. That furtive hunch. Protecting your food. Eating quickly, like someone might try to take it from you.

I turned away, and my hands shook as I examined my choices. *Prison face,* I thought. I focused on the sandwiches and picked out one filled with meat and bacon. I kept my distance from

Nathan and looked out at the skyline for awhile as I ate.

Angel sat nearby, fussing with her sandwich. "Do you . . . would you like anything?" she asked Frank.

"I ate earlier," he said. He hadn't moved from his position by the door, and his intense stare never wavered from Nathan.

There were voices in the hall, and then the door opened and Mr. Shackleton walked in. Frank straightened up a hair, Angel adjusted her clothing, and Nathan turned into a wet weasel. "Dad—" he began.

"Shut up," his father snapped. He stopped near Angel. "Ms. Chow," he said. "I'm sorry for this . . . complication."

"I've had worse," Angel said.

Shackleton's gaze hardened, but not so much that a tiny twitch couldn't work its way across his lips. "Bliss," he said, directing his attention at me. "GSW?"

"Yes, sir." *GSW* was what they wrote on the intake form at the hospital. *Gunshot wound.*

"Through and through?"

"I haven't looked."

"How's your range of motion?"

"I suspect I won't be trying out for the Lakers this year."

He focused on my half-eaten sandwich. "Appetite and attitude presenting," he said. "You'll be fine, son."

"Thanks, Dad."

Having run out of other people he could talk to, Shackleton turned his attention to the huddled figure at the end of the table. "How's the leg, Nathan?"

"It's fine," Nathan said, trying to not sound petulant, but not trying that hard.

"Any pain?"

"Yes." This came out more stridently than Nathan probably wanted, but there was no taking it back.

"Can you—" Shackleton turned his ferocious gaze toward the window. Whatever he was going to ask died in that moment.

"I'm fine, Dad," Nathan said. He sat up straighter and said it again. Mentally, I gave him a thumb's up. It wasn't easy being someone different than who your old man wanted.

Shackleton put his hands together, but having done so, he wasn't sure what to do with them next. "I've just had a call from a Detective Green, over at Robbery-Homicide, Hollywood Division. He told me a story about two idiots checking themselves out of the hospital. I didn't contradict him, because it certainly sounded like the sort of stupidity I would expect from the two of you."

Angel cocked an eyebrow at me, and I gave her a nod. *That's a fair call,* I thought.

"Detective Green requested an interview with Mr. Bliss at the earliest convenience."

"I was thinking about—"

"I told him you would be at his office first thing Monday morning," Shackleton said.

"I might be busy."

"I might not care." Shackleton showed me his teeth. "This is my polite face."

"I've seen it," I said.

We stared at one another for a moment, and then Shackleton shifted his attention to the end of the room. "Are you representing him?" he asked Nathan.

"I—I said he was a client . . ."

"Is that correct, Mr. Bliss? Are you a client?"

"I guess so," I said. "No one asked my opinion at the time, and since then, your son has been busy muzzling me."

Shackleton looked back at Frank and gave his man a nod. Frank snapped to attention and left the room. After he was gone, Shackleton put his hands on the table and gave me the full force of his attention. "Frank is fetching a standard agreement form. You will sign it. My son will sign it. And you will both agree that you signed it three days ago. Am I clear?"

"Clear," I said. Nathan echoed me a moment later.

"Good," Shackleton said. "Therefore everything said in this room is privileged information. Anything you say to my son is privileged information. You do not have to speak with Detective Green on Monday, if you do not wish to. If you do, you will only do it when your lawyer—my son—is present. Are we clear?"

"Clear," I said again.

Mr. Shackleton looked at Angel. "You should go," he said.

"I'm not leaving," Angel countered.

"My son can't represent you. There's a conflict of interest."

"There *was* a conflict of interest," Angel said. "There isn't anymore."

Something like a sob slipped out of Nathan's mouth. But it could have just as easily been a hiccup in the HVAC system. Or maybe I made the noise. It was hard to tell, and Shackleton took his time deciding whether he he'd heard it or not.

"Have the two of you had sexual relations?" he asked.

"Her and I?" I asked.

"No, her and him." Shackleton pointed at his son.

Angel nodded. Down at the end of the table, Nathan shifted in his chair. I didn't look. I didn't want to know, even though I did know. I felt something grind in my chest. Was that jealously? *Jesus,* I thought, *really?* But the feeling was there.

"You two don't understand the concept, do you?" Shackleton said. "It's even more of a conflict now that you're not together."

I put up my hands and broke his train of thought. "Look, I don't know what's going on—I rarely do, frankly—but what I do know is that Angel's here because I was given a piece of paper with her phone number on it. She's here because that was the play, and if she goes, I go too."

"My father's right," Nathan piped up. "She's not involved. She shouldn't be here."

"Why? Because you don't want her to hear about what a fuck-weasel you've been?"

Nathan banged his hand on the table. "God damnit, Bliss. I'm sick of your mouth. I'm sick of the sight of you. I'm sick of your—"

I let him rail on. By the sound of it, he'd been bottling up a lot of anger and resentment for some time. It all came pouring out now. Nathan wanted to be heard, and so we listened. And listened. And listened.

Eventually, he ran out of steam and fell back in his seat, gasping for air. Gasping with the realization of what he had done to his relationship with Angel. It was already on the rocks, but his diatribe really put it down. He hadn't realized he was doing it until it was too late, and then he had kept going. Like he could turn it around somehow, but man, there was no fixing that.

Frank had returned with paperwork and Shackleton put it in front of me. "Sign it," he said, slapping a pen down beside the document.

For a legal document, it was short. I made one addition, and then signed at the bottom of the second page. I slid it over to Angel, who raised an eyebrow at what I had written, but she signed it too. I slid both pages and the pen down to Nathan. He let out a loud squawk when he saw what I had done to the first page.

"You can't add her like that," he objected.

"I did," I said.

"I'm not—"

"Sign it!" Shackleton roared.

Nathan jumped—Hell, we all jumped—and when he had recovered, he scrambled for the pen.

Shackleton collected the document from his son, initialed both pages, and then handed the counter-signed document to Frank. "Now," he said, his tone no less a whipcrack than before. "Tell me the whole goddamned story. The both of you."

I let Nathan go first. We knew a lot of it, but it was time to hear it from the source.

CHAPTER 25

NATHAN STARTED WITH THE LACEY ACT. DURING THE EARLY PART of the twentieth century, the environmental movement was concerned about the extinction of animal species. In addition to making poaching illegal, the Lacey Act also enacted rules for transporting animals across state and national lines. It's been these rules that have been used recently to try to curb the spread of non-native species—the Burmese python in Florida, for example. They're cute when they're only a foot long, but like small children, they get a lot bigger when they grow up.

Internationally, CITIES was formed. The Convention on International Trade in Endangered Species of Wild Fauna and Flora was an effort by a bunch of governments to coordinate their efforts to control the import and export of rare species. It was a voluntary treaty, and it was a stick nation-states could use to whack animals smugglers with. It also gave agencies broad abilities to share relevant data, which made it easier to track smuggling operations.

The problem, Nathan explained, was that the penalties for violating Lacey and ignoring CITES were about as financially taxing as getting a parking ticket. You find a ticket under your wipers. What do you do? You throw it in the glove box with all the others and forget about it. If you ever get pulled over, the officer might notice your oustanding violations when he pulls your license. *Hey, you've got a lot of parking tickets.* What do you do? You beg forgiveness. Maybe even offer to write a check right then, right?

Maybe that was the way it worked in your zip code, I thought, but I didn't interrupt.

More to Nathan's point: does this incident scare you off from parking illegally? Only if you were a decent law-abiding citizen who was easily cowed by the presence of a shiny badge and a uniform.

Anyway, reptile importing was the same thing: get caught with animals on the CITES list and get slapped with a meager fine. In extreme cases, you could get sentenced to a week at a federally-sponsored country club, but that process took longer than the lifespan of many species of lizards. "US Fish and Wildlife estimate there are somewhere in the neighborhood of a million illegal reptiles coming into the US every year," Nathan said. "They don't have the staff or budget to deal with that many animals."

"You can't fund a government organization with parking tickets," I said.

Nathan gave me a 'more or less' wave of the hand. "Now, you can only be cited if you knowingly take possession of illegal animals," he continued.

Say some guy wanders into your shop. He's got a box of turtles he wants to sell you. Says they're Asian box turtles. You don't know any difference, and since he's a professional, you take his word for it. You take the turtles off his hands and dump 'em in a tub in the back room. A couple of days later, one of your eager amphibian enthusiasts says, *Hey, those aren't Asian box turtles.* Someone gets out one of those guidebooks with all the color pictures and *son of a bitch!* These turtles are actually Vietnamese leaf turtles, and you know what? They're on the CITES list of protected species.

Now, you might feel bad about having these turtles on hand, but damn, Vietnamese leaf turtles, right? You're going to quietly sell them to private collectors who are trying to fill their turtle Bingo cards. And if Fish and Wildlife happen to stop by while you've got some of these critters paddling about in that tub, what are you going to do? You're going to get all soft-eyed and

and nervous sweaty-like. *Oh, officer, I'm sorry. I didn't realize I was doing something wrong.*

Fish and Wildlife, who get to play the role of stern authoritarians, are going to shake their fingers at you. *Okay, but don't do it again,* they'll say. They'll take your turtles too, but that's better than getting thrown in jail, right?

Naturally, what Fish and Wildlife really want to know is whether you knew these were illegal turtles when you bought them, but how are they going to figure that out? The guy who sold them to you is long gone. You don't have any paperwork. If they wanted to catch you in the act, that's going to require phone taps, surveillance, and a van full of dudes breathing each other's farts for a month or more.

Even if they managed to scrape up a budget for that, all you have to do is have a good lawyer on retainer. Someone who is happy to remind the guys in the van that private individuals are innocent until proven guilty, that people are free from unreasonable search and seizure, and oh, they can freely assemble, talk about any goddamned thing they want, and they have a right to know the particulars of any accusation laid against them.

There's going to be billable hours in all that, but what do you care? At this point, you're selling so many geckos and snakes that you have more pressing concerns, like warehouse space and tax write-offs.

Meanwhile, a budget committee back in DC wants to know why Fish and Wildlife isn't showing any results for all the cash going into this investigation. All Fish and Wildlife can say is *Well, gee, investigations are ongoing.* That's not what budget watchers in DC want to hear, and so they decide Fish and Wildlife needs a trim. *Find easier targets,* they say, and that's how long-term projects involving serpent smugglers get pushed aside.

Now that the gatekeepers aren't actually watching the gates, you've got a green light to expand your inventory. You start looking for the real exotic stuff—snakes and lizards and turtles that are going to make your collectors piss themselves with glee.

Word gets around, of course. You're the guy who has the really rare critters. Your clientèle changes. You get inquiries from individuals who aren't your usual suburban reptile collector. These people work in other industries. Still the import/export business, but they traffic in a different class of commodity. And they have cash, don't they? Lots and lots of cash. You get them an albino python. Then two more. *Would you like a pig-nosed turtle from Australia?* Sure, they'll take a dozen. *How about an Old World monkey or two or six?* You don't do primates, but hey, they're not quibbling about cost and they pay promptly, so why not?

Nathan fidgeted a bit as he got to the next part, and I suspected we were done with all the deep background stuff. "One day, you get an invitation to come out to some guy's place," he said. "'Come see my menagerie,' this guy says. He's a good client. He hasn't said a word about the retainer payments he's been making, and so you think *Why not?* It'll be good for client relations. And so, you go out. You see his menagerie, and yeah, it's a lot of weird creatures you've never seen before. Stuff you never see at the zoo. He suggests you stick around for the weekend, and it's a bit unorthodox, but you're already out there, so you think, *Yeah, okay, I'll stick around.*"

Shackleton made a noise in his throat, but Nathan wasn't listening.

"This guy's place is out in the desert," he said. "He's got an open-air shooting range out back. It's totally illegal, but it's too late to be *that* guest, isn't it?" Nathan shook his head. "He offers you drugs—cocaine, E, other stuff. 'How about some girls?' You try to keep your distance, but it's a long weekend, right?"

"These things happen," I said. Not because I agreed with him, but because I wanted him to keep talking. There was a point here that Nathan still hadn't gotten too.

"Then, late one night, he wants to talk business. All these crates and suitcases that have been sailing through customs? What if they were carrying other things? Yeah, every once in a while, Customs opens a box and finds a bunch of lizards or snakes. So what? Fish and Wildlife slap your hand and tell you to knock it off, but do they notice all the coke baked into the lining of the case? It's not their remit, so . . . it's like being pulled over for a speeding ticket when you've got a dozen kilos of coke in the trunk."

"It, uh, it never works out that way," I volunteered.

"Is this guy your client?" Shackleton asked. "The snake guy."

Nathan moved his head from side to side. It was a very lawyery motion. Neither a nod nor a denial.

"Cut the bullshit," Shackleton snapped.

"Trevellian," I said. "His name is Jack Trevellian."

Nathan tried to wave me off. "Mr. Trevellian has been unduly harassed by Fish and Wildlife," he said angrily. "It's been going on for years. Sure, he's been cited a few times, but he's always paid his fines and cooperated with any agent who has wanted to look at his inventory or operation. But he's been investigated more than all the other herpetological businesses in the state of California combined."

"Is he running drugs?" Shackleton asked.

Nathan spread his hands like the question was outside his expertise.

"Do I need to ask Frank to break your other leg?" his father asked.

"Dad! That's . . . that's—"

"I don't give a shit what you think it is," Shackleton said. "Answer my fucking question."

Nathan's eyes flickered toward Angel, who wouldn't look at him.

"I'll break your other leg if Trevellian hurts Pen," I said. "And I'm not as practiced at it as Frank, so it'll hurt more when I do it."

"He's not running drugs," Nathan said. He slouched down, sliding toward a major sulk.

"Not yet," Angel said.

That got everyone's attention. "Do tell," I said.

"About six months ago, Nathan and I were supposed to spend a weekend in Monterey," Angel said. Her gaze lanced toward the end of the table. "He left me a voice mail midmorning on Friday. He was supposed to pick me up after my eleven o'clock class because we wanted to get out of town before the freeways jammed up. I was going to skip my afternoon classes. But no, he left voice mail. Saying he said he couldn't do it. Something had come up."

She toyed with the bottle of fizzy water she'd been drinking. There was a film of condensation on the bottle, and she ran her finger through it and then smeared it on the polished wood of the table. "I was pissed," she continued. "I went by his house to confront him. He'd been erratic recently, and I was getting tired of it. It wasn't the first time he'd canceled, and I know that happens when you work at a firm like SG&B—billable hours are important, after all—but not this time. We'd been planning this trip for months, and he'd promised me he wouldn't get called in. He said he had made sure his schedule was clear."

"Angel," Nathan whined. "I couldn't get away. There was a major—"

"You weren't at the office," Angel snapped, cutting him off. "I went by your house. I saw you there. I saw you talking with those—those men."

"Which men?" Shackleton asked.

"Government men," I said, making an educated guess. Things were starting to fall in place. "The DEA was putting a squeeze on Nathan."

Angel nodded. "I'm not a naïve little girl who doesn't know about this sort of thing, about who does it and when and how much. You told me that clients sometimes pay you with product, and I let myself believe that. *Just because they're paying him this way doesn't mean he's doing it.* That's what I told myself. God, I was an idiot." She threw up her hands. "I wanted to work here. I wanted to be part of a firm that was making a difference. And they wanted me. Me! Bernstein himself said they were going to offer me a job as soon as I had my degree. I worked real hard to convince myself, didn't I? If your client pays you in coke, you don't ask yourself whether or not you should be having this person as a client. No, you ask yourself: am I doing all that I can to make sure his rights aren't violated. Otherwise . . ."

An awkward silence filled the room. Nathan wouldn't look at Angel. Not that it mattered, he was invisible, as far as she was concerned. Frank, usually immune to what was going on around him, was studying the ceiling tiles. Shackleton's jaw moved up and down, chewing on what he had just heard. Eventually he looked at everyone in the room in turn before settling his gaze on me.

"What? Just because I've actually done time for trafficking in narcotics doesn't make this my fault," I said.

"No," he said, "but you're going to fix it."

I cocked my head at him. "How does that work?" I asked. "Because there's a train of thought that went seriously off the rails in your head."

Shackleton nodded toward Nathan. "Do you want him to fix this?"

"Oh, hell, no," I said.

He nodded at Angel. "What about her?"

"It's not her—" I looked away. Angel's involvement wasn't my concern. Yes, I had called her, but only because Frolic had put me in that position. And why had she done that? Mrs. Chow had known. That's why we had gone driving around to all the salons. So that I could figure it out. Angel was going to be in trouble—not because she was involved in the smuggling, but because she was involved with Nathan. Guilt by association.

I was here because I owed the Chow family a debt, and that meant making sure *favorite daughter* didn't go to jail.

"Goddamnit," I said quietly.

Angel started to reach for me. "Butch—"

I shook my head. "No, no. He's right. I need—" I glared at Shackleton. "I'm not doing this for him," I said, jerking a thumb toward Nathan.

"I'd have Frank stop you if you were," he said.

I looked at Frank. Frank shrugged. It wasn't up to him. He just did as he was told. He didn't care one way or another.

"Just a hot dog," I said. That's all I ever wanted.

"What's that?" Angel asked.

"Nothing," I said. I ran my hands over my face. "Okay," I said, putting away all the bitching and moaning. "So, the DEA caught you with coke," I said to Nathan. "Is that it?"

Nathan did that head motion thing again. Neither confirming nor denying. *You're the one who is crafting a narrative. Whatever choice works for you.*

Fucking lawyers.

"They made you a deal," I said. "They would forget whatever they had on you if you helped them out." I drummed my fingers on the table. "Fish and Wildlife didn't have the budget to catch Trevellian. The man was too crafty for them. They needed help, but the only way they could get help was if they could get another agency involved." My fingers stopped. "Snakes and coke," I said. "That's what Trevellian talked about that weekend, wasn't it? Smuggling drugs along with the snakes. That was the angle that got Fish and Wildlife excited, wasn't it? Yeah, they don't care about the drugs, but the DEA does. If they busted Trevellian for illegal animals *and* drugs, the DEA would get involved. It wouldn't be their bust anymore—we know how the DEA doesn't like to share—but Fish and Wildlife could live with that. The SoCal Snake King would be out of business. That was the important part. If Trevellian could be busted, DEA,

Fish and Wildlife—whoever—they'd misplace that evidence they had on you. Was that it? Something like that?

Nathan fingered the paper wrapper of his sandwich. "Yeah," he said quietly. "Something like that."

Another piece fell into place. "Cock Robin," I said. "He got you into this, didn't he? He set you up."

"Who?" Shackleton asked.

"Some guy named Rob," I said. "He's your son's investigator. Serves papers. Does peep work. That sort of stuff. I bet he's the sort of guy who knows where to find coke when you need some, isn't he?"

Nathan wrinkled his nose, but he didn't deny anything I had just said.

"Turns out Cock Robin was more connected than you knew." I laughed. "God, the DEA probably turned him years ago. Kept him on a string. Just in case. You know how high these high-flying Century City lawyers like to get."

Nathan finally showed some emotion. A brief spurt of anger in his face. He didn't like the idea that Cock of the Walk had been playing him. But his outrage didn't have any fuel, and the flicker died as quickly as it had been born.

"You took his keys," I said to Angel.

"Whose?"

"Rob's. When you came to my place. That set of keys with the rooster. You took them."

"Why does she have his keys?" Shackleton wanted to know.

"That's how I come into this story," I said. "Cock Robin was supposed to take a snake down to Tijuana. Some kind of intro-duction between parties. A tree python." I glanced at Nathan. "Or was it an emerald tree boa? I get them mixed up."

Nathan shrugged. "I . . . I don't know. It was a snake. I didn't want to know."

I finally felt like I had all the pieces to the puzzle and they were starting to fit together. "Rob was brokering a meeting between Trevellian and some drug guy in Mexico. But they were being cautious about it. Rob wasn't directly connected to Trevellian, and the guys in Mexico probably aren't connected to whoever is on the other end. Everyone has deniability." I glanced at Nathan. "Everyone didn't want to know, except they did. If the trade worked out, then Trevellian and this guy could move forward. If it went to shit"—I nodded briefly to skip over that part of the story—"they wouldn't be tied to it."

"You still haven't said why Angel has his keys," Shackleton reminded me.

"Something happened to Rob, and I got picked to make the run instead," I said. "In his car. With his keys."

"Why you?"

I gave him a tired smile. "The DEA doesn't like me," I said.

"Why don't they—" Shackleton shook his head. "Never mind. I don't want to know."

"I saw Cock Robin at the reptile show," I said. "He didn't look like he had been roughed up. I thought the DEA—or whoever is running this scheme—had pinched him, and that they were trying to preserve the meeting by sending someone else. But if that was the case, then why was he wandering around the convention center, keeping an eye on me?"

Shackleton motioned for me to get to my point.

"Rob's playing for more than one team," I said. "Look, Trevellian called Nathan and said he had Nathan's girlfriend, but since Angel is sitting right here—"

"I'm not his girlfriend," Angel said.

I tried to keep the smile off my face. It would have been difficult to explain at the present time. "Nathan says Trevellian isn't very good with names, and yes, I know that 'Penelope' and 'Angel' are as different as 'succotash' and 'palm tree,' but let's take this out a step or two and consider who else is involved."

"I do wish you would," Shackleton said.

"Pen was grabbed by two of the guys I saw in Mexico."

"What?" Angel exclaimed. "Why didn't you say something earlier?"

I waved a hand at Nathan. "I tried to, but your ex-boyfriend didn't want to talk about anything until we got here," I said. "Now that we're here, I'm telling you."

Shackleton figured it out. "The drug connection in Mexico is in contact with Trevellian," he said.

I nodded. "Rob's the key, isn't he? He set up the meet in Tijuana. He knows these Mexicans. There are layers of deniability, but that's all smoke and mirrors. Rob knows Trevellian. He knows this drug guy. He's merely pretending he doesn't know either end. More importantly, he knows who Angel is. They might not have met, but come on, he's Nathan's investigator. He's been turned by the DEA. Of course he knows who Nathan is sleeping with." Angel moved to speak and I held up my hand. "*Was* sleeping with," I corrected. "My point is he knows whoever these guys grabbed at the convention center isn't her, but Trevellian's in a mood, isn't he? He thinks Nathan is screwing him—"

"I'm not!" Nathan interrupted.

"It doesn't matter. Rob tells him Pen is Angel. Or maybe he doesn't say it outright. He suggests it. Whatever. The point is that he wants Trevellian to spook. To do something stupid."

Shackleton nodded. "Because if Trevellian spooks, then maybe he'll do something that will allow the DEA to move in."

"Or it'll make the drug guy in Mexico make a move," I said. "Either way, all the government folks are excited that this might turn into a bust. Meanwhile, Trevellian is going to figure out Pen isn't Nathan's girlfriend, and when he does . . . " My hands tightened into fists. "We need to find him before that happens," I said. "Angel has Rob's keys. You have to know where he lives. I want to pay him a visit."

Shackleton narrowed his eyes. "If you aren't up for trying out for the Lakers," he said. "You're not up for putting the hurt on someone."

"I know," I said. "Which is why Frank is coming along."

Frank was surprised to hear his name. "I am?" he asked.

"Frank's been itching to hit someone," I said. "We might as well let him."

CHAPTER 26

SG&B Payroll had an address in Canoga Park for one Robert Robinson—the name Cock Robin's mother knew him by—and that was our destination when we left Century City an hour later. Angel had gone down to a haberdashery on the second floor and picked out suitable attire to brace someone in their own home. I napped in the passenger seat while Frank drove. I was the brains of this operation. It was important for me to be rested.

The sun was straining toward the western horizon when we reached the Western Arms Apartments in Canoga Park. The lengthening shadows gave the apartment complex a rumpled look, like a week's worth of stubble and sleeping in the same clothes for most of that time sort of look. A sign at the entrance proclaimed that we were in the presence of *Fine Apartment Living!*, but the place was about as "fine" as two-weeks-past-their-sell-by-date pork chops. Each apartment had a weak porch light—not very inviting illumination—but it made it easy to read unit numbers. Rob's apartment was in the back of the complex. Downstairs. On the left of a broad staircase that connected a group of four units.

Frank backed his black SUV into an open spot of the bumpy parking lot. We sat in the car for a minute, waiting to see if anyone noticed our arrival. When nothing changed, we got out and casually strolled across the lot. I had checked over Rob's keyring and I guessed right which key would work the front door. There was a deadbolt too, but it was keyed the same. Frank crowded behind me as I got the door open, and we slipped inside like we knew what we were doing.

Frank sidled to the right as I closed the door quickly. A dim light came from the kitchen, which was partially hidden behind a wall that broke the apartment into two halves. The main living area bumped out to the left, and it contained a sprawling leather sectional, a rectangular coffee table, and an enormous TV on a heavy stand. The area to the right was the dining room, but there was no formal dining table. There was a small table with a single chair against the outside wall, and something that looked like a homemade cat stand behind it. In front of long curtains was a wire cage with plastic tubes running out of it.

Something rattled in one of the tubes, and in the kitchen, the refrigerator hummed to itself.

"No security system," Frank whispered.

"No dogs," I said.

"Gerbils," Frank said.

"What?"

He pointed at the tubes. One of them ran across the floor and then curved around what I had thought was a stand for cats. The tubes ran to separate cages on two different levels. When I went over and took a closer look, something popped out of the tube connected to the lower cage. It scrambled across a floor covered in shredded newspaper and nosed at the wire mesh. I tapped the top of the cage and the critter spooked a bit, but it didn't flee. "He's got a rodent farm," I said.

I was talking to myself. Frank wasn't in the living room. *Checking out the rest of the apartment*, I thought, as I wandered into the kitchen. The decor was either retro '70s, or it had literally been that long since the place had been remodeled. The counters were bare. The sink was empty. I looked in the refrigerator, which was about as empty as mine: a couple beers, some condiments, and a box from a local pizza delivery place.

"Gun safe in the spare bedroom," Frank said when I closed the refrigerator door. He was standing right there. I hadn't heard him come into the kitchen.

"Jesus," I said. "You're going to give me a heart attack."

He checked out the cupboards while I did my own reconnaissance. The apartment was a long rectangular box, with rooms on one side and the kitchen and a bathroom and utility room on the other. The doors to the two bedrooms and bathroom were open. All very utilitarian, though the gun safe in the spare bedroom was an unusual upgrade for this zip code.

When I returned to the kitchen, Frank had stacked several boxes of .45 ammunition and shotgun shells on the counter. "Where did you find those?" I asked.

"Behind the baking supplies," he said.

"Cock Robin bakes?"

"They were camouflage," Frank said. He hefted one of the boxes. "This is safe, but dumb."

"How so?"

"Guns are in the safe," he said. "Ammo is out here." Having inventoried Rob's stash, Frank put the boxes back in the cupboard. "Keeping them separate means the guns can't be used against you if someone broke into your apartment."

"Like us," I said.

Frank lifted his jacket and showed me the gun holster attached to the back of his belt. "We brought our own," he said.

I nodded sagely. "So now what?" I asked.

He dropped his jacket. "We wait," he said.

"For how long?"

"As long as it takes." He shrugged at my expression. "This was your idea," he reminded me. "He'll come back here eventually. We'll be waiting."

I tapped the refrigerator. "Things could get dire if we have to wait long," I said.

Somewhere in the next hour, I fell asleep on the leather sectional, which made for an awkward moment when Rob unlocked the front door and came into the apartment. He flipped one of the switches next to the door, which turned on the light in the dining room.

"What the hell—" he started when he saw me. That's when Frank stepped out of the kitchen, his gun pointing at Rob.

"Don't," Frank said as Rob's hands started to dip toward his waist. Rob made a quick assessment of Frank and decided to listen to the man.

"Way to keep us waiting," I groused.

Frank waved Rob away from the door, and when Cock Robin got to the center of the room, Frank indicated he should turn around. He did, and he glared at me while Frank patted him down. Rob had a gun, and Frank made it disappear into his jacket pocket. "Sit," Frank said, shoving Rob toward the table next to the wall.

"Who are you assholes?" Rob asked as he pulled the chair out and sat down. He was a wiry fellow, and the overhead light gave his eyes an oily chemical gleam. His pompadour was sagging, and on the shoulder of his Army surplus jacket was a patch showing a red-combed rooster giving us a knowing wink and a thumbs-up. He was trying to look bored, like home invasions were a weekly occurrence for him, but there was a nervous jitter to his frame that he couldn't suppress.

"You don't recognize me?" I asked.

His eyes flicked in my direction. "Yeah, yeah," he said. "I've seen you on TV or something," he said.

"What's my name, then?" I asked.

"What?"

"My name," I said. "If I'm famous, you must know my name, right?"

"Uh, it's—" Rob gave Frank a *Do I get a hint?* look. Frank's face was all *I will beat you with your own leg*. Rob swallowed nervously. "You're, uh, that guy from that show," he said.

"*That* guy from *that* show," I said. "Way to narrow it down."

"No, wait. You're Chuck. Chuck Dangers. You do stunts and stuff."

I rubbed my jaw. "Stunts," I said.

"Yeah," Rob said. "Stunts."

I glanced at Frank. "Show him a stunt," I said.

Frank hit Rob in the face with his left hand. A quick pop to the nose. He was good and fast. I was impressed, and a little intimated.

"Son of a bitch." Rob's voice was muffled by his hands. When he moved them away from his face, we saw a trickle of blood inching down from his nose.

"I saw you at the LA Convention Center yesterday," I told him. "The reptile show. You saw me. You recognized me, in fact, and it wasn't because you thought I was some jackass celebrity."

"I don't know what you're talking about," he muttered.

Frank hit him again, and Rob's head snapped back. The front legs of his chair rocked off the floor, and there was more blood coming out of his nose this time.

"Who told you what I looked like?" I asked. "Who told you to watch for me?"

Rob wiped the blood from his face with the back of his hand. "I don't—"

Frank tensed like he was going to hit Rob again, and the wiry man flinched in the chair. "Hey, man, don't—" He held his hands up in front of his face.

I wandered into the kitchen and splashed some water on a towel. I tossed it to Rob. "Here," I said.

"Oh, so you're the good cop," he sneered. He gingerly swiped the towel across his face.

"No," I said. "We're not cops."

His eyes widened, and when he looked at Frank again, there was a different gleam in his eye. This wasn't the game he had been expecting. I noted that he wasn't more afraid. He was merely making a different assessment of the situation.

"Where's the girl," I said.

"What girl?"

"The one Jack T. has."

"Jack who?"

Without waiting for a signal from me, Frank smacked Rob again. This time he popped Rob in the left eye.

We waited for Rob to stop swearing.

"I'm getting bored," I said. I wandered over to the gerbil habitat and flicked the wire cage a few times. "Should I cut to the chase and have him put a bullet in your kneecap? Would that help your memory?"

"Oh, man," Rob moaned. "You don't have to do that."

I pulled out Rob's ring of keys. "You recognize these?" I asked.

He got angry when he realized what I was holding. "Hey! Those are mine."

"They are," I said, dangling them just out of reach. "How do you suppose I got them?"

"I lost them," he said. "No, wait. They were stol—" He put up his hands as Frank made a fist. "Hang on! That's not what happened," Rob said quickly. "It's—okay, okay. I'll tell you. I'll tell you what you want to know."

"Good," I said. I swung the keys into my palm and closed my fingers around them. Two of the keys stuck out between my knuckles. "Because I was going to hit you next."

"Jesus Christ, man! I'll talk. Okay? I'll talk."

I tightened my grip on the keys. "Start talking," I said. "And don't forget to tell us about the snake."

It took a little coaxing, but Rob got on the right track eventually. I wasn't surprised when he said the whole snake swap had been Nathan's idea. Nathan had approached him about getting a snake and taking it down to Mexico. He wanted to make a connection between one of his clients—*gee, I wonder which one?*—and some guy down in Mexico who was looking for an independent pipeline into the US. Rob swore that was all Nathan told him. "I was supposed to deliver a snake. They were going to pay me," Rob said. "That's it."

"How much?" I asked.

Rob leaned away from Frank. "Nathan didn't say," he said.

"You expect me to believe that?"

Rob put up his hands. "He's a fucking lawyer, man," he said. "I assumed it was going to be drugs. That's what it always is when lawyers don't want to tell you."

"And you were going to haul those drugs across the border?"

"It's not that hard if you know what you're doing," he said. "Especially if it's just a kilo. There are easy places to hide a key in the car. You just gotta keep your cool."

"Really? Is that all it takes?"

Rob's gaze went back and forth between Frank and I. "Am I— am I missing something?" he asked.

"Nah," I said. "It's not worth getting into."

Frank remained inscrutable. I wondered how much he knew about my past.

"You didn't make the meet, though," I said to Rob. "What happened?"

Rob's face got red. He didn't want to tell us, but he caved after a few seconds of bluster. "I got jumped in a bathroom," he said.

Frank snorted. It was the first bit of commentary we had heard from him.

"No, seriously, man," Rob whined. "That's what happened. After I got the snake, I stopped off for gas at this place in Woodland Hills. Near the 101 interchange." He wiggled his hands. "I didn't want to make the drive without a full tank, you know? And while I was filling the car, I went to take a leak. The place had one of those bathrooms on the outside. I was the only one there. I was standing at the urinal, doing my business, when the door opens and some dude comes in. I thought I had locked the door, but—yeah, whatever. I look over to tell him that the room's occupied, and he's got a black mask on. Some kind of ski mask or something. He hits me with a sap, and—dude, it wasn't cool. I had my—you know—I had it in my hand, man."

"A man can lose a lot of dignity when he's got his pants down," I said.

"Damn right," Rob said. "It wasn't dignified."

"Regardless, when you wake up, your car is gone, right?"

"Right, man. That's what happened." Rob's leg started to dance. "I had my . . . I was peeing . . ."

I sighed. "What kind of snake was it?" I asked. "The one in the box."

"It was an emerald tree boa," he said.

"Really?"

"You want to see the receipt or something?"

"You got a receipt?"

"Damn right, I did. I could expense it."

"And the kilo of coke you figured you were going to be paid? What were you going to do with that? Put that on the expense report too?"

"That's not how expense reports work," Rob said.

Frank shrugged when I looked at him. It wasn't his fault I didn't know how expense reporting worked.

"So, a man in Mexico was going to give you a kilogram of cocaine for an emerald tree boa," I said.

"Yeah, he was."

"How much did that snake cost you? A hundred bucks? Maybe one-fifty?" I shook my head. "They're not even native to the US. They come from South America, for crying out loud. This guy could have gotten one for a lot less from some importer in Mexico. Why was he giving you a key for this one?"

"It was some kind of rare breeder," Rob said. "It was supposed to make white snakes or something. Albinos."

The snake I had taken across the border had been a green tree python. Not the same snake at all. Who was lying? My pal from the pet store? Rob? Whoever had sold Rob the snake? Had the contents of the box been switched between when Rob had gotten smacked in the bathroom and when I got the car?

"Where did you get the snake?" I asked.

Rob got very interested in our shoes. "I got it from Reptile World," he said eventually.

"Ah," I said. "The place owned by Jack Trevellian."

"Yeah," Rob said quietly. "It is."

"So when I mentioned Jack T. earlier, you knew who I was talking about."

Rob swallowed visibly. "Yeah, I did."

I looked at Frank, who shook his head slightly. He wasn't going to smack Rob around for telling the truth.

"Who did you call when you realized your car had been stolen?" I asked.

Rob's lips firmed into a thin line. A gerbil scampered through one of the tubes of the habitat. Its tiny nails made a *clickity-clickity* noise on the plastic tube. Frank and I waited, listening to the gerbil scamper around its sprawling habitat.

"I called Nathan," Rob said finally.

"And what did Nathan say?"

"He said he'd take care of it."

"What does that mean?"

"I don't know, man. He said I should get a cab. Go back to my place and wait for him to call."

"Did he?"

Rob shook his head.

"How about the police?" I asked. "Did you call them about your car?"

He shook his head again.

Something had been bugging me about all this, and it suddenly came clear in my head. "If your car was stolen, how are you getting around?"

"My truck," Rob said.

"What truck?"

"It's an F150. A Ford. I use the station wagon—the car that was stolen—when I'm working."

"So you weren't worried about it being gone?"

"No, man, I was worried."

"But not so worried that you called the cops."

He didn't reply.

"Who did you call?" I asked. "When Nathan didn't call you back."

"I didn't call anyone."

It was a lie, and I thought about hitting him, but beating answers out of someone is exhausting and it never gets you what you really want. "All right," I said to Frank. "I guess we can dump him and the car somewhere."

"What?" Rob's head came up. His eyes were wide.

I shrugged. "It's been a long day," I said.

Frank raised his gun, and Rob put up his hands. His right leg danced really fast. "No, wait. I remember now. I called him. I called him a couple days later."

"When?" I asked. I didn't ask who. I had a pretty good idea

"Uh, Thursday. Yeah, it was Thursday."

"And what did Jack say?"

Rob didn't even flinch. "He said he knew what was going on. We were going to talk about it later."

"He wasn't angry?"

"Dude is always angry about something. He's got—he's got his own way of looking at things, you know?"

I didn't, but I could imagine. "He said there was something you could do for him, didn't he?"

Rob nodded, suddenly very eager to be helpful. "You can never tell with that guy," he said. "But yeah, he said I could be helpful. I could make things square between us."

I had been assembling a fairly speculative narrative of this past week, and while Rob's story didn't mesh with all of it, there was enough confirmation in his side of things that I was getting more confident that I knew what was going on.

"Talk to me about the girl," I said. "What happened there?"

"What girl? Do you mean Nathan's girlfriend?"

I almost believed him.

"No, the girl I was with at the convention center."

He stared at me for a long moment, trying to decide if he had any stomach left for lying. "I wasn't there," he said. "I heard the shot, and I—all I saw was these two dudes arguing about something. And I saw the girl—the one you were with. Those two dudes, they—they nearly shot me when I came around that corner. But I—I talked them down. I got them to put their guns away. I told them they had to get out of there before security showed up, man. It wasn't good. You were lying there, bleeding all over the place. People were going to show up. They had to go."

"And so you showed them where to go, didn't you?"

"No, man, I—it wasn't like that. Jack said—" He stopped.

"What did Jack say?" I asked.

He shook his head.

I looked up the ceiling. "Come on, Rob," I said. "We're almost there. Don't dry up on me now."

Rob fought with his sense of dignity for a minute or so. His sense of self-preservation won out. "Jack said to take them to his place."

"Which place?"

"The place where he keeps all the snakes and shit. This ranch he has. Near San Bernardino. Past Nealeys Corner."

Frank and I exchanged glances. "You took them there," I said, making sure I had heard him right.

"Yeah," Rob sighed, his confession complete. "I did."

CHAPTER 27

ROB OFFERED TO GIVE US THE ADDRESS OF TREVELLIAN'S PLACE, which was the funniest thing he'd said all night.

"You're coming with us," I said, and when he started fussing about that, I turned to Frank and asked him about the best way to mess up the bones in Rob's legs without getting blood all over the apartment.

"The trick is to not break the skin," Frank said without an ounce of humor. "You need a hammer." He looked thoughtfully at the kitchen. "Maybe a meat tenderizer," he offered. "Or a rolling pin."

"Okay, okay." Rob put up his hands. "I'll go. Just—can I pee before we leave?"

"You got a gun taped to the back of the toilet?" I asked.

"What? No!"

"You going to jump out the window?"

"No, man. I gotta take a leak." He looked at Frank with a frantic gleam in his eye. "You don't want me go all over the back seat of your car, do you?"

Frank's look said: *You pee in my car and I'll shove your—*

"I'll go check the bathroom," I said.

I didn't find anything that could be used as a weapon, and the window didn't open enough for a rabbit to sneak through, much less a frightened man with a pompadour like Cock Robin. "All clear," I said.

Rob came down the hall. He squeezed past me, and when he started to close the bathroom door, I shook my head. "It stays open," I said.

"Man, I can't go while you're watching," he whined.

"You shouldn't be looking at us when you're doing your business anyway," I said. "Just get it done, all right?"

Grumbling, Rob faced the toilet. He fumbled with his belt, and then stood there. Waiting for something to happen.

Frank and I stood in the hall. Neither of us looked directly at Rob, but we were both watching him out of the corner of our eye. Just in case he tried to squeeze himself through that window.

"What do you think?" I asked Frank, keeping my voice low.

"I think he's full of shit," Frank said. "But Trevellian is our next step, so . . ."

I nodded. "We're just going to go take a look," I said. "We're not going to shoot the place up or anything."

"I've sat through God knows how many mission briefings, and you know what? 'Let's not shoot the place up' was always the part that didn't work out."

"Well, how about we try to break that streak, okay?"

Rob put his head back and stared at the ceiling. Trying to ignore the fact that we were standing behind him. That his bladder muscles weren't cooperating.

"What does Trevellian want?" I asked. "What's he really after?"

Frank shrugged. "Those questions are above my pay grade."

"Could you, maybe, show a little enthusiasm about rising above that level?"

Rob managed to find his happy place, and he visibly relaxed as his bladder loosened.

"Should I go in and spook him?" Frank asked.

"He'll never pee again if you do," I said. "Getting jumped twice when you're taking a leak will scar a man for good."

"If he even got jumped the first time," Frank said.

"Yeah, well, it takes some serious balls to claim that was the case when it didn't actually happen. He couldn't come up with a better story? One that wasn't so . . . emasculating."

Frank shook his head. "People will say anything to not get hurt," he said. "They'll readily debase themselves if it makes you see them as weak. They're trying to get you to make a mistake."

"Is that the way you see the world?"

"It's the way it is," Frank said.

I shook my head. "You must be a lot of fun on a first date."

"Whatever," Frank said. "He's going to rabbit on us, you know. The first chance he gets."

"I know," I said. "But we need to get to that ranch. We need him to tell us about the place. After that . . . Well, I probably don't need to know, do I?"

Frank nodded curtly as Rob flushed the toilet. "Wash your hands," he said out of the side of his mouth. When Rob was done, Frank jerked his head toward the front of the apartment. "All right," he said. "Let's go. Nice and easy."

The three of us left Rob's apartment. I turned off the light and locked the door, and then followed Frank and Rob across the parking lot. When we reached Frank's car, Frank instructed Rob to put his hands on top of the car. When Rob did, Frank put his gun away and produced a zip tie from the pocket of his jacket. He grabbed Rob's wrists and yanked them down. He slipped the noose over both wrists and yanked it tight before Rob could react. Frank unlocked the car and opened the back passenger side door. He shoved Rob in, and then told me to go around to the other side and make sure his seatbelt was on. "We don't need him flopping around back there," he said.

I did as Frank asked, and when Rob was all nice and tight, I came back around the car and got in the passenger seat. Frank circled the SUV and climbed in behind the wheel. He didn't turn on his lights until we were out of the apartment complex, and he wasted no time getting on the freeway and heading west.

I kept an eye out for someone following us, thinking either Detective Green or one of Frolic's black sedans. I only relaxed when we passed Pasadena and got on the 210.

My shoulder was starting to throb, and there was a thin film of sweat on my forehead. I closed my eyes, promising myself that I would only rest for a few minutes. I fell asleep almost immediately, and didn't wake up until we really did go off-roading.

We wound up on a dirt track that wasn't much wider than Frank's SUV. We bumped and careened along the road's tumbling course, and it felt like we were moving uphill more often than not. Scrub and the occasional tree popped up in the gloom beyond the headlights.

I ran my tongue around the inside of my mouth. "Where are we?" I asked.

"Heading north from Sierra Lakes," Frank said. "Mt. Baldy is over there, somewhere."

My shoulder ached. All this bouncing around wasn't helping. I twisted in my seat and checked on Rob. He had a pained expression on his face. Sitting with his hands cuffed behind his back as we bounced over the uneven road wasn't what he had in mind for this evening.

"How much farther?" Frank asked.

"A couple of miles," Rob said. He sounded a little queasy. "There will be a gate on your left."

Soon enough, a barbed wire fence started paralleling the road. The strands were new and tight, and after a mile or so, the posts got thicker. Frank slowed the car to a lurching stop as we came abreast a gate. Before we could look more closely, a spotlight came on, blinding us. Frank stomped his foot down on the accelerator, and the SUV bounced and became airborne as it rocketed on past the gate. He ran the car a hundred yards or so past the gate before he slammed on the brakes. The car shook and bucked, and our seatbelts held us tight against the seats.

Frank was out of the car in a flash. Before I could fumble with my seatbelt, he had come around the car and opened up the back door. Rob yelped as Frank hauled him out of the car. By the time I got my seatbelt off, Frank had knocked Rob to the ground.

I put myself between the pissed ex-Green Beret and the whimpering sniveler. "Don't," I said.

Frank got close to me. There was murder in his eyes. "Goddamn motion-sensitive light," he snarled. "He knew it was there. He didn't warn us."

On the ground behind me, Rob groaned.

"It's just a light," I said.

"Is there a fucking camera?" Frank snapped at Rob.

Rob made some noise that didn't answer the question.

Frank pushed past me. He ignored Rob. His gaze was on the cone of light streaming down on the ground in front of the gate.

"There's a camera or there isn't," I said, coming up behind him. "They're paying attention or they aren't. Nothing we can do about it now."

"We have to assume there is and they are," Frank muttered. He turned and looked at me. "'We'll just go out and take a look,'" he said, quoting me. "How's that plan sound now?"

"Fine, you were right," I said. "Can we move on to Plan B?"

Rob grunted behind us, and I turned around to see what he was doing. I didn't spot him right away, and as I was looking around for him, I heard a ping of metal. Like a strand of wire being plucked.

"Son of a bitch." Frank darted toward the fence. Rob was squirming under the lowest strand of the barbed wire, and he got through as Frank reached the fence. Frank got a hand on his leg, but Rob kicked at him with his other foot. Frank tried to hold on, but Rob wrenched himself free. His hands still bound behind his back, he stumbled to his feet and disappeared into the darkness beyond the fence.

"Get that wire," I said to Frank as I rushed over. "I'll go after him."

Frank grabbed the middle strand of barbed wire and tugged it up. I bent over and ducked through the gap. Something tugged at my shirt and I felt cloth tear, but I made it through.

Frank let go of the wire and it made the pinging noise. "Come on," I said, gesturing in the direction Rob had gone. "We can still catch him."

Frank shook his head. He pulled out his gun and offered it to me. "Safety's on. There's one in the chamber."

I hesitated. "What about you?" Did I have to take the gun?

"I'll be right behind you." He hooked a thumb at the SUV. "I have some stuff in the back. I'm going to find some higher ground. Give you overwatch."

"Overwatch?"

"Just keep your head down if you get into trouble, okay?"

"Is this Plan B?"

"Whatever," Frank said. "I'm not keeping track."

I took off after Rob. The ground was as rocky and uneven as the road. I would have put the gun down the front of my pants to leave my hands free, but safety or not, it seemed dangerous to be running around in the dark with a loaded gun pointed at my crotch.

A sliver of a moon wandering around the eastern horizon gave me enough light to avoid the big rocks and the giant gopher holes. I caught sight of indistinct movement that I assumed was Rob, and I angled toward it.

He heard me coming and he tried to run, but with his hands tied behind his back, all he managed to do was look like a wounded bird trying to get off the ground. When I caught up with him, I whacked him on the side of the head with Frank's gun. He cried out and went down, face-first.

I tried to catch my breath as he struggled to roll over. "Goddamn it," he spat. "You goddamned goat fu—"

I clucked my tongue. "Let's watch it with the language," I said.

It wasn't my tone that brought him up short as much as it was the sight of the gun in my hand. Glaring at me, he managed to sit up on his knees. "You're not going to shoot me," he said.

I hate it when dudes go for the tough bluff. It puts everyone in an uncomfortable position. He didn't want to be shot, but if he didn't call my bluff, he was admitting that he was my bitch. He didn't want to be my bitch either, and so, in some warped way, it made sense to dare me to do it. If I didn't, well, then why was I pointing the gun at him? We both knew I wasn't going to use it, and that made me his bitch. This is what you learn in prison. This is how power works. You have it and you use it, or you don't and you're fucked. There's no middle ground.

I thumbed off the safety.

A bank of bright lights blew up the night. Rob shied away, like the light was physically hurting him. I didn't blame him. I could almost feel the heat off the lamps on my back.

"Drop the gun," someone said, and to punctuate their command, they worked the action on a shotgun.

I knew that sound. The guards at Tehachapi carried pump-action shotguns, loaded with bean bag rounds. *Non-lethal deterrent* was the official verbiage. Useful for crowd control and keeping the unruly at bay. Everyone had been shot once or twice with a bean bag round. Not officially, of course. That sort of news would agitate all kind of human rights advocacy groups. But how else did prisoners develop a Pavlovian response to that distinctive sound?

Reluctantly, I put my hands up, the pistol pointing toward the sky.

"Took you long enough," Rob gasped.

CHAPTER 28

I HEARD SOMEONE COMING UP BEHIND ME, AND EVEN THOUGH I knew what was coming, I was unprepared for the sudden shock of getting hit in the back of the head. I stumbled forward, trying to keep my balance as the world spun. I lost the gun, which was for the best, anyway, and the ground came up fast all of a sudden. As I tried to get up, someone hit me in the kidneys. The next shot lit up my spine with pain, and I dimly felt my arms get yanked behind my back. By the time they hauled me upright and marched me toward the bright lights, I was seeing stars and donkeys with halos and lightning bolts raining down from the heavens.

I was thrown in the back of a dirty pickup, and I lay still, my face numb against the dusty truck bed. Distantly, I heard Rob's voice, and the tiny part of my brain that was still ticking and working, noted that he was in full Cock Robin mode. Running his mouth. Talking all sorts of shit. The truck started up, and as it bounced toward what I assumed was Trevellian's ranch, he went on and on about how clever he'd been. *Lured him out here all by myself*, he was crowing. *Had him thinking he had me all trussed up, like a turkey. Gobble gobble. Like a dumb bird. Going to its death. But not this bird. This bird was smarter than that.*

Something wasn't quite right about his story, but before I could figure it out, another part of my brain flipped a switch. That was that. I was out.

Why are you trying to rescue her? Mr. Chow asked. He was sitting in the back of the rowboat, holding a pink parasol with red flowers on it. The sun was bright, its light reflecting off the surface of the lake around us, but his face was in shadows. *What are you compensating for?*

My shoulders ached from rowing, but I wasn't sure where I was trying to go or how far we had to travel. Or why I was having a vision about rowing someone across a lake again. Who had it been last time? I leaned my arms on the oars. *I'm not trying to compensate,* I said.

Mr. Chow and I had conversations like this. I had gone to a therapist a couple of times since he had died. Not because I had been worried about anything, but I had dated a woman for awhile who worked for a non-profit. She had gotten me connected to a state-funded program for rehabilitating ex-cons—helping them adjust to the stress of reentering society. I hadn't felt particularly stressed, but signing up with the program had made her happy and I liked making her happy. During the six sessions I had been allocated, my therapist and I had talked a lot about Mr. Chow. Father figure. Savior. Idealized adoration. Manifestation of personal conscience. *Mr. Chow is a visualization of your own internal moral compass*, the therapist had said.

You feel responsible, Mr. Chow said. *And when you feel responsible, you act contrary to your own self-interests.*

I believe that's called compassion, I replied.

There was no room for compassion at Tehachapi, he said.

Mr. Chow twirled his parasol, making the flowers spin. I looked out across the lake, squinting against the light. I couldn't see a shore in any direction.

Are you sure this is a lake? Mr. Chow asked. *Maybe we're in the middle of the ocean. You're never going to make it to shore.*

Or maybe it was all a metaphor, I thought. *Ferrying someone somewhere else. Never reaching the destination. Never knowing how much farther we had to go.*

I closed my eyes, and when I opened them again, the lake and the rowboat were gone. I was in a simple guest room. The walls were uniform and dull. Several cheap western art prints hung on the wall opposite the bed. Light bled through thin curtains. It didn't look like daylight. It was too pale and artificial.

"Oh, thank God," someone said. I wasn't alone in the room. Someone had been sitting in a wicker chair near the window, and as I started moving, they sprang up and came over to the bed. "I was so worried."

I recognized the voice before I could focus on the face. "Pen," I croaked.

Her hair was disheveled and her mascara was streaked. Otherwise, she looked magnificent. I managed a weak smile. "My plan worked," I whispered.

"Plan?" Pen stared at me. "This was planned?"

I managed a shrug. "We're in the same room, aren't we? I found you, didn't I?"

Pen shoved me. If I wasn't already lying down, I would have collapsed. "This?" she said, her voice rising. "This isn't a plan."

"There's another part to it," I said.

"What? Where we walk out of here and no one stops us?"

I nodded. "Basically."

"The door's locked, you idiot."

I nodded sagely. "That's good," I said. "Because I'm not ready to get up just yet. Maybe in a few minutes."

She made a sound halfway between laughing and crying as she sat on the bed. Her hip pressed against mine. "I like you," she said. "But you never take anything seriously. And this is serious, Butch."

I lifted my hand and let it fall on her thigh. "I know," I said.

She looked at my hand, and her own crept toward it. "I was worried about you," she said quietly. "When the gun went off, I thought—I thought you were dead. It was so loud. I couldn't hear anything. I didn't know what to do." I let her ramble. She needed to get it out. She needed to let go of all the worry she had been carrying. "You were lying on the floor, and there was—there was a lot of blood. The two guys panicked. I panicked. They started yelling at each other. I—I tried to run. I didn't want to, but I didn't know what else to do. It didn't matter. They came after me. I didn't get very far."

She turned on the bed, and her leg pressed against me. Her hand had found mine. "There was another guy. He had this funny hair . . . I felt like he knew me. Like he had been watching me."

Her fingers slid into mine, and I let her squeeze my hand. "He and the two Mexicans argued, and then they took me through another door. Out to the parking lot. Before I could figure out a way to get someone's attention, the guy with the stupid hairdo drove up in his truck. They threw me in it and . . . and drove out here. They put me in this room. I screamed and yelled. I beat on the door. They just laughed. It didn't matter, they said. No one would hear me."

"I heard you," I said.

She managed a tiny smile. "How could you hear me?"

"I was listening really hard."

"You're so full of shit, Butch."

"And you've been really brave," I said.

"My heart has been racing—" She lifted my hand and put it against her right breast.

I tried not to notice the firm flesh under her shirt. She was warm too. Warm and inviting. "That's not where your heart is," I pointed out.

She moved my hand over to her other breast. It was just as warm, though, this time, I could feel her heartbeat.

She closed her eyes and inhaled deeply, pushing out her chest as her lungs filled with air. "I'm feeling calmer already," she said. "Can you tell?"

Her nipple was firm against my palm.

It would be easy to slip my hand around her breast. Let her know I was aware of her arousal. That I didn't mind. That I was feeling my own arousal. It would lead to other things, and briefly, I let myself imagine those things. Her top coming off. Those jeans sliding off her hips. My own clothes coming off. Pen, crawling on top of me. Her lips finding mine. Her hands exploring. My hands exploring. Our bodies, moving together.

My hand tightened a little, and she let out a tiny sigh. She relaxed against my hand. Her lips parted.

I slipped my hand free. She stiffened as she felt me move, and I put my hand on her thigh. "Pen," I said gently. I gave her leg a squeeze. "I like you too, but this—it's like you said—this is—"

She opened her eyes, and they were filled with such fierce light that my words left me. Her mouth twisted for a moment, becoming something hard and mean, and then she leaned over and grabbed either side of my head with her hands. "Kiss me," she said. "Just once. Just so I know . . ."

I did, and her mouth was hard at first, but then she let go of all the hurt and rejection she thought she had to have. She melted against me, her mouth open and inviting. We let our feelings play out for a minute—teeth nipping, tongues exploring—and then she broke contact.

"Now," she said, patting me on the chest. "You need to come up with a better plan than the one you had."

"Why is that?" I asked.

She ran her hands down her body, shivering with the intensity of the memory of our contact. "If you're not going to get naked with me, then you need to get us rescued," she said. "Because I want to fantasize about what might have happened for many years to come."

I explored our situation. The room was four by six paces, and it contained just the bed, chair, and cheap art prints. There was no closet, and the window looked out on a central courtyard. It was illuminated by a number of heavy lights mounted along the roofline of the horseshoe-shaped ranch house. There was a dust-choked fountain in the courtyard, along with a big truck with a rack of lights and two other cars. The security lights were bright and they made it hard to see anything beyond the courtyard. The sky overhead was a diffuse darkness.

Two guys wandered around the courtyard. One had a shotgun, and he carried it like he was eager to use it. The other guy's weapon, which looked like an assault rifle, was lying on the hood on the smaller of the two cars. Unlike the other guy, he was more interested in smoking a cigarette than he was blowing away a nocturnal rodent. Both looked alert enough to catch Pen and I if we tried to climb out the window.

I checked the door of our spartan suite. Locked. The hinges were on this side of the door, but I didn't have any tools to pop them off.

That was about it. Sure, we could make a bunch of noise— my brain got distracted for a second thinking about the sorts of noises we could make—and maybe someone would show up, but there weren't many options. Throw the wicker chair at them? Hit them with a pillow? Leave the window open and hide under the bed?

None of that was going to work. We were stuck here until someone came and got us. Which meant I had some time to think of what might happen when they did.

Pen and I played our individual games over the next hour or two. I paced, pretending to give a lot of thought to escape. She alternated between the bed and the chair, squirming and wiggling as she tried to find the best pose with which to distract me. Finally, she took off her top altogether, and I stopped pretending to think about escape plans.

The growling noise of a heavy engine reverberated in the courtyard, and I tore myself away from the luscious woman on the bed and went to the window. I watched a late-model Plymouth Barracuda rumble into the courtyard. It was painted a color usually reserved for Slurpee machines at 7-11, which was akin to a zit-faced adolescent screaming "Look at me! Look at me!"

The driver was wearing a dark cowboy hat, and when he got out of the card and started talking to the guards, I caught sight of his face.

"Our host is here," I said.

Pen came up behind me, and as she peeked out the window, her breasts pressed against me. A little reminder, in case I had forgotten.

"That's the guy from the reptile show," she said.

"Yeah, that's Jack Trevellian."

When I moved my arm, she snuggled closer. "Look," I said. "I'm aware of what you have there, and I'll be happy to inspect them later, but in the meantime, could you put your shirt on?"

"Why?" she asked. "Won't they be a good distraction?"

"They are a marvelous distraction," I said. "But that's not going to help us right now."

"Why not?"

"Because Jack wants to talk, and we should let him talk."

"How do you know he wants to talk?"

I smiled at her. "Because if he didn't, they would have shot us both and dumped our bodies in a shallow ditch somewhere," I said. I kissed the top of her head. "But they didn't, and now Jack is here, which means he's got something on his mind."

She looked up at me. "You expected this, didn't you?"

"I did," I said. Which was mostly true. I knew Jack would show up sooner or later. Pen had been bait, I had fallen for it, and now, Jack held all the cards. He was in charge, and he was going to tell us how it was all going to work out for him.

CHAPTER 29

We didn't have to wait long before someone came and got us. The only warning we had was a brief wiggling of the doorknob before the door unlocked. A sandy-haired guy with a downturned mouth and thick eyelashes pushed the door open. He remained in the hall, the shotgun in his hands. "Mr. T wants a word," he said. "With both of you."

I followed Pen out of the room, and the guy stepped to the right, indicating we should go to the left. We walked a short distance to a wide staircase that doubled back on itself as it led us to the first floor of the ranch house. I looked around briefly, noting a large kitchen, a sprawling living room, and an expansive dining area with big windows that looked out on the courtyard. There were a couple of guys in the kitchen, but I didn't get a chance to look at them closely. .

"This way," our guide said. We went down a hall, passing closed doors on either side, until we reached a broad room that had a big screen TV, an expensive looking leather couch, and a number of taxidermied animals mounted on pedestals. The animals had all been posed to look menacing, but the lighting in the room made me think they all looked more frightened than fierce.

Jack Trevellian was standing near a set of French doors that led to a patio. He had a heavy crystal glass in his hand, filled with several fingers of bourbon. He was wearing a t-shirt that had a road printed on it. It split into two directions, and just before the fork, there was a snake coiled up. The caption read: "Fork in the road." You had to notice the snake's tongue to get the pun.

Droopy and Twitch sat on the couch. They weren't drinking.

"So, these two," Jack said, like he was continuing a conversation that had been started an hour ago.

"Yeah," a voice said behind us.

It was Cock Robin. He pushed past Pen and I. He had a beer in his hand, and it was a toss-up whose face looked worse: his or Droopy's. He took a long swig from his beer as he wandered over to stand next to the stuffed coyote. "That's Butch Bliss," he said, lowering his beer. He belched and indicated Pen. "And that's whatshername."

"She's not who you think she is," I said.

"Who do I think she is?" Rob shot back.

"She doesn't know Nathan."

"Who's Nathan?" Pen asked.

"See?" I said.

"Why would she know Nathan?" Trevellian asked. An oily grin spread across his face.

I waggled a finger at him. "You said—on that message you left for Nathan—you said you had his girlfriend."

Trevellian shook his head. "Why would I say that?"

"Because you wanted Nathan to panic and—"

"Nathan doesn't need any help panicking," Jack said. "If I wanted to see him, I would have just said so."

"So it wasn't about getting Nathan out here," I said.

Twitch laughed. Beside him, Droopy nodded, a sick smile on his face.

I looked at Rob, who shrugged and drank more beer.

"Well, here I am," I said. "Whoops. You caught me."

Trevellian eyed me for a minute. Then he drank some of his bourbon, before staring at me some more.

He's stalling, I thought. *He has no idea.*

"You don't know who I am," I said.

His glass paused on its way to his lips, but only briefly.

"Jesus Christ, Rob," I said, turning to the pompadour-wearing beer drinker. "What the hell is going on?"

Trevellian finished off his bourbon. He looked at the bottom of his glass, as if he might find some insight there. But when nothing was revealed, he tapped the glass against the palm of his hand. "Let's go outside," he said. "I want to show you something." He turned and opened up the French doors. The guy with the shotgun indicated Pen and I should go first.

We went, filing out into the night air. Shotgun followed us, and Droopy and Twitch came behind him. Trevellian came out after Rob, who had a queasy look on his face. He flinched when Trevellian clapped him on the shoulder. The other guys who had been in the kitchen with Rob filled out last. Pen stood close to me, and I felt her arm shivering. She had seen the guns too. We stood around on the stone patio like we were early to an industry cocktail party and no one had recognized anyone else as a power player in Hollywood.

Motion-activated lights lit up the area. Beyond the patio, there was a pitiful attempt at a yard. There were a pair of outbuildings that were too large for garden sheds, but didn't have garage doors on them. Farther back, there was a two-story barn with a hay loft that looked like it predated every other building by a decade or more. It hadn't been used for horses for a long time. A stone ring sat out in front the warehouses. It looked like an above-ground pond or a fountain, but there was no statue in the center.

"Over there," Trevellian said, indicating the stone ring. When we got close, we realized it was a pit and not a pond. It was deeper than I expected, though not much more than six feet or so, and it was filled with—

"Rattlesnakes," Trevellian said when he heard Pen gasp. "They're all over the desert I pay out a bounty. Five bucks a snake. They all go in here. Every once in a while, I have the guys toss in a bag of mice, just to keep them from eating each other."

I peered down at the slow slither at the bottom of the pit. "Ever toss in something bigger?" I asked.

"A goat, once," Trevellian said. "Just to see what would happen."

Rob tried for a polite laugh, but it came out like a dying man's wheeze.

Pen stood back from the pit, her arms wrapped around her body. Her face was pale.

One of the guards picked up a long pole with a noose at the end of it. He handed the pole to Trevellian, who stepped up to the pit and dangled the noose end over the edge. "I don't like surprises," Trevellian said. He tried to slip the noose around the head of one of the snakes. Warning rattles came from the pit.

"Who does?" I said. I looked at the two Mexicans and then at Rob. "You should ask them," I said.

"Ask them what?"

"It's their party," I said. "I showed up late."

Trevellian jerked the rope, taking up the slack in the line. "Was there a party? No one invited me."

"That's a shame," I said. "You seem like the sort of guy who would be a lot of fun at a party."

He gave me a side-long glance, and then turned on the showboating smile he had been wearing at the NARC booth. "Tell me about this party," he said to Rob.

"Man, I told you already," Rob said. "These guys . . . these guys here—Hector and Pedro—they represent a business opportunity in Mexico. I was trying to get an introduction for you—"

"For me?" Trevellian feigned surprise, which was about as honest an expression as his shit-kicking show grin was. "Who do I need to know in Mexico?"

I glanced at Pen, whose expression said everything that needed to be said about doggerel-spouting snake-handlers.

"No, man," Rob said. "A *business* connection."

"I don't have any business in Mexico," Trevellian said. "I get my snakes directly from South America and Africa. Why do I need someone in Mexico?"

"It's a different sort of business," Rob said.

Trevellian raised the stick. Dancing on the end was the writhing shape of an angry rattler, its head neatly caught in the tightened loop. "Are you suggesting I need to consider diversification?"

Rob held up his hands. "That's not what I'm saying," he said.

Trevellian slapped his palm against the stick, making it bounce. Making the snake mad. "What are you saying?"

"Hector and Pedro are in the cocaine smuggling business," I said, trying to move this conversation along. "Cock Robin here thinks you should be in that business too."

Trevellian frowned as he swung the pole around. Everyone took a step back. "Why would I want to be in that business?" he asked.

Rob was too busy glaring at me to answer. Between the pair of them, Twitch looked like he was enjoying the snake-handling routine. Droopy was having a flashback to another snake encounter.

Trevellian slid the pole under his arm and grabbed the angry rattler behind the head. He squeezed it at the hinge of its jaw, and the snake opened its mouth. It fangs sprang out, forced forward by Trevellian's pressure. "If you know how to handle them, they aren't dangerous," he said. The snake, feeling very disagreeable, whipped its tail. "Snakes don't like it when you hold them. They're used to being treated with more respect." Trevellian squeezed harder, and a tiny drop of venom appeared at the tip of the snake's fangs. He held his finger under the fang, and we all held our breath as the bead swelled and then fell. Trevellian raised his finger to his mouth and sucked off the venom.

Beside me, Pen made a noise in her throat. I reached over and gave her hand a squeeze. Her fingers were cold.

Trevellian moved his tongue around his mouth, playing up the moment, and then he swallowed. "What doesn't kill you, makes you stronger," he said. "You know who said that? Nietzsche. You know who Nietzsche is?"

He wasn't asking anyone in particular, and I seized the moment. "I do," I said.

"He was afraid of snakes. Did you know that?"

"I did not."

Trevellian nodded. "He knew they were aliens. They didn't come from this planet. They were sent here to spy on us. Their overlords"—he lifted his chin toward the sky—"they're waiting. They're waiting for their spies to tell them when the time is right. When they can harvest us. Because we're cattle."

"I—I must have missed that part of Nietzsche."

He gave me a feral grin. "Nietzsche couldn't see past the failings of humanity," he said. "He got too wrapped up with stuff in his head. He thought the snake was a test. It was meant to make us evolve into something better. But he got it all wrong. We're not going to get better. We're going to get fatter. That's what the snakes want. They want us fat and compliant. Docile."

"Like cows," I said, just so he felt like someone was keeping up with him.

Trevellian released his hold on the snake and swung around toward Rob. The snake on a stick made a wide arc too. It wiggled around like he was dowsing for water. Or testing for sanity. "Do you know the truth?" he asked.

"I . . . I don't know what you're talking about," Rob said.

Judging by the range of expressions on everyone else at this backyard party, he wasn't the only one.

"The truth of the serpent," Trevellian said. "I'm talking about the fang and the rattle. Which do you prefer?"

"I prefer the one that doesn't kill you," I said.

When Trevellian turned toward me, bringing the snake with him, Rob's shoulders slumped. He had been spooked.

Trevellian narrowed his eyes, trying to decide if I was playing with him. Unlike Cock Robin, I did a better job of keeping my cool. "That's not the right answer," Trevellian said after a long examination of my face.

"There is no right answer," I said. "It's all bullshit. What Rob's been telling you. What those two over there have told him. What Nathan's been saying. It's all bullshit."

"Except you," Trevellian said. "You're the only one who has been telling the truth."

"I'm the only one who doesn't want to fuck you," I said.

Trevellian licked his lips, and it was an oddly serpentine gesture. He eyed Pen. "You fuck her?" he asked.

"It doesn't matter if I did or not," I said.

That struck him as extraordinary profound, and he lapsed into thought. Or maybe he was staring at Pen's chest. It was hard to tell, and I didn't want to be rude and ask.

"You don't want to fuck me," Trevellian said quietly. There wasn't regret or disappointment in his voice. It was something else. *He's thinking this through,* I thought.

"US Fish and Wildlife Service wants to fuck you," I said, trying to be helpful. "Your lawyer rolled over for the DEA, and you know they're going to fuck him. Cock Robin over there wants to set you up a date with a drug kingpin in Mexico. I dunno. Maybe he wants to fuck you. Or maybe the DEA wants to take pictures of you fucking each other." I went for the eloquent shrug. Might as well after all the salty language I had just used. "Me? I've got no interest in you. I'm just here for the girl."

Trevellian chewed on the end of his mustache. "Just the girl," he said. He squinted at me.

"Just the girl," I said. "She shouldn't be here. Let us go home."

"And everything else?" He gestured at the Mexicans and Rob. "All this—this talk of fucking . . ."

"It's none of my business," I said. "You can have your boys toss them in the snake pit for all that I care."

"Why?" he asked.

"Because they—" I shook my head. "They wanted to use me. They thought I would be their lapdog, but I'm not. I did my time. I don't owe anyone. I'm my own man."

His eyes flicked toward Pen. "If he gets you out of here, are you going to fuck him?"

She didn't say anything out loud, but I knew she was nodding.

Trevellian swiped at his mustache with the back of his hand. "You think that's fair?"

"It sounds fair to me," I said.

He brought the stick close and grabbed the snake's head. He forced its fangs forward. A drop of venom swelled at the tip of the fangs. "You're crazy," he said.

I held out my hand. "No more than you, King of the Road."

A smile tugged at the corner of his mouth. He nodded as the bead of venom dropped onto my palm. I raised my hand, and ignoring Pen's sudden intake of breath, I licked my palm clean.

I didn't feel anything as I swallowed. Nor did I expect too. Snake venom is a neurotoxin. It's only dangerous if it gets into your bloodstream.

I had read a book in the Tehachapi library about writing mysteries. It shouldn't have been there. People would get the wrong ideas. One of the sections was about poisons: how they worked, how they didn't, and how to safely handle them. The sort of thing an earnest writer of mystery novels would want to know.

Trevellian knew this, of course. Not because he was a budding crime novelist, but because he made a living of handling snakes. As long as you didn't have open sores in your mouth or have an ulcer, the venom wasn't going to harm you. Your stomach acids would break it down before it could do anything.

Trevellian watched me closely, and when I didn't start spasming or vomiting blood, he nodded. He plucked at his shirt, as if he had just noticed the design. "Snake road," he said.

"Snake road," I said. You had to make a choice. That's what the 'fork in the road' was all about. It's what Robert Frost was talking about in that old poem of his. And it's what the snake represented in the Garden of Eden. In the beginning, when man and woman were without sin, they couldn't choose right or wrong, good or evil. They didn't know any better. There were no choices to make. But then the snake came along. Offered them temptation. Pick a path, it said. The future forked, and who knows if Adam—or Eve—picked right, but they made a choice. That was what mattered.

"All right," Trevellian said. "You two can go."

"Thanks, Jack," I said. I backed away, pushing Pen into motion.

Trevellian released his grip on the snake. It started thrashing, and he turned toward Rob, holding the stick out. "What's this about the DEA?" he asked. His back was to us. We were no longer on his mind. We were free to go.

"One moment," one of the Mexicans piped up. It was Droopy. "I'm not done with him."

CHAPTER 30

SHOTGUN SWUNG HIS WEAPON TOWARD ME. COCK ROBIN, WHO had been backing up from Trevellian, changed his direction, putting distance between himself and the Mexicans. Getting distance from everyone. Trevellian paused, the tip of his tongue touching his bottom lip. He regarded Droopy, seeming to notice the man's taped nose and bruised face. "Is there a problem?" he asked.

"*Si,*" Droopy said. "*Uno problema.*"

Trevellian pointed at the tape. "He do that to you?"

"*Si,*" Droopy said.

Trevellian frowned. He swiped at his mustache. "Didn't you shoot him?" he asked.

"Hector shot him," Droopy said. That made him Pedro, though I was inclined to stick with my nickname. This didn't feel like a real *Get to Know Your New Pals* moment.

"Seems like you might be even," Trevellian said. "Not that I give a shit one way or another." His face grew thoughtful, and I nudged Pen to keep moving. *Slowly*, I thought. *Let's not draw attention to ourselves.*

Trevellian's goons were looking at one another. They didn't like the situation. I didn't blame them. I didn't like it either.

"What do you think?" Trevellian suddenly turned toward Cock Robin.

"About what?" Rob was startled to be drawn into this conversation.

"What do you think, dipshit?" Trevellian's voice had lost its casual drawl. There was an edge to it now. An edge I had been hoping to avoid.

Rob's hands fluttered nervously, and his eyes couldn't stop moving. "I don't know, man," he said. "I don't know anything about these guys."

"No, you don't, do you?" Trevellian said. He shook his head. "They turn you, Cock Robin?" he asked. "Did you let those scaly motherfuckers put their snake babies in you?"

"What?" Pen couldn't help herself.

Trevellian seemed surprised to hear a woman's voice. His head came around, and his eyes focused on me. Bright. Dangerous. "That's how it happens," he said, his lips sliding along his teeth. "They slip them under your skin. When they're smaller than the hairs on your arm. They burrow and eat, and when they're done eating, they nest in your gut. When they grow, when they shed their layers, you shit snake skin."

"I'm going to side with Rob on this one," I said. "I don't know anything about that."

"I've been telling you. I've been telling everyone, but no one listens." Trevellian shook his head. "None of you know anything about snakes. You don't know what they are capable of. What they are doing to us. You're not going to be ready when their masters come."

"Unlike you," I said. "You've got hundreds of them in an open pit. You've studied them. You know their ways."

"I do," Trevellian said. He tapped the side of his head. "I know how they think. I know how they move. I know how they talk to one another, in their snake tongue." His tongue flicked out and ran across his lips. "I know their serpentine ways."

I side-eyed Hector and Droopy. They weren't following all of what Jack was spouting, but it was becoming clear to Droopy that he might not get what he wanted. That was going to be an issue for him.

I looked at the rest of the players, gauging distances. Between us and them. To the ranch house. To the warehouses. And the barn—*no, the barn was too far away.*

The hay loft door was open. Had it been open earlier? I wondered. I tried to remember, but I hadn't been paying close attention to the old barn. It was abandoned. *Why would—*

My brain spun for a second. What had Frank said before I had gone through the wire?

Overwatch.

Droopy came to a decision. He pulled a gravity knife out of his back pocket and shook it open. "He owes me," he said, pointing at me with the tip of the knife.

Trevellian lifted his shoulders and then dropped them. "Yeah, okay," he said. "You can have him." His mustache twitched at my expression. "Did you really think I was going to let you walk out of here?" he asked.

"I thought we made a pretty good argument for it," I said.

"It was a fucking dumb argument," he said. Without looking, he jabbed the pole in Rob's direction. "Where's my breeder?" he snapped. "Terry here"—and he pointed at one of the guards—"says he gave you a female breeder. You told him that I told you to come out here and get it." The tip of the pole swung toward the Mexicans. "Did you give it to them? Was that the deal? Did you give them my snake?"

"No, man, he stole it." Rob pointed at me.

"You?" Trevellian's mustache bristled as he looked at me. "You did fuck me." He seemed pained by the realization.

"I didn't steal it," I said. "I never saw it. All I saw was a green tree python, which isn't the same thing. I know."

"Yeah, no shit, it's not the same thing," Trevellian said. "Where's the boa?"

Rob spread his hands. "I don't have it, Mr. Trevellian. I swear."

Trevellian looked at the Mexicans. "You two have it?" he asked.

Hector pointed at me.

"Oh, no," I said. "I was the delivery guy. I delivered. You're the idiot who shot it. And it was a python. It wasn't the damn boa."

"What? You shot a snake?" Trevellian couldn't decide if he was pissed or delighted. I didn't really want to stick around until he figured it out.

"Rob'll feed you a bullshit story about being jacked in the bathroom at a gas station," I said. "According to him, both his car and the snake were stolen."

"Did you steal them?"

I shook my head "I was given the car and a snake, but it wasn't the same snake."

"Who gave them to you?"

I raised my hands. "The DEA. Who do you think?"

Rob opened his mouth to contradict me, but decided against it. I may have been the only one who noticed his reaction.

Trevellian shook his head. "This is some seriously fucked up shit," he said to his men. "You believe this guy?" he asked Pen, indicating me.

"I do," she said quietly.

"You sure?" he asked.

"Uh huh."

Trellevian stared at her, his tongue worrying the inside of his cheek. "Well, that's too bad," he said finally. He nodded, making a decision with himself. "Okay, do it," he said to Droopy. "Let's get this over with."

"No, wait—" Pen started.

Droopy came at me, leading with his knife. He had a loopy grin on his face. He had been waiting all night for this. I moved away from Pen, to my left. Closer to the pit. Trevellian moved out of the way. He wasn't going to get caught up in a scrappy knife fight. That put him closer to Rob, which meant I had those two on my left, the three guys with guns between me and the house, and Hector and Pen on my right. It wasn't the best arrangement, but at least I could keep an eye on everyone.

Not that I was paying them much attention. Droopy and his knife had to be dealt with.

"Gonna take my time, *imbécil*," Droopy cooed as he got closer. "Gonna cut you slow."

I waited for him, hands hanging loosely at my sides. His smile got bigger as he made the blade dance. It was all flash. He wasn't in range. His arms were shorter than mine, and even with the knife, he was going to have to get closer than that to cut me.

He was a jabber too. Not a cutter. When he made his move, all I had to do was twist my body to the right, putting my face out of the path of his blade. I raised my hands—*plucking a sparrow's tail feathers*—and my forearm caught his forearm. The tip of the knife went up as I slid my arm up past his elbow. I reached past the knife with my other hand—my shoulder twinged, but I ignored it. I caught his wrist and pulled him. He was already moving in that direction and all I did was keep him moving. Overextended, he stumbled off balance. That's when I slipped my arm out from under his, and backhanded him in the mouth.

I still had his wrist in my left hand, and I pulled my right arm back and shoved my palm against the spot where his arm joined with his torso. Twisting his wrist and shoving with my right hand drove him in the direction I wanted. Right into the stone wall of the pit. His head bounced off the rock wall, and when his legs went all rubbery, I gripped the back of his shirt and tossed him over the wall.

He yelled as he fell into the snake pit, and he kept on yelling as the snakes started to bite him.

No one moved. We didn't want to listen, but we couldn't help ourselves. We all stood there and listened to the terrible noises of a man being snake bit to death. Eventually, he stopped screaming and the only sound was the disturbed rattle of a hundred snakes.

Trevellian spoke first. "God damn," he said. "That was something."

Rob was close enough to the pit that he could look in. I don't know why he felt like he needed to, but he did. He paled at what he saw. "I wish you hadn't done that," he said. His voice was quiet enough that I was the only one who heard him.

"I thought you might feel that way," I said, knowing the other shoe had finally dropped. Rob was playing all sides against each other, because that's what the DEA did.

"What? Thought what?" Trevellian snapped out of his reverie.

Hector complicated everything by pulling a gun. I couldn't blame him. Things had taken an unexpected turn for him and Droopy. He started jabbering at me in Spanish. I caught one word in six, but the wild gesturing with the gun was plain enough. Trevellian's goons were nervous about all the gun pointing, which was making me nervous, because I didn't think Hector was that good of a shot. He had missed me from closer range not too long ago. No, the guards had shotguns, and you didn't need to aim those in order to make a mess of things.

I kept my hands where Hector could see them and waited. It took all my resolve, but I figured since he hadn't shot me instantly, he wasn't going to. That's the thing about men with guns, right? If you don't use them right away, you're probably not going to.

"Hold on! Hold on!" Trevellian had his hands up too, and the pole with the snake was clenched between his arm and his body. "Let's not get too uptight," he said. "Let's just chill out for a minute. We can be civil about this."

I wasn't so sure about that, but Hector stopped waving his gun around. It was pointed at *me* now, but if that's what it took to make everyone relax, I could live with it for the time being.

"Look, your pal wanted a piece of him and he got his chance," Trevellian said. "It didn't turn out good for him, and that's too bad, but this doesn't have to reflect on you, amigo. Okay? You understand what I'm saying?"

"Pedro was my second cousin," Hector said. "On my mother's side."

"Ah," Trevellian said. He nodded as if he understood the dilemma. "Family."

"*Si. Familia*," Hector said.

"Well, shit," Trevellian said. He looked at me. "Family messes up everything, doesn't it?"

"You were going to shoot me anyway," I said. "This way, it's not your problem."

"It's still my problem," Trevellian said. "I've got to get rid of your body." He nodded toward Pen. "Hers too."

"You could still let us walk out of here," I said.

"Yeah," he said. "But this fellow's not going to like that, which means I'm going to have to shoot him. And his fucking second cousin has to come out of the pit. God damn it. This is becoming a real pain in the ass." He waved a hand at his goons. "Shoot them all. Fuck it. We'll dig one big hole." He pointed at Rob. "Him too. For being—"

"Wait! Wait!" Rob stepped away from the pit. His hands were up, but his face wasn't the face of a frightened man. His eyes were alight with outrage—fear giving way to anger. "I'm working with—"

One of the guards got tired of listening to all this back and forth. His shotgun boomed, and Rob was lifted off his feet by the blast. He slammed against the snake pit wall, his chest a mess of blood and bone. Pen screamed, and the muscles in my lower back and legs got tight. Sphincter-puckering tight.

Trevellian stared at Rob's bloody body, tongue working his lower lip. Hector was back to waving his gun around, but he couldn't decide which of the three goons to shoot first.

"Shut her up," Trevellian snapped, and I motioned for Pen to come over. She rushed into my arms, and I held her tight as she sobbed wildly against my chest.

"What was he talking about?" Trevellian muttered. "Did you hear what he was saying?" His goons looked at each other, and the guy who had fired his gun had a guilty look on his face. Trevellian whirled around, his face bright with rage. "Who was he working for?" he shouted.

He noticed Hector and he blinked heavily as he focused on the gun in the man's hand. He frowned. "You going to use that?" he snarled. When Hector didn't respond, Trevellian snapped his fingers. "Use it or lose it, *amigo*." *Snap. Snap.*

Hector licked his lips, his eyes flicking back and forth between Trevellian and the three guys with guns. The odds weren't good. He flicked his wrist, taking his finger away from the trigger of his gun. "Okay, okay," he said. Moving slowly, he crouched and put the gun on the ground.

I spotted Droopy's knife. He had dropped it when I had bashed his head against the brick. I looked away so I wouldn't stare at it. No one had seen me notice it. I looked past Rob's wrecked body, and my breath caught in my throat.

There was something in the barn. Up in the loft. A tiny red light. I stared, not sure I had seen anything, but then it blinked again.

Overwatch. It was one of those words military guys used.

Trevellian stared at Hector, a look of disgust on his face. "Fucking pussy," he said when the Mexican abandoned his gun. He turned toward his men.

"Wait," I shouted.

He frowned at me. "What the fuck do you want now, Bliss?"

"Let me do it," I said.

"Do what?" He laughed as he understood what I wanted. "Do you think I'm that stupid?" he asked. "I'm not giving you a gun."

I shook my head. "I don't need a gun," I said. "I'll do it with my mind."

"Your what?" Trevellian gaped at me.

"The power of my mind," I said. Pen tensed against me, and I gave her an encouraging squeeze.

"What the fuck are you talking about?" Trevellian asked.

I took a step to my left. Closer to the knife. Away from Pen. I didn't look at the barn. I didn't want to give anything away. "You were talking about Nietzsche earlier," I said. "Remember? Before we got to the part about the snakes and and how they were going to, uh, come down and impregnate us with their snake babies. That's why we drink their venom, isn't it? To get stronger. To overcome the things that could kill us." I was babbling, but all I had to do was hook him. Get him to listen for a few moments, just long enough for me to figure out how to signal to Frank.

He was up there in the barn. He had to be. Otherwise, we were all dead.

"You keep talking, don't you, Bliss? It's always going to be like this, with you, isn't it? You are always going to be selling some sort of shit."

"Nietzsche had a theory about supermen, didn't he?" I said, ignoring him. "The uber race, right?"

"*Übermensch*," Trevellian said, instinctively correcting me. It was enough. I knew I had his attention.

"Right, *übermensch*. We gotta be one these dudes if we want to beat the snakes. If we want to find them when they hide among us. Kill 'em before they do . . . whatever it is they're going to do to us."

I had him now. There was a fervent light in his eyes.

I raised a hand and tapped my fingers against my forehead. "This is how we'll do it," I said. "With our minds." I pointed my fingers, thumb raised, toward Hector. "Like this."

Hector didn't understand what was happening. Was I going to shoot him with my finger gun? Was he supposed to fall down when I said *Bang!*

Trevellian looked a little skeptical too. "Are you going to make his brain explode?" he asked. "Like in that movie?"

"Yeah, sure," I said. "Like in that movie." I didn't know what movie he was talking about, but whatever. If the analogy worked, I wasn't going to fuss.

Trevellian tugged his mustache. "All right," he said. "This I gotta see." He waved a hand at his men. "And when this guy's head doesn't explode, shoot them all."

While everyone's attention was momentarily on Hector, I shifted my aim. I pointed at the guy closest to Pen and did the thing with my hand. Finger gun go boom.

And then I dove for the knife in the dirt.

Hector starting yelling and pointing. Trevellian sensed something was happening, and all too quickly, everyone's attention came back to me.

There was a funny zip of noise, like a bee traveling past at a hundred miles an hour, and the guy who I had pointed at lost his head. Just like in the movies.

I pawed around for the knife. Got my hand on it.

Hector went for his gun, picked it up and got one shot off before a shotgun blast blew him off his feet.

The third guard was trying to decide who to shoot, and the next round from Frank's sniper rifle blew the decision right out of his head. Most of his brains too.

Trevellian dropped his snake pole and clawed at the back of his pants. He had a gun back there. I charged him, keeping low so that the remaining guard couldn't get a clear shot at me without wiping out his boss. I slammed into Trevellian, who took the blow well. He was scrappier than I expected, and he gave up on his gun and grappled with me instead.

I wasn't interested in grappling. In prison, I had learned a few things about using a knife. Trevellian made a funny noise the second time I stabbed him. The light started to fade from his eyes, and he sagged against me.

I didn't bother trying to hold Trevellian up. I wanted the gun he was carrying. I had to get to it before the last guard decided to shoot me.

The bee buzzed again, and the guard coughed. He stumbled, spitting out a lot of blood. He twisted as he fell, and the final act of his life was a minute pull of his finger. A last twitch of a dying nerve ending.

His shotgun boomed.

CHAPTER 31

I WAS NEXT IN LINE FOR A HOT DOG AT THE CORNER OF VENTURA and Las Mercados, and when the couple in front of me got their food and left, there was no one between me and the cart. But it wasn't Horatio behind the cart. It was Mr. Chow, a pair of silver tongs in his hand. *The usual?* he asked as he got a bun out of the warmer and put it on the metal rack.

Sure, I said, wondering if he knew what the "usual" was.

He tapped the side of his head. *Of course I know what it is,* he said. *I'm in here, aren't I?*

Then you know I got shot, I told him.

More than once, he noted. He used the tongs to get a hot dog out of the steamer. *Did it hurt?*

Yeah, I said. *It hurt quite a bit.*

Worse than that time when you got shanked in your cell?

I tried to remember, but the memory had gone soft on me. The details were vague. *No,* I admitted.

He smiled as he put chili and cheese on the hot dog. *Good,* he said. *You're getting tougher.*

I'm not sure I want to get tougher.

He dismissed my concern with a wave of his hand.

No onions, I pointed out, but he ignored me.

You can't always get what you want, he said. He put the hot dog in a paper tray and set it in front of me. It smelled great.

Mr. Chow turned into Jack Trevellian. Blood ran out of a stab wound in his neck. It stained his t-shirt, obscuring the design. The roads were gone. All that was left was the snake, its forked tongue flickering. Telling me to make a choice. Telling me that was how we figured out who we were. How we moved on.

Trevellian leered at me. When he stuck out his tongue at me, it was forked too.

I woke up in a hospital room. It was bigger than the last one. It had another bed, in fact, though there was no one in it. The sheets were tightly wrapped around it, and there was a light blanket tucked in tight. A cardboard filing box sat in the middle of the bed.

I knew someone had brought that box. Just as I knew they were still in the room. But as my senses came back, all that mattered was what I was smelling.

There was a hot dog on the bedside table next to me. It was piled with chili and cheese, and I could see steam rising from it. My mouth watered as I looked at it. I started to sit up, but my chest didn't like that motion. I tried to reach for it, but my hand was brought up short by a metal handcuff.

I stared at the handcuff. I jerked it a few times. It was really there. And so was the hot dog.

The person in the room came around my bed and nudged the bedside tray closer. "Here's your hot dog," Frolic said.

I fell back against my pillow. My chest ached. My hand was cuffed to the bed. I settled for glaring at her. "You should eat it while it's hot," she said, unmoved by my stare.

"What did you put in it?" I managed. My mouth wanted that dog, but I was too angry to put food in my face.

She drifted out of reach. "Oh, chili, cheese, relish," she said. "No onions. I don't like onions."

"Nothing else?"

She stopped at the foot of the bed. I had been restless during my dream, and I had kicked loose the covers. My left foot was sticking out. She looked down at my painted toenails, and then lightly covered my foot with the loose blanket. "You let the girls at Mrs. Chow's salon put that on you?" she asked.

I swallowed my first retort. "Yeah," I said. "I did." I struggled to reposition myself on the bed. Having a plaster around your chest and being handcuffed makes that difficult.

"Maybe I'll try that next time," she said. "What is it?"

I struggled to remember. "Hungarian Death Nun," I said.

She gave me a smile that went all the way to her eyes. "I like that," she said.

I stared at her for awhile. She didn't look away. "You should eat," she said. "Before it gets cold."

"Fuck you," I said. I rattled the handcuff.

She sighed. "You can thank Detective Green for that," she said. "He has no case against you, but he's not quite ready to let go."

My stomach growled noisily. It, at least, was done being pissed at Frolic. For the time being. I reached for the tray and pulled it against the bed. She had laid out napkins too, and I managed to get my left hand around the hot dog in a way that would expedite it into my mouth.

I made an involuntary noise as I tasted beef and cheddar and chili. It was really good.

"There," Frolic said. "All better. We square?"

"No," I said around a mouthful of hot dog.

She pursed her lips as if she was disappointed, but I could tell she did it mainly to hide a smile. "I'm impressed," she said. "It was quite brilliant how you managed to pull that off."

"Pull what off?"

"Getting the girl involved like that. I had no idea who her parents were. Well-respected Beverly Hills cosmetic surgeon. Emmy-award winning daytime soap star. Talk about impeccable character witnesses."

"What are you talking about?"

"She drove you to the hospital in San Bernadino. By the time LAPD got there, she had gotten ahold of her parents. They showed up with their lawyers. Had a press conference right out in front of the hospital. Mom told a tearful story about how her daughter had been abducted by cultists during the reptile convention. You had taken her there on a date. It was—what was it?—your second date." Frolic cocked her head at me. "So very sweet."

I continued to devour the hot dog, even though I didn't like the taste in my mouth. I didn't care. How long had I been dreaming of this hot dog?

"And you went out there to rescue her," Frolic continued. "All by yourself. Such a stupid thing to do, really, but oh, Natasha Verlaine is a very good actor. She sold it to the press. Boyfriend takes it upon himself to rescue his new girlfriend. Maybe he did to atone for his past sins? Maybe he wanted to show her that he was a good man, after all. That prison hadn't made him a monster."

"She's not my girlfriend," I protested.

Frolic waved a finger at me. "Don't ruin the story," she said.

I settled back against my pillows. There was extra chili still in the wrapper. I dragged it over and, without any shame whatsoever, lapped it up.

Frolic continued her story. "Meanwhile, San Bernardino Sheriff sends out a full response team, and what do they find? Well, it's a real mess. Blood and death and snakes. That was the headline I saw, in fact." She repeated the headline, tapping my covered foot with a long finger on each word. "And that's that," she said. "Nothing about drugs. Nothing about any pending investigations by the US Fish and Wildlife Service. Nothing about the DEA or entrapment or any of those things that make everything much more complicated than they need to be. Just a tear-jerker story about a boy and a girl and some snakes." She smiled at me. "It was so well played, Butch. I'm very impressed. But then, I knew you'd take care of everything for me."

"What the fuck are you talking about?"

"Fish and Wildlife wanted Trevellian, but couldn't make anything stick. The DEA got to his lawyer, and they hatched a plan to get Trevellian to smuggle snakes and drugs. One of theirs could broker a connection with a known Mexico drug dealer—a guy who has a thing for exotic pets, in fact."

"Cock Robin," I said.

She nodded, and there was a hint of regret—remorse, maybe?—in the motion. "They were going to get Trevellian and this dealer in the same room with a lot of coke and a lot of snakes, and then they were going to bust everyone."

"But you intercepted Rob," I said. "You sent me instead. Why?"

"They had a good plan. But it wasn't the right plan."

"And why was that?"

She shook her head. "The drug dealer works for us."

"Us?"

She nodded.

"Who's 'us'?" I asked. "The United States? CIA? Who the fuck is 'us'?"

Frolic adjusted her coat. "Well, I really must run along," she said. "I shouldn't be here."

I rattled the handcuff and kicked my feet under the blanket. "Who the fuck are you?"

She put her hands on my feet to quiet them, and when I stopped thrashing, she smiled at me. It wasn't a patronizing smile. It was an unexpected smile. A brief window into her that I didn't expect, and what I saw made me settle down. "I brought you a present," she said. She nodded at the box on the other bed as she strode toward the door.

She stopped and looked back before she left. "For the record," she said. "My parents really were into French soft-core porn."

I stared at the door after she left, my brain reeling with what I had seen in her eyes. Everything she had told me. Or not told me. Can you ever really trust anything a spook says?

And then something moved in the box.

☆

More Bliss

Building a relationship with my readers is one of the marvelous parts of being a writer, and the best way that relationship grows is through interaction. The only way I know these stories are making you laugh, cry, or shake your fist in joy is by hearing from you. The easiest way you can let me know that you'd like to see more Bliss is to leave a review.

Reviews don't have to be complicated. All you need is a place to leave a few words about the book (the retailer where you purchased this book, an online review site, or—heck!—even a hand-drawn sign works). Let me know what you think about Bliss!

Also, the Harry Bryant mailing list is very low-traffic. It's the best way to stay informed, and signing up lets me know that you're a fan and you'd like to see more.

http://www.harrybryantwriter.com/mailinglist.php

Thanks for your support!

ACKNOWLEDGMENTS

Many thanks to Nancy Ekse, Richard Choate, and Evelyn Nicholas, who provided encouragement along the way. An additional tip of the hat to Evelyn, who kept an eye on my extra letters and skewed phrasing.

ABOUT THE AUTHOR

Harry Bryant lives in the Pacific Northwest with a house full of pretty books.

Find him on the web at http://www.harrybryantwriter.com